A Natural Killer?

Tracy Gorman

World Castle Publishing, LLC
Pensacola, Florida
Copyright © Tracy Gorman 2018
Paperback ISBN: 9798891263819
eBook ISBN: 9781629899015
First Edition World Castle Publishing, LLC, April 16, 2018
http://www.worldcastlepublishing.com

Licensing Notes

Cover: Karen Fuller
Editor: Maxine Bringenberg

Table of Contents

CHAPTER ONE

Elise Sampson sank into her favorite armchair. Her lips were trembling, and there was a tingling in her bones that hadn't been there before. She folded her hands together, interlocking her fingers in a cat's cradle. She'd never been afraid of anything, yet tonight a deep sense of foreboding clutched at her chest. She couldn't pinpoint the source of her unease, but it seeped through her body like oil through a well.

She rose from her seat and drifted across to the window. The driveway was dark and quiet, a murky void of shapes and shadows. Her eyes fixed upon a distant streetlight. Its fluorescent glow was little more than a dull haze from where she stood. Nevertheless, its presence was oddly comforting. It reminded her that there was a world beyond her curtains.

The light flickered, and Elise shuddered involuntarily. There was a chill in the air that her trusty wood burner couldn't seem to quell. It added to the darkness of her mood. She pulled her cardigan tightly across her chest. Perhaps it was just the cold that was unnerving her. After all, the temperature had dipped considerably in recent days.

She retraced her footsteps, sinking easily back into her seat, just as the grandfather clock in the hallway chimed a quarter past nine. Usually at this time of the evening she'd engage in a little knitting, or tackle one of her many puzzles. It was her way of winding down...a little end of the day treat. But tonight, not even the promise of such pleasures could placate her.

An idea struck her, and she pulled herself up, heading purposefully toward the kitchen. A nice cup of hot cocoa would do the trick. It would soothe her uneasiness *and* warm her bones. She didn't know why she hadn't thought of it before. Cocoa was the perfect antidote for the winter blues, and once it was inside her, she'd be back to her normal self in no time.

Her joints creaked as she moved slowly through the darkened space, reminding her of the disadvantages of age. If it wasn't for the fact that every bone in her body now groaned, she'd still feel twenty-one. She shuddered at the thought. Where the hell had the years gone? It was as if she'd blinked and turned the corner into God's waiting room...an unsavory maze of creaking joints, sleepless nights, and sympathetic looks. God, how she hated those sympathetic looks.

The thought brought a brief smile to her dry lips. At least she had no regrets. A stab of conscience prickled the back of her neck. OK, everyone had *some* regrets. Bad choices they'd made, things they wished they'd done differently. But they were the traits that defined a person, the scars that ensured they never make the same mistakes again...and at least hers had been made with the best intentions.

She reached the kitchen and flicked on the light switch. When nothing happened, her uneasiness returned. She'd changed the bulb less than a week ago. Surely it couldn't have burned out already. She craned her neck to see behind her. The lounge light was still on, so it couldn't be a problem with the circuit breaker.

A cold sense of dread ascended her spine, a visceral awareness that she wasn't alone. She shook herself firmly. She *had* to get a grip. She was eighty-two years old, for heaven's sake. If someone had wanted to send her to an early grave, they'd have done so long before now.

The thought appeased her, and she stared ahead into the gloomy kitchen. Without the light, it was impossible to see more than five feet ahead. Still she persevered, forcing her eyes to focus. There was a set of spotlights right above the cooker. They'd provide ample illumination for her to replace the bulb. And when it was done, she'd make that cocoa.

The kitchen tiles were cold against her bare stockinged feet. Still, she propelled herself forward, again scolding herself for her foolishness. It wasn't as if her house wasn't secure. She had the tallest fence in the street, not to mention the latest in burglar alarm technology. Christ, she was practically living in Fort Knox. Houdini himself would struggle to get in. Not that he or anyone else would want to.

She was about to reach for the spotlights when a loud shuffling stopped her in her tracks. It was so unexpected, she instantly felt her heart quicken. She made to turn, but before she'd gotten all the way around, something had gripped her legs and was pulling her backwards. Her face hit the kitchen worktop with such force it took her breath away and sent shockwaves of pain surging through her skull.

Confusion prevailed. Elise opened her eyes, desperate for some form of clarity. But the room was spinning, and she was forced to close them again. She tried to lift her head, but something or *someone* was holding her down. Then a warm, moist liquid trickled down her cheek, and she could taste the sharp, salty tang of blood. She opened her mouth to speak but nothing came out, and her head felt so fuzzy she wasn't sure if she was standing of her own accord or if someone was propping her up.

In the seconds that followed, she was aware of something

cold piercing her neck. Its icy bite sent a shiver along her spine. Then it was no longer icy. It was a red-hot fire, streaming through her body like lava through a volcano. Its tortuous heat taunted every inch of her tender flesh, scorching her from the inside out, and the pain was excruciating.

More seconds passed, and Elise's body contorted in agony. She tried to scream, but the torment had taken such a hold, she no longer had control over her mortal functions. All she wanted was for the pain to be over. She longed for death, prayed for it with every inch of her being. But the release she craved eluded her.

A faint murmur escaped from her lips, finally fading to a dull whisper. Then a bright light flashed before her, followed by a deep, impenetrable darkness. Her head jolted backwards, and a solitary voice echoed from within. The devil had come for her, and the fiery furnace of hell awaited.

A sudden sharp pain stabbed at her chest, the definitive act in her torment. Her body convulsed and, as her heart struck its final beat, the figure behind her breathed a sigh of relief. It reverberated through the darkened space like a faint whistle, then retreated back into the blackness from which it had come.

CHAPTER TWO

Detective Inspector Anna Rose leaned against her locked Mitsubishi Shogun. It was 5 a.m., and she was tired and cold. A combination of over-work and lack of sleep had driven her virtually insane these last couple of weeks. So much so that she was beginning to wonder if she'd ever feel rested again.

She glanced up, raising a hand to her aching temples. The sun hadn't yet pierced the lead grey sky and a thin, thread-like mist veiled the nearby street lamps. She shuddered, crossing her arms tightly across her chest. Her black leather jacket clung to her body like a chrysalis to a moth, accentuating her slender frame and shielding the dark trouser suit beneath it. The ensemble cut a stark contrast against the light blonde of her hair, which, as always, had been tugged into a tight pony tail.

A chill breeze ruffled the nearby hedgerows and Rose lifted the collar of her jacket. The weather had turned colder in the last few days. An icy December wind was slowly gaining momentum, its rhythmic thrashing targeting loose fence panels and gate posts. Before long the snow would arrive, and the streets would be gridlocked, making her job even harder than it already was. She cringed at the thought. She'd never been good with the cold. Maybe, when she retired, she'd move to warmer climes. It was

9

a scenario she pondered often. The problem was, she still had twenty years of service to get through. If the job didn't kill her first.

A further sound fractured her thoughts and her partner, Detective Sergeant John Stipes, emerged from the doorway of the nearby building. He'd hung back to remove the tapes from the property's security cameras, and he now held them in his hands, wrapped in familiar plastic evidence bags.

Stipes paused to inhale a breath of air before continuing his ascent along the driveway. He was a good ten years younger than Rose, but in outlook there was little between them besides the obvious gender difference. They shared a mutual love of Italian cuisine and a deep-seated passion for rock music. Beyond that, neither had married. Both had become firmly wedded to the job, a choice that, however clichéd, had instilled a firm bond between them.

Stipes continued his ascent along the driveway, shoving the two small packages into his jacket pockets. Rose watched him in silence. She knew what was going through his mind. It was the same thought that had been plaguing her own mind these past fifteen minutes. Who in God's name could've been capable of inflicting such violence upon a fragile old lady? But even as the question presented itself, she knew she wouldn't like the answer.

Stipes reached the car's passenger side and Rose disabled the central locking and climbed inside. Once seated, she took a last look into the now animated street. The incident had occurred in one of the most prestigious parts of Brackley. It was an area she rarely had cause to visit; yet, when she did, she was always surprised that such affluence sat so closely beside the city's more deprived neighborhoods. It was as if the residents were deliberately flaunting their wealth...putting the proverbial middle finger up at their less privileged counterparts.

Of course, it wasn't the residents who'd built these magnificent structures. It was the planners, architects, and officials. They were the ones who'd come up with the bizarre notion of social integration. Not that it made the reality any more palpable. She shook her head and pulled on her seat belt, wondering if social politics had anything to do with the incident they'd just witnessed. It seemed unlikely. So far there were no signs of forced entry or burglary; nothing to indicate that the perpetrator hadn't been invited in, other than the open gates.

Rose turned the key in the ignition as Stipes shuffled in his seat. There were beads of sweat on his forehead, despite the cold, and an unhealthy pallor tainted his cheeks. She focused her attention on the road ahead, pretending not to notice. The scene they'd just witnessed *had* been particularly gruesome, with the age of the victim making it even less palpable. If she was honest, she was still reeling from the discovery herself.

The realization sent her mind drifting back to their arrival at the scene. The victim had been lying on her front, her head resting face down in a pool of her own blood, her body contorted in an unnatural pose that appeared to have resulted from her fall to the floor. Her thick pink nightgown had risen to above her knees, revealing deep red markings where, according to the pathologist, she'd likely been grabbed and thrown off balance.

Rose shuddered as the image replayed in her mind. The victim's head had made contact with the kitchen work top as she'd fallen and had possibly been held there for quite some time. A thick pool of blood had seeped onto the smooth black granite, leaving a macabre stain that would taint the stone for many years to come.

Stipes pulled on his seat belt and a stab of annoyance prickled her senses. What was most disturbing was the pathologist's reluctance to postulate cause of death, a sure and certain sign

11

that things weren't as they appeared. It was never a good omen when a pathologist withheld such thoughts. More often than not, it threw all sorts of ominous questions into the mix.

She pushed her foot down on the accelerator, discreetly viewing her partner through the corner of her eye. His face was slowly regaining color, though he hadn't spoken since entering the car. She shrugged it off. Contrary to public opinion, murder wasn't something you became desensitized to, just because you happened to witness more of it than was normal. Besides, a bit of emotional attachment was healthy. It helped stimulate the appetite for the job.

When Stipes finally found his voice, it voice was thin and dislocated. "What do you think, Guv?"

Rose ran her hands along the smooth leather steering wheel. "At this point in time, I don't know *what* I think. I can't imagine how anyone could do that to an elderly lady. Then again, I can't imagine how people commit child abuse or bomb innocent bystanders. But we both know those things happen."

Stipes leaned back in his seat, her answer clearly not quenching his curiosity. "But what possible motive could they have to do *that* to an old lady? I mean, she was hardly likely to have been much of a threat."

Rose sighed. "That depends. This could've stemmed from something that went way back. It could've started as a heated debate and gotten out of hand. How many murders have begun as a simple dispute and escalated?"

Stipes shrugged his shoulders. "True. But that doesn't change the fact that the victim was a defenseless old lady."

Rose let out a deep, frustrated sigh. She hated playing devil's advocate, but all possibilities *had* to be considered. She pushed her foot down harder on the accelerator. "She might not have been defenseless. Not all threats are visible. That old lady could've

12

had sensitive information on our killer. She could've been blackmailing him or her. Or she could've committed horrendous crimes in the past. Until we run a background check, we should probably reserve judgement."

As they pulled out of the street, a van Rose recognized as a mortuary vehicle pulled in. Rose nodded her head. Even so, when the vehicle had passed, she visibly shuddered. Soon the victim would be sealed in a body bag and transported to the path lab, where science would reveal the last few moments of her life. She found the process sickening, despite its necessity.

A few minutes later, all thoughts of the mortuary having dissipated from her mind, Rose was heading along Main Street in the direction of the station. Even though it was still dark, neither she nor Stipes would want to be anywhere else. The station was where they did their best thinking, and at this time of the morning it would give them the peace and quiet they needed. Besides, she wanted to get a head start on the case before the rest of her team arrived, for something told her this one was going to be complicated.

CHAPTER THREE

Thirty minutes later, having turned the office into an incident room, Rose and Stipes sat staring at the newly constructed murder board. At present, there was no photo of the victim to take pride of place at its center. It could be a couple of hours before the crime scene pictures filtered through. In the meantime, they needed to take stock of the information they'd acquired so far. Which, by all accounts, was very little.

It was Stipes who broke the tense silence. "At least there's no next of kin to inform."

Uniform had already run a brief background check. The victim, eighty-two year old Mrs. Elise Sampson, a former obstetrician who'd dropped her title on retirement, had no remaining family. She'd lived alone at her address in Amber Court for the last twelve years, since the death of her husband, and appeared to have enjoyed a fairly uneventful life. Not that official records necessarily provided an accurate depiction of a person's private endeavors. Mrs. Sampson could've committed any number of crimes and, unless they'd been uncovered, Joe Public would be none the wiser.

Rose ran her fingers along the arch of her brow. Lack of information regarding cause of death was still frustrating her.

Until they had that, they had nothing to help them construct a profile of the killer. It was a major setback. She leaned forward, scrutinizing the scant black writing on the murder board. The pathologist had promised to begin work on the autopsy ASAP, whatever that meant. But that didn't help them now.

She fumbled with the tapes Stipes had retrieved from the surveillance equipment. They'd played them the minute they'd gotten back to the station, but they'd apparently been disabled at 8:15, most likely by the killer. According to the pathologist, death had occurred less than an hour later. She turned belatedly to her partner.

"I'm not sure how much of a blessing that is. Still, this lady must've had acquaintances. Friends, ex work colleagues, neighbors...people she spent time with, who might yield some insight into why she was killed. We need to construct a list of everyone who knew her, plus an itinerary of her movements these last couple of weeks and any regular routines she had. We need to know where she went, with whom, and why."

She slouched back in the cold metal chair, her mind ticking over like a clock on speed.

"And we should consult with her doctor. A lady of that age is likely to have had regular appointments. We need to know if she had any unusual conditions. Or medication. Perhaps she chose to self-medicate, which could've put her in contact with some very unsavory characters."

Stipes pulled a note pad from his pocket and began jotting down potential lines of inquiry. It was his way of generating ideas. Plus, it would give him something to refer to later, when the rest of the team arrived.

Rose closed her eyes, her mind drifting once again to the crime scene. When they'd left, the house had been filling up with SOCOs (scenes of crime officers) and Forensics. With any luck, they'd find something that would help. The guys were miracle workers these days. Even the tiniest of anomalies could yield vital clues to a killer's identity.

Stipes leaned forward in his seat, purposefully eyeing the tapes. "At least the recordings should help us identify visitors. Who knows? One of them might be our guy."

"Or girl."

Stipes shrugged. It was true. The female perps were as violent as the men these days. If not more so.

Rose hunched her shoulders, cradling her chin in the palms of her hands. "The question still remains; how did the killer get in? Was it someone the victim knew? Did she let them in, perhaps even invite them over? They would've had to have known the exact location of the security cameras, so if they weren't acquaintances, they'd have had to have staked the place out beforehand. Then there's the light bulb...."

Uniform had discovered that there was no bulb in the main kitchen light fitting, a strange coincidence considering the old lady had been killed in there. Normally she'd have concluded that the killer had removed it prior to the attack. The problem was, if the killer was already inside the house, as preliminary findings suggested, why the need for such a measure?

She fumbled with the tapes again. "You're right, these might be of more use than we thought. We'll get Willis to check them out."

Willis was a member of Rose's newly constructed homicide squad. Like the other members, he'd been contacted shortly after their arrival at the station. Willis's area of expertise was finding the most obscure of details, however small, amidst the most mundane of material. It was a highly specialized skill.

Rose pushed thoughts of the tapes aside, her mind turning instead to the lavish property they'd recently visited, and to the seemingly elaborate security system surrounding it. "I still keep thinking about the amount of security Mrs. Sampson had. It seemed a lot for one old lady. The fences were huge. Then there were the electric gates and the security cameras. Was all that just a deterrent for potential intruders? Or was there more to it? Was Mrs. Sampson *waiting* for someone to come after her?"

The question hung in the air like a stale odor. The likelihood of this having been a random killing was slim. Apart from there having been no obvious signs of a break-in, nothing appeared to have been taken. Not that that they had any kind of inventory, but if anything specific *had* been taken, that still pointed to the killing having been premeditated. Plus, whoever had entered the building had already assessed the security cameras and knew how to disable them without alerting the owner. It appeared that Mrs. Sampson had been deliberately targeted. The question was, why?

By the time Rose's team began filtering through the door at seven thirty, they were no further into unravelling the complexities of the case. Still, they'd viewed the evening's recording again and ascertained the length of the security tapes, which was approximately four months in total. Presumably, the previous tapes had expired at that time and had been replaced with fresh ones. Rose made a mental note to find out where the victim had archived used copies, and to establish whether or not the security company had them backed up.

They'd also been in touch with Forensics, though initial findings pointed to there being very little, if anything at all, to help identify the killer. On the plus side, the crime scene photos had been faxed over. They now decorated the murder board like some gruesome jigsaw puzzle. Rose ran her eyes along the well-defined images. If nothing else, they conveyed the severity of the attack.

As for cause of death, there'd still been no news from Pathology, though Rose knew that was to be expected. Post mortems took time. She didn't even want to contemplate the complex procedures that bodies went through on those cold stainless-steel gurneys. Sometimes ignorance really was the best policy.

There were a few moments of muddled confusion while everyone found their places. When they were all seated, Rose positioned herself beside the murder board. Aside from herself and Stipes, her team consisted of five individuals of varying skills and abilities. Each had been assigned to her following her recent promotion to detective inspector. Most she'd worked with before, but two were new to her: Detective Constable Willis and Detective Constable Reece. Both had recently transferred from Vice and considered Homicide and Special Crimes an upgrade. Which, for Rose, was an asset.

Silence descended, and Rose began trailing through the details of the case so far, which sadly took less than five minutes. When she was done, she looked to her team for inspiration.

Willis was first to contribute. His thick Irish accent reverberated throughout the modest room. "If you ask me, this has the markings of a revenge attack. The level of brutality way exceeded what was necessary, especially considering the age of the victim…I mean, who could *do* that to an old lady…?"

His words echoed Stipes's earlier sentiments, and Willis looked around the room as if to reaffirm his point. When he turned back to Rose, there was an edge to his voice. "Are we really ruling out the head injuries as cause of death?"

Rose tried hard to keep the sarcasm from her voice. "At present, we're not ruling out anything…we're waiting on confirmation. As for the revenge theory, I'm inclined to agree with you. At first sight, this doesn't seem like a random attack, unless we're missing something. The killer doesn't appear to have forced entry; the alarm was still intact and there were no obvious signs of burglary. Plus, he or she was probably familiar with the security cameras." She took a deep breath. "Still, we can't afford to be complacent. We've had nothing back from Forensics or Pathology yet, and we all know how quickly things can change. So, for the time being, let's just stick to the facts. If it turns out the killer had an agenda, we'll get to it soon enough."

She draped her arm over the murder board, more for support than anything else. She was so fatigued she was starting to feel light headed, and the fact that she hadn't eaten since early yesterday evening wasn't helping. If she didn't get sustenance soon, she was likely to pass out. A voice detracted her from her thoughts.

"And this was called in by a neighbor? I thought those houses were so far apart, they were practically on different streets."

DC Matt Banks, a short, stocky man with spiky red hair and a head that looked too big for his body, was peering up at her through his thin rimmed glasses. Rose managed a fleeting smile. She'd worked with Matt on numerous occasions in the past, and knew he was reliable and thorough, even if he *did* sometimes have a tendency to be obnoxious. She turned back to the murder board, realizing she should've given her team more time to examine its contents.

"They are. But fortunately, the lady at number eight works nights. She passed the victim's house around 4 a.m. and noticed that the gates were open, which seemed odd. So, being a good neighbor, she decided to check it out. When Mrs. Sampson didn't answer the door and she found it unlocked, she ventured inside. And when she saw her neighbor lying on the kitchen floor...."

Banks sank back into his chair. "Must've been one hell of a shock. But why would the killer leave the gates open?"

19

Rose shrugged her shoulders, the complexities of the case again compounding her. "That's anyone's guess. Maybe they wanted the victim found. Or maybe they were just in a hurry to leave. Either way, they wouldn't have expected anyone to find the body 'til morning."

She stepped away from the murder board and began slowly pacing the small area of carpet in front of it. "I'll be honest with you. Right now, we don't have a great deal to work on. Uniform started work on house to house last night, and they're following up today on anyone they couldn't get hold of. But so far no one seems to have seen or heard anything untoward." She paused to convey the gravity of their predicament. "So we need to find out what we can. Cover the ground work and see what comes up. Firstly, we need to compile a list of Mrs. Sampson's known acquaintances. Friends, neighbors, old work colleagues. Anyone she had contact with over the last five years. We also need to establish whether she'd been involved in any quarrels or disputes, and if she had any regular routines or appointments the killer might've used to determine their time slot."

DC Reece raised a hand. "I'm on it, Guv."

Rose nodded. "Good. On top of that, we need to access the victim's financial and medical records. If she made any large deposits into her bank account, or suffered from any condition that required costly, perhaps even illegal medication, it could've provided our killer with a motive. And we need to check her phone records. I don't know if she had a mobile, but there's definitely a landline."

DC Grace Sherman nodded her head in acceptance of the task. Aside from Rose, Sherman was the only female member of the team.

Rose smiled before continuing. "We also need to ascertain who the estate falls to now that Mrs. Sampson is dead, and whether or not there were any unusual caveats in the will."

DC Banks conveyed his acknowledgment.

Rose glanced back at the murder board. She was keen to get this wrapped up quickly, so she could get back to the business of detecting. Besides, all this talking was making her throat dry. She kept up the momentum. "In addition to those tasks, the victim was formerly an obstetrician. We need to ascertain if there were ever any cases of negligence brought against her. Banks, can I rely on you for that one, too?"

Banks mumbled in response and Rose continued pacing, finally halting beside Willis. "Willis, I'd like you to take a thorough look through the surveillance tapes. If you find anything in there that looks unusual, anything at all, let me know ASAP."

"Right, Guv."

She placed the tapes on his desk. "Plus, I want pictures of all visitors to the Sampson property enhanced. They can then be cross-referenced against the database to see if anything comes up. And get copies of the images to Reece. He might be able to identify some of them as friends, work colleagues, neighbors, etc. If not, we might be able to ID them throughout our inquiries." She went to turn, then remembered something. "And find out if there's any CCTV in the street, will you? In an area like that, you'd expect at least one camera. If there *is* CCTV, get as much footage as you can."

Willis nodded, sliding the first of the tapes into a small black machine on his desk. Rose stepped back, her attention drifting to the final member of the team, DC Jack Blake. At twenty-four, Jack was the youngest member. Nevertheless, his talents couldn't be underestimated. In Rose's opinion he was a born detective, a natural to police work, and if he hadn't chosen a career in law enforcement, he'd probably have made a pretty good criminal. A fact that wasn't lost on her.

21

She stopped beside his table, resting the palms of her hands on its only available space.

"Blake, I'd like you to look into the people involved in the area's development. I know it was a while ago, but I've always found the location a bit odd. Plus, if my memory serves me correctly, there was a lot of opposition to it in the early days. I know it's a long shot, but if Mrs. Sampson or her deceased husband had any links to the development process, it *could* provide grounds for revenge." She paused for a moment, considering the implications of what she'd just asked. "But keep it on the low, will you? We don't want to go ruffling any feathers. At least not yet. Like I said, it's a long shot. But seeing as though we don't have much else at the moment, we'd might as well explore the possibility."

Blake smiled reassuringly, turning to his computer. Rose straightened herself up and clapped her hands together in a "let's get moving" gesture. "OK guys, that's it for now. Once we get cause of death, we'll have more to go on. In the meantime, let's keep all lines of inquiry under wraps. One whisper of the 'm' word and the media will be all over it."

Even as she said it, she wondered how long they had before details of what had happened became common knowledge. A bulletin had been released a short while ago, relaying news of a death in the exclusive Dahlia area of Brackley. But so far, details had been sparse. Once the word "murder" was bandied around, it would be a different story. The media would be out in droves. Not to mention the crime nuts who hoped to become the next Sherlock Holmes. It was then that the mayhem would really begin.

Bodies gradually dispersed, and Rose scanned the room for her partner. Stipes was leaning against the far wall, apparently deep in thought. She considered giving him a moment's repose. He looked calm and pensive, serene even. But they had work to do and peace was a luxury they couldn't afford. Besides, there'd be plenty of time for reflection on their forthcoming journey.

Stipes sensed her presence before she got to him. "Guv?"

"I guess we should head back to the crime scene. SOCOs should be done by now, and we might pick up on something we missed. There *has* to be something there that could help us."

Stipes grabbed his coat from the back of a nearby chair, and together they headed for the door.

CHAPTER FOUR

On the journey back to Amber Court, Rose stopped for a snack at Diego's Drive-Through. She'd been craving a strong cup of coffee and a warm toasted bagel since she'd left the station, but in the end, she had to be satisfied with a dry Danish pastry and a cup of lukewarm tea. She grimaced as she forced the cake along her throat, washing it down with the uninviting beverage. If nothing else, at least it would sustain her until she could get a proper meal.

When they arrived at Amber Court, she slowed the car to a virtual standstill. Inquisitive neighbors would be on the lookout for any sign of police activity, and in the event of an ambush she wanted to be prepared. She scanned each property's meticulous façade, along with the row upon row of pretty Georgian windows. Suspicious deaths in this neck of the woods weren't an everyday occurrence. The Sampson house would be a source of curiosity for many years to come, its victim more notorious in death than in life.

Seeing nothing untoward, Rose parked the car outside number six and killed the engine. After placing the keys in her jacket pocket, she pulled two sets of boot covers and gloves from the glove box and handed a set of each to Stipes, shoving the remaining items in her pockets. She'd put them on just before entering the house, thereby minimizing the chances of cross-contamination.

When she was done, she stepped from the car into the quiet street. For a few moments she simply stood there, eyeing the property as if for the first time. When she finally gained the impetus to move forward, Stipes stepped up alongside her. His long black coat billowed in the breeze, and his heavy black boots tapped noisily against the hard pavement. Like Rose, he was tall and slim. But there the similarity ended. His hair was as black as ink, and he had a rugged, square jaw that tended to jut out when he spoke. His shoulders were unnaturally broad, and he had the hands of a builder, sizeable and strong. On the outside he was the archetypal detective. On the inside, he could be as soft as butter.

Rose lifted the collar of her jacket. The weather showed no sign of improvement. A relentless drizzle trickled icily from a dull grey sky, its spindly fingers coating every surface in a fine, freezing mist. It added to the coldness of her mood. She propelled herself forward, her enthusiasm dwindling with every step.

When they reached the house, it was cordoned off by crime scene tape, and they had to duck beneath it to access the gates. Rose punched in the four-digit security code she'd gotten from the tech guys. As she did so, she wondered if the numbers had been significant to Mrs. Sampson. The first four digits of a specific date, perhaps. Or part of a memorable number or password. If they *had* been significant, that might have made them easier for the killer to ascertain.

Once they were in the driveway, they watched the gates close behind them and cast a good long look at the house. Somehow it looked bigger than it had earlier...more formidable. Rose scanned its magnificent façade, along with its seemingly impenetrable boundary. Even from a distance it had a rigid, almost military

25

look about it. It was the kind of place one retreated to, to escape the outside world. A fortress. The words Fort Knox suddenly sprang to mind.

The analogy made her question the killer's instincts. When he or she had targeted Mrs. Sampson, had they known how seriously the old lady took her security? If they had, then they'd risked a great deal in the pursuit of their plan, and that either made them desperate or careless.

She stepped forward, viewing the house as the killer might've viewed it on their first visit. She was looking for any sign of vulnerability...a chink in its outwardly perfect armor. Nothing leapt out. She walked further forward, craning her neck to see around the corner where the driveway led to a tall side gate. It had been dark when she'd last been here, and there were many details she hadn't noticed. Like the thick poison ivy that trailed the walls, and the tiny wooden building that sat almost camouflaged at the property's periphery. It looked like the sort of thing that might be used for garden tools and other miscellaneous items. She wondered if the victim had used it recently and made a mental note to check it out when they were done in the house.

When they finally approached the doorway, the sickly scent of chemicals was so overwhelming it struck them like a bolt of lightning to the chest. Rose felt her gag reflex jolt and took a deep breath to stem it. Forensics might have left the building, but their presence lingered. She pulled on the gloves and boot covers and shot a glance at her partner. As always, Stipes was ready and waiting. She reached into her pocket for the small silver key she'd placed there earlier, and seconds later they were standing in the property's immaculate foyer.

Once they were inside the chemical smell intensified a hundred-fold. It hit the back of Rose's throat with the force of a thousand angry bees. She wished she'd brought a face mask, then realized she probably had a spare one in the car if she had the patience to go back for it. She decided she didn't. Patience was a virtue that seemed to elude her these days. Besides, it was too late now anyway. The smell was already within her.

She shot a glance at Stipes and they moved forward, their steps silent against the plush cream carpet. When they reached the hallway, Rose hesitated. Her gut directed her to the kitchen, but she hung back. She was still deliberating over the killer's mode of entry. If they *had* been invited in, they'd have walked this exact route just hours earlier, and if there was the slightest possibility that both she and Forensics had missed something, she wasn't about to make the same mistake twice.

When they finally reached the kitchen door, Rose again considered the possibility of a break-in. Even though the property's exterior and garden had been thoroughly checked, the killer might've been clever. They might have penetrated the property in such a way that it would be virtually impossible to detect. She recalled a case she'd worked on a few years earlier, where a similar incident had baffled detectives. It had turned out that the owner had left an old outdoor drain cover, which had led to a downstairs cellar, unlocked. The killer had managed to squeeze through it undetected and later cover his tracks. It was a shrewd, if uncommon, tactic.

She shook the thought off. This hadn't been a break-in. Everything about it pointed to the contrary. Plus, the fact that Mrs. Sampson had been attacked from behind appeared to further corroborate that theory. If the killer had been known to the victim, it would've made it harder for him or her to initiate a head-on attack.

Rose let out a deep sigh. Now she was taking things too far. A lot of killers attacked their victims from behind, simply because it was the best way to catch them unawares. Besides, anyone with a conscience would surely have been incapable of committing such an act in the first place. She was giving the killer more credit than they deserved…but what about the light bulb?

Not for the first time the anomaly taunted her. Was she simply reading too much into it? Coincidence or not, perhaps the light bulb had simply become loose and fallen. The victim *was* elderly. She might not have been able to replace it.

The theory temporarily placated her, and her mind flashed back to the image of Mrs. Sampson lying motionless on the kitchen floor, her thin white hair infused with blood. It had been a shocking sight; unnatural on so many levels. She pitied the poor neighbor who'd stumbled upon it. That image would probably haunt her for the rest of her life. Rose promised herself she'd check with the neighbor at the earliest opportunity. Even though the woman had already been interviewed, things were often missed in the confusion of the moment. In calmer circumstances, she might recall a seemingly minor yet vital detail. It would certainly be worth a try.

Rose turned the corner and stepped into the kitchen, almost snagging her jacket on a nail protruding from the wall. At some point it had probably been used to hang a calendar or some other practical item. She wondered if fragments of the killer's DNA might've inadvertently adhered to it. Like every other facet of her theory so far, it was a long shot. But, more often than not, it was the long shots that broke a case. She made a mental note to check with Forensics that the nail had been dusted and subsequently tested for DNA.

When she was barely a foot from the door Rose paused. Sometimes the only way to tell if something was off kilter was to examine a scene in its entirety. So she stood perfectly still, her eyes following every line of the modest space. Stipes remained behind her. Being familiar with the subtle nuances of her routine, he knew better than to disturb her at such a crucial juncture.

When she'd completed her initial inspection, she took one step forward. Nothing struck her as obviously out of place; but then nothing struck her as particularly *in* place either. The room was a mish-mash of miscellaneous cooking implements and utensils, none of which appeared to be stored in order. Mrs. Sampson had clearly held no interest in things culinary. Either that or she'd possessed an unusual method of composition. Even the small white labels that had been left by Forensics blended into the chaos.

Rose switched her thoughts from the victim to the killer. It was most likely they'd followed Mrs. Sampson into the kitchen and struck when she was at her most vulnerable. A dark kitchen with granite surfaces would provide a perfect backdrop.

She re-thought the implications of what she'd just surmised. Perhaps the killer *had* removed the light bulb after all, even if it wasn't necessary. Perhaps it was the first time they'd done anything like this, and it just made it easier for them to carry out what they'd planned. After all, it wouldn't have been difficult. They could simply have pretended to be using the facilities and made a quick detour. She smiled to herself. It made some semblance of sense, even if it was just conjecture.

Stipes patted her shoulder and she moved slowly forward. For a house so large, the kitchen was relatively small. A long oak table took pride of place at its center, and a large, old fashioned larder occupied the far wall. This was flanked on either side by a succession of mahogany cabinets with granite worktops. Her eyes drifted to the surface where the victim had hit her head. A layer of stale blood still clung to its surface, like marmalade to toast. She turned away. The pastry she'd eaten earlier was already making her stomach churn, and she had no intention of revisiting it.

Stipes closed a nearby cupboard and Rose lowered her gaze to the tiled floor. A white chalk figure now occupied the space where the victim had lain. It sent a shiver along her spine. Nevertheless, her attention remained fixed on it for a long time. It was the reason she was here. If only it could tell her what had happened.

Again, the ambiguity surrounding the victim's demise niggled at her. Once cause of death had been established, she was certain other irregularities would fall into place. She glanced at the clock on the wall above her. If it was right, it was only eight forty-five. It could be a good few hours before they received any news from the pathologist. She had a sudden urge to call him, then decided against it. If he was busy, the interruption wouldn't be welcome. Besides, by the time they'd finished checking the house, examined the out-building and followed up with the neighbor, they could probably drop by the lab. A congenial visit had to be better than an impromptu call.

She reached the room's center and raised her head to examine the small glass light shade. It possessed a standard fitting, the type that required a screw cap bulb. It would've taken little effort to remove the bulb and dispose of it. She scanned the kitchen for a bin, finally discovering one wedged between two small units. Placing her foot on the pedal, she popped the lid. It was empty, and there was no bag inside. As ever, SOCOs had been thorough. They'd have to call them to see if a light bulb had been discovered amongst its contents.

Stipes stepped up beside her. Until now he'd remained silent, allowing them both to gain an objective interpretation of the scene. Now it was time to share those thoughts. "What're you thinking, Guv?"

Rose arched her neck, raising her head to the smooth cream ceiling. "I'm thinking the killer was someone Mrs. Sampson knew. Or at least knew *of*. She lets them in and probably leads them through to the lounge." She walked forward, leading the way to a large room situated almost directly opposite the kitchen. It was tastefully decorated in rich reds and browns and had a cozy ambience that radiated comfort and warmth. "They talk, perhaps regarding the reason for the visit, and the killer excuses themselves for a few minutes, probably on the pretense of using the bathroom. But instead they head to the kitchen and remove the light bulb; either that or the light bulb simply slipped from its casing and has no relevance whatsoever. Maybe we'll never be able to answer that conclusively. Anyway, when the victim later offers to make a cup of tea, they seize the opportunity to follow her out and...." The end of the sentence eluded her. They still weren't certain what had happened next.

There was a moment of silence which Stipes soon broke. "So we're definitely ruling out an intruder?"

"We can't totally rule it out. At least not until we have all the evidence. But the signs *do* point to the killer having been someone the victim knew." Rose leaned back on her heels, silently surveying the room. "There appears to have been little resistance. I know the victim was elderly, but you'd still expect to see at least *some* sign of a struggle. Plus, the burglar alarm wasn't disabled. Then there's the light bulb. If the killer *had* already planned to kill her in the kitchen, it's likely they knew the house's layout."

Stipes shook his head, which immediately set alarm bells ringing.

"What is it?"

"I'm not sure. Something just doesn't feel right. This whole light bulb thing...."

Rose was glad she wasn't the only one who had an obsession with the anomaly.

"What if the killer had a way of disabling the alarm? In this day and age, it wouldn't be difficult to access the technology. And we already know he or she was clever enough to tamper with the security cameras." Stipes stared through the large bay window into the quiet street beyond. "If the killer *had* been invited in, why kill her in the kitchen? Why not kill her in the hallway? Or the lounge? Surely the most likely scenario is that the killer was already in the house. They could've removed the bulb and lain in wait. There'd be little disruption because they'd have utilized the element of surprise. The victim wouldn't have known what hit her."

Rose nodded. It was a valid explanation, particularly as Mrs. Sampson had been seen leaving the house earlier that evening, and there was no footage of her returning. They could check the alarm's usage with the security company, but evidence of tampering was often difficult to prove. She looked around the room for inspiration but found none. "I guess it's possible. It would've achieved the same end result. Perhaps we should focus on looking for motive for the time being."

A search of the downstairs proved fruitless. Other than the usual extraneous artefacts amassed throughout the victim's lifetime, there was nothing that might help them resolve what had taken place. A search of the upstairs proved similarly unrewarding, until Stipes discovered a small wooden box in the bottom of Mrs. Sampson's wardrobe.

On initial glance, it appeared to possess a compilation of files. Stipes ran his eyes along the first of the neatly typed papers. It looked like some kind of medical itinerary. But other than name, date of birth, and a list of unticked medical conditions, it contained very little. He scanned furtively through the others, ten in total. Each subject was female and appeared to have been pregnant at the time the file was created.

He lifted the box onto the bed and Rose stepped up alongside him. There were no contact details or dates on the files. They'd probably been created years ago, when Mrs. Sampson had been at the height of her career.

"What do you think, Guv? Ex patients?" He looked relieved to have found something.

Rose leaned forward and picked up one of the files. "More than likely. As an obstetrician, Mrs. Sampson probably cared for scores of pregnant women. The question is, what made these unique?"

Stipes shrugged. "Perhaps they were special to her."

"But how?"

Rose scanned the documents again. At face value they contained nothing remarkable. It looked like Mrs. Sampson had created them herself, perhaps as a reminder of particular cases or achievements. She placed them back in the box. With any luck, further research would reveal something their initial analysis couldn't.

When they were finally finished with the property, Rose led the way to the small out- building to the side of the driveway. They couldn't find a key to open the padlock, but finally it yielded to Stipes's sheer brute force. At the end of the day, most things did.

Once the padlock was removed, they stepped back to examine the building's contents. It was pretty much as Rose had anticipated. The walls were lined with garden tools and other practical implements, and there was a long oak table containing a selection of hacksaws. At some point, they'd probably been used in the preparation of logs for the wood burner she'd noticed earlier.

She stepped inside. The building was full of insects and cobwebs and had the musty smell of a space rarely used. Mrs. Sampson had probably taken to buying her logs prepared these days. Rose added another item to her "to do" list. If the logs *had* been delivered, they needed details of the delivery company she'd used. After all, they'd have had regular access to the property *and* its owner.

She took another step forward. A small box on the floor in the building's far corner caught her eye. At first glance it looked remarkably similar to the one Stipes had found in the bedroom, and she wondered if it might contain more files. She moved towards it, crouching down to remove the lid. Her fingers were trembling, and she took a deep breath to help steady them.

When she'd finally removed the lid and placed it on the floor, she leaned forward and peered inside. The box contained numerous cassettes identical to the ones Stipes had removed from the cameras. She glanced up at her partner. If they were what they appeared to be, they *could* contain valuable footage of comings and goings to the Sampson house in recent months. They might even possess footage of the killer. She pulled herself up and continued her search, resolving to take the box with her when they left.

Despite their successes in the house and out-building, a third accomplishment wasn't to be. A knock on the door of number eight revealed that the neighbor, a middle-aged widower named Ms. Andrea Mills, wasn't home. Rose stepped from the doorway, pausing to glance through the large front window. It was partially obscured by thick net curtains, and she could barely see more than three feet inside. Still, there were no signs of movement. Perhaps the stress of the morning's events had proven too much for Mills and she'd chosen to take temporary respite with a friend or relative. Rose just hoped she'd followed instructions and notified the station.

With their time in Amber Court momentarily at an end, Rose suggested a visit to the pathology lab. There was a chance the pathologist might have something by now, even if it wasn't conclusive. Stipes tossed the box of tapes onto the car's rear seat, and they both climbed in out of the hostile weather.

CHAPTER FIVE

It was ten minutes to eleven when they reached their destination. The pathology lab was a surprisingly modern-looking building, with a façade consisting almost entirely of glass. Rose supposed it was appropriate for a team that operated at the forefront of science, even if it *did* briefly house dead bodies. She found a space in the parking lot and they stepped out into the blustery air.

When they arrived at the building's entrance they were greeted by a tall, middle-aged receptionist, who, after phoning the pathologist, led them down a narrow corridor to a spacious autopsy suite. Rose peered through the wide glass door. The pathologist appeared to be cleaning up. She noted the polished surfaces and immaculate stainless-steel bowls. They brought to her mind images of severed body parts and displaced organs. She shook them off before she started feeling queasy again. The receptionist left, and she knocked on the door.

Dr. Malcolm Weller was a short, stocky man with a full head of chestnut brown hair and unusually long arms. Rose had often wondered if they aided in the undertaking of his professional duties. Though on reflection, she couldn't imagine how. Weller stepped towards them, wiping his hands in a huge paper towel.

"Good morning, detectives."

Rose walked forward. On the outside she was smiling, but on the inside her stomach was churning like butter. "Good morning, Dr. Weller. I'm sure you know why we're here."

"Indeed. Mrs. Elise Sampson. I've literally just finished her post mortem...an unusual case."

He tossed the paper towel into a large stainless-steel bin and Rose felt her spine tingle. "Unusual in what way?"

"Well, when I first opened her up, there appeared to be nothing out of the ordinary. I removed the organs and, after examining the heart, I almost recorded cause of death as a simple case of heart failure due to cardiac arrest. Not an unusual symptom for an elderly lady who was under attack. That was before I noticed the tiny puncture wound at the back of her neck. It was so minute, I almost missed it."

Rose shot a glance at her partner. Just when they seemed to be making progress, something had arisen to throw a spanner in the works. "So she was injected with something?"

The doctor nodded, causing a thick flap of hair to fall onto his forehead. He pushed it away. "It appears so. Though, at the moment, I have no idea with what. There was no residue left on the surrounding skin, and there appear to have been no visible side effects."

Rose felt a surge of optimism. "So the puncture wound could be unrelated?"

"It's unlikely. It's fresh, and its location would've made it very difficult for the victim to have made it herself."

Rose ran a finger along the arch of her brow, a habit she'd adopted to help her think straight. "What if she had someone who came in and injected her? Say, with something she was prescribed." She hadn't seen a copy of the victim's medical report yet.

"Again, it's unlikely. I can't think of anything that would need to be injected in that area. Plus, most prescribed drugs would leave some trace, even something as innocuous as smell. And I managed to access her medical records. She was remarkably healthy for a woman of her age."

"And it's definitely a needle mark, as opposed to something she might've done by accident?"

"It's definitely a needle mark."

There was a moment of silence while they all considered the implications of the doctor's find. It was Stipes who broke it.

"So what happens now?"

"I'm submitting blood, bile, and urine samples for analysis. Some tests will take longer than others, but I'm hoping to have the first few back by the end of the day. A guy down at the lab owes me a favor. I'll call you as soon as I have something."

Rose shuffled her feet against the smooth tiled floor. This case was getting more complicated by the minute. "So just let me just clarify things. Are you telling us you're not *sure* if the victim died of heart failure?"

Weller appeared to suppress a smile that pushed at his lips. "The victim died of heart failure. It's what precipitated it that I'd like to establish."

A middle-aged man wearing what appeared to be a cleaner's uniform poked his head around the door. Weller ushered him away.

Rose stepped forward slightly. "Is that why you were reluctant to comment on cause of death at the scene?"

The doctor sighed. "As I said, I didn't notice the puncture wound until I had her on the table. I was reluctant to comment on cause of death at the scene because, to put it bluntly, I wasn't sure how she'd died."

Rose fiddled with the mobile in her pocket. She couldn't

help feeling she was missing something, but she had no idea what. "What about the head wound? Might that have been a contributory factor?"

Weller stepped back, placing his hands on his hips like a petulant child. "Are you telling me how to do my job now, Detective?"

Rose held up her hands in apology. "I'm sorry. I'm just trying to figure out what happened."

"As am I. The head wound would've caused severe problems, essentially due to loss of blood. But there was no hemorrhaging, so it wasn't what killed her. Let's run the tests and see what comes up."

Rose turned to leave, then had second thoughts. "Is there anything else you can tell us? Anything at all?"

The doctor scratched his head. "I've confirmed the marks on her legs as finger marks, though unfortunately there are no prints. Her attacker must've worn gloves. Also, the nasty gash on her head is consistent with contact with a hard surface. Forensics have confirmed that the blood on the worktop was hers, so that fits with our assumption that she was grabbed from behind and her head hit it as she fell. As I stated earlier, the amount of blood left behind suggests that she was then held there for quite some time. Possibly to enable her attacker to perform the injection."

Again, a moment of silence prevailed. An image of the elderly Mrs. Samson being brutally attacked and tortured wasn't pleasant in anyone's books. Rose silently considered the implications. It was sounding more and more like a revenge killing. But revenge for what? Perhaps there was something in the old lady's past that had finally caught up with her. Perhaps it had something to do with the box of files Stipes had discovered. One thing was for sure...at the moment there were more questions than answers, and if they didn't start unravelling some of them soon, the media would be baying for their blood. Not to mention the chief. She sighed to herself. It was just her luck that her first assignment since her promotion was "unusual."

She thanked Weller, unable to keep the frustration from her voice, and headed back the way they'd come. What had begun as a godawful day was showing no sign of improvement, and her mood was steadily becoming blacker. Once back in the corridor, she took a long, deep breath. If nothing else, she was relieved to be free of the harsh chemical odors. She closed the door behind her. Stipes was waiting.

"Fancy a coffee, Guv? I spotted a machine on the way in."

The statement temporarily appeased her. "Stipes, you read my mind."

The coffee machine was ten meters or so along the corridor, positioned alongside a small seating area. Stipes reached into his pocket and pulled out a handful of change. Rose sat on one of the small blue seats. It was barely even lunchtime, yet already it felt much later. She fiddled with her hands on her lap.

"What the hell's going on here, Stipes? A little old lady murdered in her own home; and as if that's not enough, she was possibly drugged and tortured first."

If Stipes had heard her, he didn't comment. Instead he handed her a polystyrene cup and she placed her hands around it, absorbing its comforting warmth. But it didn't detract her from thinking aloud.

"We need to take a closer look at those files. There might be something in them that can tell us what Mrs. Sampson did to warrant such a brutal death. Who knows, one of the people in there *might* even be our killer."

Stipes turned his body to face her. "D'you really think we'll get that lucky?"

"Who knows? Something's got to turn up sooner or later. Let's just hope it's sooner, for everyone's sake."

CHAPTER SIX

When they got back to the incident room, only half the team was in situ. The other half was out gathering information. Rose walked inside and poured herself a cup of water from the dispenser. The coffee had left a sour taste in her mouth. Having downed the water, she turned to the remaining members. "So, what do we have so far?"

Sherman looked up from her computer screen, her face unusually flushed. "The victim had no significant medical conditions, Guv. There was nothing out of the ordinary in her financial records either. She was financially stable, with a healthy pension and a well-stocked savings account. She also had a couple of ISAs with a few thousand in each. She withdrew funds frugally, probably because she had a simple lifestyle. She had no mortgage and no visible debts. She rarely touched more than the pensions."

"How far did you go back?"

"Five years, like you asked."

"Go back another thirty."

"Guv?"

Rose thought back to the files Stipes had found in the victim's wardrobe. If one of the individuals listed there *was* their killer,

41

Mrs. Sampson's transgression could've occurred years ago.

She took a deep breath. "We have reason to believe that, as we suspected, this might've been a revenge attack. If that turns out to be the case, it *could* be related to something the victim did in her past. Possibly during her professional career." She explained the discovery of the files, and the pathologist's confusion as to cause of death.

Banks cut in. "Well, there were no cases of negligence brought against her. In her professional capacity or otherwise. So if she *did* do something to piss someone off, it was kept quiet."

Rose felt the hairs raise on the back of her neck. "And settled privately. But not necessarily amicably." She glanced at the murder board, which hadn't yet been updated with all the new information. "What about the will?"

Banks glanced at the paperwork on his desk. "She left everything to the NSPCC. I guess, since her husband was dead, and she had no children of her own, it was a natural choice. And there's something else."

Rose was all ears.

"She made quite a deal of dropping her title on retirement. She even redrafted the will to change it. Seems an unusual move for someone who should've been proud of their career."

Rose shrugged the fact off. "OK, well, that's unusual, but not unheard of. Is there anything yet on potential friends, ex-work colleagues, or relatives?"

Banks ran his thumb along the brink of his chin. "Reece is still out chasing that one. Apparently, there's an estranged sister, but she moved abroad years ago. Other than that, I think she was pretty much a loner."

Rose left Banks to his computer and turned to Willis, who appeared to be still trawling through the video tapes. "Any luck?"

He pushed a piece of paper across the desk towards her. "I'm still printing off images of all visitors to the property, and I've refined the ones you gave me. And guess what...I've found one who's in the system."

Rose picked up the paper and read the individual's details. "Mrs. Sampson's gardener?"

"It appears so. Though it doesn't look like she called on him very often. I'm halfway through the first month and he's only turned up once. But I've looked up the company, and they appear legit."

Rose studied the document again. Twenty-two year old Andrew Dyer had served a stint in a juvenile unit five years ago, when he was seventeen. Shoplifting and anti-social behavior were listed amongst his offenses, but there was nothing to indicate he'd ever been violent.

"Keep a special lookout for him during your observations, will you? See if he shows an unhealthy interest in the security cameras, or in any other area of the property."

Willis nodded. "Will do."

She placed the paper back on the desk. "What about any other CCTV?"

Willis wiped his brow as though the weight of the world was upon him. "There's one camera at the entrance to the street. I've arranged to collect the tapes later, but it'll take time to rule out the victim's visitors from anyone else going through, if it can be done at all. Most of the arrivals will be by car."

Rose shot him a sympathetic look. His was no doubt the most mundane of tasks. "OK, well, just keep hold of it for now. If you find anyone of interest on the Sampson tapes, we can go from there."

Willis nodded, and she headed back towards the murder board. The team was getting restless, clearly anxious to address their tasks. She cleared her throat. The water hadn't succeeded in quenching the taste of the coffee. "Is there anything else from Forensics yet? Or anything from the house to house?"

Again, it was Sherman who responded. "Not yet."

"OK, well, can you chase up Forensics? If they haven't got anything useable, it would be nice to know for certain. And can you find out if SOCO found a light bulb in the kitchen bin?"

Sherman reached for the phone on her desk, but a look from Rose stopped her in her tracks.

"What about the phone records?"

"She had no mobile, at least none that was listed, and she received very few calls. Most were just sales calls and the like."

"And outgoing calls?"

"There were a couple to her dentist and one to the chemist over the last month. She didn't really use it. Seems sad really. Like she was all alone, just waiting to die."

Rose ignored the comment. This wasn't the time for sentiment. "What about a computer?" She hadn't seen one during her search of the property, but that didn't mean Mrs. Sampson hadn't possessed one. She was an intelligent lady. Or at least she *had* been.

"Again, no sign of one, Guv."

Rose drifted away, leaving Sherman to the tasks she'd been set. Her mind was on the box of files Stipes was already beginning to go through. It would give them something to work on. Hopefully, since the individuals appeared to have been patients, it shouldn't be difficult to access their hospital records. Whether or not they still resided at their previous addresses was another matter…that was, if they were even still alive.

CHAPTER SEVEN

It wasn't until three hours later that Rose finally received a call from Doctor Weller. Both she and Stipes had been busy trying to attain the addresses of the seven surviving individuals in the box of files, none of whom had any visible reason to hold a grievance against the victim. They'd also begun attaining details of the individuals' families, insofar as they were able, along with their financial records and medical histories. Now it was time to set up appointments with the three they knew to still reside in the country, and to establish whether or not they'd had any contact with the former doctor in recent months. Only one of the women had so far proven elusive — a Miss Abigail Ross — but that was hardly surprising after such a long period of time.

Rose had headed into a small side room to take the doctor's call, more to avoid interruption than for privacy. She wanted to have this discussion with a clear head. Plus, she had questions she didn't want to forget. Now she sat with one leg crossed over the other, the side of her face pressed firmly against the phone's receiver.

"Good afternoon, Doctor. Do you have cause of death on the Sampson case yet?"

Weller cleared his throat. "Indeed, I do. I can tell you

conclusively that the victim's heart failure was induced by an unusually high dose of potassium chloride."

Rose shifted uneasily in her chair. "Potassium chloride? Isn't that a natural substance?"

"Yes. But so's marijuana, and so are many other drugs which, in large enough doses, can be just as lethal."

Rose felt her self-esteem shrink to the size of a pea. She tried to overcome it. "So can you tell me a bit about potassium chloride? So I can get an idea of why the killer might've chosen it."

The doctor took a sharp intake of breath. It was clearly audible through the phone line.

"Well, as you quite rightly point out, potassium chloride is a substance that occurs naturally within the environment. It's a form of mineral that is water and alkali soluble, and it can be found within a variety of mineral combinations. In addition to that, potassium is inherent within every cell of the human body. It's a necessary component, like salt. Occasionally people found to suffer with low potassium levels may be given small amounts of potassium chloride to replenish them." He paused for a moment and, when he spoke again, his tone of voice had dropped a few octaves. "However, taken in large doses, potassium chloride *can* be lethal, particularly if taken intravenously. This allows the chemical to bypass the digestive process and increases its potency…it's one of the three chemicals that form the lethal injection in executions. Its purpose, in that instance, being to stop the heart."

Rose carefully digested the doctor's words. "And have you come across anything like this before?"

"Not at all. This is the first case I've ever come across, thank heavens. Though the chemical *has* occasionally been linked to suicide, and I'm certain there've been many cases in the past where cause of death has simply been recorded as heart failure when, in actual fact, it was potassium chloride that caused the heart to fail. If it's not specifically tested for, it's virtually impossible to detect."

"So what made you test for it?"

There was a moment's silence before the doctor continued. "As it happens, I've just finished reading an article on it. If I hadn't, I may not have realized the significance of her raised potassium levels. Then again, I'd seen the needle mark, so her death was always suspicious."

Rose deliberated over her next question. "So if the needle mark was well enough hidden, potassium chloride *could* be described as the means to commit the perfect murder?"

The doctor sucked in a breath. "Yes. In fact, it *has* been referred to as such." He paused before continuing. "What we have to consider in this instance is that the killer's use of the chemical was unusual. He wasn't trying to pass the death off as natural causes, which would be the obvious reason for its use. If he had been, he wouldn't have initiated such a violent attack. No, in this instance the killer had no aspiration to create the perfect murder. In fact, I'm wondering why he used it at all. Another blow to the head would probably have finished the old lady off."

Rose felt a coldness ascend her spine. "So the injection didn't play a role in disabling her?"

"Not at all. The head wound would have done that."

Rose considered the implications of the doctor's last statement. If the injection hadn't been necessary, that put a whole different spin on things. She fiddled with the phone against her ear. "So are you saying the killer might've had a specific reason to use potassium chloride? That it might even have been symbolic?"

Weller made a loud tutting sound. He was clearly uncomfortable with where this was going. Finally, he added, "I'm simply stating the facts. I leave those assumptions to the likes of you."

Rose smiled. The doctor was being unusually modest. She pressed on. "So how does it work, this kind of poisoning? Would death have been instantaneous?"

Again, Weller coughed to clear his throat. Rose wondered if it was a habit he adopted in circumstances such as these.

"Unfortunately not. Death would've taken several minutes, and, during that time, the victim would've experienced severe pain. It's why it's the *third* of the chemicals used in the lethal injection. The other two possess anesthetic properties and induce muscle paralysis. In other words, they make the process more humane. To say that an overdose of potassium chloride alone would be unpleasant is an understatement."

"So the killer wanted Mrs. Sampson to suffer?" Rose shifted uneasily in her seat.

"He doesn't seem to have been averse to it. As I said, the victim would've been in considerable pain before her heart finally stopped."

Rose's mind drifted back to an image of the elderly lady, lying on the hard kitchen tiles of Six Amber Court, and her heart went out to her. She quickly brushed the feeling aside.

"OK, so just to sum up, the killer's use of potassium chloride in this instance was both uncommon and unnecessary. But it *was* what ultimately killed her."

"That's correct."

Again, a moment of silence prevailed as Rose went over the doctor's words in her mind. When she spoke again, she'd recovered her professional demeanor. "Is potassium chloride hard to get hold of?"

Weller's response was immediate. "Not necessarily. Most things are accessible these days on the World Wide Web. But the killer would need to know the exact quantity required to produce a lethal dose; and we have to bear in mind that this is not a chemical that's widely used or written about, at least for the purposes of murder. The average Joe wouldn't bother with something so ambiguous. Most people probably aren't even familiar with its properties."

Rose knew *she* wasn't. "So the killer is likely to have had some knowledge of the chemical?"

The doctor sighed. "Now you're putting words into my mouth. I'm not saying that at all. As I said, there've been instances where it's been used before; and in those cases, the killer hasn't always been predisposed to it. What I'm suggesting, however, is that whoever injected it may have had a specific reason to use it."

Rose shook her head. Frustration was gnawing away at her like rats at a cable. When she'd suggested earlier that the killer might've had an agenda, Weller had brushed the idea aside.

She leaned back in the hard metal chair and raised her eyes to the ceiling. Doctors had a knack of delivering responses without actually saying anything. She tried to get a handle on what that reason might have been. Perhaps its significance lay in its relationship with the lethal injection and with the notion of justice, though they'd found nothing in the files or anywhere else to suggest that Mrs. Sampson had actually sinned. She searched her mind for a way to get something more from Weller but found nothing. Finally, she gave up.

"Thank you, Doctor. If I need anything further, I'll call you back."

Weller sucked in another breath, clearly relieved that their conversation was ending. "Sure. I'll have the report sent over to you as soon as I get it typed up."

When she finally returned to the incident room, Rose was pleased to discover that both Reece and Blake had returned from their travels, having attained sufficient information to have made their absence worthwhile. After a brief catch-up, she headed to the murder board, which had recently been updated.

"OK guys, listen up. I've just had the pathologist on the phone, and we finally have the full low down on how Mrs. Sampson died."

She explained the killer's use of potassium chloride, a slow and tortuous method of inducing a cardiac arrest and, by all accounts, one of the most painful ways to die. She also explained the use of potassium chloride in the lethal injection.

Banks leaned forward in his chair. "What I don't understand is why the killer made things unnecessarily complicated. I mean, Mrs. Sampson was an elderly lady. It wouldn't have taken much to kill her. Why the need for all the drama?"

Rose was glad he'd come to the point. "That's exactly what we need to find out. It's possible that the mode of death had some significance for the killer. And, since potassium chloride is used in the lethal injection, perhaps this was some kind of private execution."

She let the theory hang in the air. It was Sherman who chose to drag it back down.

"Are we still going with the theory that the killer was someone the victim knew?"

Rose fiddled with a stray lock of hair. "Either that or someone she'd pissed off in her professional capacity. So we need to run thorough checks on any acquaintances, neighbors, and ex work colleagues Reece can come up with, and any others we can ascertain. Plus, we need to identify all the people on the video tapes. Stipes and I will check out those in the files. It appears that Mrs. Sampson didn't have any regular routines. The neighbors rarely saw her. So it's unlikely the killer was someone she'd made contact with socially. Did you get anything back from Forensics?"

Sherman lowered her eyes to the table. "I'm afraid not.

Nothing useable."

"And the light bulb?"

"SOCOs *did* find a light bulb in the kitchen bin. It was a screw top which matched the kitchen fitting, and it was still working, so it hadn't blown."

At least that answered one question. Or did it? There was still the possibility that it'd fallen of its own accord.

"And there were no prints?" Rose already knew the answer.

"Nothing, Guv."

The sound of a mobile ringing disrupted proceedings and Reece shot a hand into the pocket of his rucksack. Rose tried to ignore it.

"OK, well, Blake has ruled out any connection between the Sampsons and the development of the Dahlia project, so there appears to be nothing worth chasing up there. And the lack of any significant withdrawals from the victim's bank account appears to rule out blackmail. So we're back to the drawing board, and to good old fashioned interviews. Hopefully Willis will have some luck with the tapes."

She glanced across at Willis, who still had one hand on his computer mouse. He showed no sign of any such breakthrough yet. She turned her attention back to the briefing.

"The chief will be issuing a press release later today, meaning it's likely we'll be getting more media interest, which isn't going to help us. So, as I said before, we need to be as discreet as possible. Keep all inquiries on a personal level; don't use a squad car unless you have to, and only distribute information on a need to know basis. If you have anything come up, anything at all, let me know ASAP."

When she was done, Rose walked back to her desk and raised her eyes to the one small window. The day was drawing to a close and, so far, there was no sign of a suspect. A dull ache descended in the pit of her stomach. The first forty-eight hours of any investigation were crucial. After that, it would be harder to decipher any tracks the killer may have left behind.

She ran a finger along the arch of her brow, wondering if there was anything she could've done differently. There wasn't, she was sure of it. This case was just destined to be complicated. It had layers that delved deep below its surface, but once they'd been exposed, she was certain that a logical pattern lay beneath.

Her eyes fell on the box of files. Stipes had already arranged appointments with the three individuals who were still in the country. Fortunately, they all still lived locally, so logistically, things couldn't be better. The problem was, she wouldn't get to meet them until tomorrow at the very earliest, a detail that did little to ease her frustration.

She folded her legs beneath the narrow chair. All she could do now was re-examine the information they had so far. She fiddled with the growing pile of paperwork on her desk. It wasn't necessarily a bad thing. Sometimes a second look yielded details that hadn't been delved deeply enough into the first time around. She drummed her fingers against the cluttered desk. If only she had more to go on.

A thought struck her, and she twisted in her chair. "Willis, can you get me copies of those tapes? I'd like to take another look myself."

Willis shot her a look that said, "You're wasting your time." Nevertheless, he rose from his seat and began fumbling with the wires on his desk. "Sure thing, Guv. Just give me ten minutes… but just to warn you, there's a lot of tape."

CHAPTER EIGHT

Three Violet Crescent stood in total darkness as Zack Finlay approached from the road. He halted his four by four barely three meters from the property's front door and jumped out onto the smooth concrete drive. As his boots clipped noisily against the solid surface, his whole body quivered with relief. It'd been a long day, and he craved the peace and quiet of an empty house; that and the uncomplicated solitude of his own company.

He closed the car door behind him and switched on the central locking. A moist cloud erupted from his mouth as the cold air mingled with his warm breath. It made him shudder. He thought back to a time when he'd been quite fond of the cold. Even the harshest of winters had never bothered him. But now it was different. Since he'd turned sixty, it seemed to seep into his very bones, chilling his body to the core.

He headed for the door, unfolding his arms to remove the keys from his pocket. He plunged the largest of the bunch into the lock, twisting it in a counter-clockwise direction, and a few seconds later, the door lurched forward.

Once inside the foyer, Finlay reached for the light switch. Nothing. Either the bulb had gone, or the circuit breaker had tripped. He cursed himself for having purchased such a sensitive system. If it *was* the circuit breaker at fault, it'd be the second time this month he'd had to reset it. The first time had cost him a whole freezer full of food.

He stepped forward. The darkness was so intense, it was a struggle to find the next light switch. When he finally located it, he pressed it on. Again, nothing happened. It *had* to be the circuit breaker.

For the first time since his arrival, Finlay almost regretted coming home. He brushed the thought aside. Switching the power back on was hardly a big deal. It wasn't as if he was in any hurry. And once it was done, he'd put his feet up and relax with a nice cool beer. He had a case in the car, straight from the chiller of the local mini-mart.

The circuit breaker was in a small cupboard just off the hallway and, as on the previous occasions, Finlay hadn't brought a flashlight. He scolded himself for the oversight, reaching into his pocket for his mobile. The light it emitted wasn't great, but it was enough to help him negotiate his path along the hallway. He raised it up, his arm outstretched as though he were carrying an Olympic baton.

Shapes altered, and shadows shimmered beneath the phone's flickering light. Finlay squinted his eyes, unused to seeing such a distorted version of his sanctuary. It was strange how different things looked in the dark. It was as if he'd stepped into another world, one infinitely more sinister and complex than his own.

He'd barely made it a few steps from the door when something caught his attention…a sign of movement in the lounge to his right. At first it was nothing more than a brief flicker in the corner of his eye, but its significance seemed to grow. He stepped towards it. He couldn't be sure that it wasn't the darkness playing tricks on him. Then there it was again. A distinct shift in the shadows.

He stepped closer, the phone trembling in his hand. Its light

54

wasn't strong enough to illuminate what he wanted to see, so he continued on, his movements slow and shaky. Every nerve in his body was tingling, and his heart was beating so fast he had to take deep breaths to slow it.

In the few seconds it took him to enter the room, Finlay considered using the phone to dial for help, then decided against it. After all, it probably *was* just the darkness playing tricks on him. That or a stray cat that had smuggled its way in during his last visit. It wouldn't be the first time. Nevertheless, he moved tentatively, half expecting some ghostly apparition to leap out at any moment.

When the shadows finally lifted, and he realized that the source of his curiosity was a figure, Finlay momentarily froze. Its identity was too hazy to make out, its features still cloaked in darkness. But its presence in the room was unmistakable. It filled the modest space with the vile, cloying essence of evil.

Finlay halted in his tracks, uncertain how to proceed. His limbs felt like lead, and he was breathless and vulnerable. He opened his mouth to speak, but nothing came out. Then, in the blink of an eye, the figure had dissolved back into the darkness.

Confusion flooded Finlay's veins. He twisted his head this way and that, unsure if what he had seen was real or if it had simply been the figment of his imagination. When the figure didn't re-appear, he turned to retreat, but his legs wouldn't move fast enough. It was as if he were trapped in a murky void and he couldn't break free. He felt a presence behind him and an icy draught grazed the back of his neck. Then a sudden sharp pain pierced the base of his skull, and a dense, overwhelming blackness consumed him.

CHAPTER NINE

When Rose opened her eyes that following morning, her eyelids felt heavy. Her sleep had been restless and sporadic, fractured by dreams of dark cloaked executioners armed with needles. She lay there for a moment, silently contemplating the day ahead. It was still dark outside. The first flash of early morning light hadn't yet filtered through the thin beige curtains, and not a sound arose from the street below.

Her alarm sounded, and she reached out to stop it, the palm of her hand striking its icy surface. The coldness startled her, and she shuddered, collapsing back into the soft pillow. It was at times like this that she could almost forget the horrors that taunted her daily life. Not that the reprieve ever lasted long.

She closed her eyes again, reveling in the magic of early morning. This was her favorite time of day, probably the only time she ever felt free of the pressures of her job. She lifted her eyelids, savoring the comfort of her warm, double bed.

A horn beeped somewhere outside, and Rose's mind drifted to her choice of vocation. It was just as well she'd become firmly wedded to her career. What man on earth would want to live with someone so unnervingly familiar with death? Not to mention a hopeless insomniac, who found it impossible to separate her personal life from her professional one. If she wasn't actively investigating a murder, she was dreaming about one.

The thought made her giggle, and she realized it was the first time she'd done that in a long while. She tried to hang on to that feeling, just long enough to feel revitalized. Then memories of the previous day washed over her, and a tortuous weight pushed heavily against her chest, restricting her breathing and casting a thick black shadow over all thoughts of the day ahead.

She placed a hand at the nape of her neck. She hadn't found anything remarkable in her brief look through the surveillance tapes yesterday. As hadn't Willis. Gradually all the visitors were being identified, though none of their visits appeared suspicious. Not that the arrival of a killer would exactly scream "It's me! I'm the one you're looking for!" What they needed was a witness, someone who might have inadvertently seen Mrs. Sampson's deadly visitor without realizing it. But as yet, no one had come forward.

Her attention shifted to Stipes's theory. It had taken her a while to get hold of the security company, and when she had, they'd informed her that there was no evidence of the system having been tampered with. However, according to Willis, that wasn't necessarily proof that tampering hadn't taken place. In the modern-day world of new technology, many hackers could operate with virtually no visible footprint, especially in cases where the systems weren't exactly state of the art. The security company *did*, however, possess back-ups of the surveillance tapes, a fact that could prove useful if the box of tapes they'd found in the out-building proved to be unreadable.

She rose from her bed and headed to the shower, her earlier enthusiasm having already evaporated.

Thirty minutes later, when she finally reached the office, Rose was surprised to find Stipes already there. His clean white shirt looked immaculately starched, and he seemed surprisingly fresh for a man who'd worked late into the evening. She wondered how early he'd arrived. It was still only a little after seven, and two polystyrene cups already littered the desk beside him. If he wasn't careful, he'd become as much of a workaholic as she was.

She shrugged her shoulders and stepped inside. Stipes was staring at the murder board, as if somehow it might yield the answers he was looking for. He was so immersed in thought he didn't even notice her come in. When he finally realized she was there, he clutched his chest as though he were having a heart attack.

"Jesus Christ, Guv. I didn't hear you come in."

His reaction made Rose laugh for the second time that morning. She leaned forward, tapping her partner firmly on the back. "Christ Stipes. If you can't even sense *me*, what kind of a detective are you?"

All joking aside, Rose walked to the coffee machine to pour herself a drink. As she did so, a thought struck her. If the killer *had* somehow managed to gain entry when the victim was out, how could they have known when she'd be back? Or had they been content to simply lie in wait, for however long it took? It seemed a very haphazard way of carrying out something that appeared to have been so meticulously planned. Also, how did they know for certain that she'd return alone? Or that the gardener or a cleaner didn't have access to the property?

There were too many variables for the killer not to have done their research. They could've been stalking Mrs. Sampson for months and, even if they'd never actually met her, they could've surveyed her activities from afar, memorizing her routines and assessing any acquaintances. Rose fiddled with the coffee in her hand. It was time the neighbors were questioned again. The killer might not have been an infrequent visitor to the neighborhood after all. He or she could well have become a familiar fixture.

She was about to put her thoughts to Stipes when her mobile sounded in her trouser pocket. She placed the coffee cup on the table beside her and pulled it out. "DI Rose."

The caller was an officer from uniform. She pushed the phone closer to her ear, though, a few seconds later, she wished she hadn't.

"Guv. There's been another murder."

Rose physically felt her heart sink. It was enough that she already had one of the most complicated cases this year to deal with. But another murder? It felt as though she was being deliberately targeted, if only by fate itself. She digested the details and placed the mobile back in her pocket.

Stipes was sitting at his desk, silently perusing a file from the box. No doubt in preparation for their forthcoming meetings.

Rose walked over to where he sat and leaned her elbows on the desk's sticky surface. "There's been another murder. We need to go."

Stipes looked up from the paper, but the significance of what she was saying didn't seem to register. She leaned in closer, mouthing the words as though she were addressing a child.

"Stipes. Let's go."

CHAPTER TEN

When they got to Violet Crescent, it was easy to see where the incident had occurred. Two squad cars took pride of place at the property's periphery, their blue flashing lights piercing the air like warning flares. Rose smiled to herself. It was amazing how fast the troops could mobilize when the department's reputation was at stake.

She found a parking space opposite the house and pulled into it. Again, once parked, she reached into the glove box for boot covers and gloves and handed a set of each to Stipes. They'd barely spoken during the fifteen minute journey. The implications of another murder in Brackley weighed heavily on both their minds, and not just because of the political implications. She took a deep breath and opened the door into the busy street.

The moment she stepped outside, a blast of freezing air struck her in the face with the intensity of mini tornado. She raised the collar of her jacket, lowering her head to the dull grey pavement. If it wasn't the job working against her, it was the weather. She quickened her pace, skillfully negotiating the clusters of icy puddles that lined her way.

When they were few meters from the property's boundary, Rose noticed Weller's distinctive white van standing at the roadside and cursed under her breath. Whoever was distributing information had their priorities back to front. Didn't they realize that a scene needed to be thoroughly analyzed before the world and its dog traipsed through it?

She stopped a uniformed officer as he was heading for the doorway. He wasn't a member of her team, but he was familiar nonetheless.

"Any info on the victim?"

The officer nodded. "Sixty year old man living alone. At the moment that's all we have."

"Do we know who called it in?"

"Anonymous tip-off…. Sorry, that's all I know."

The officer turned to walk off and Rose grabbed him by the shoulder. "Do we know if it was a man or woman…the caller?"

This time the officer merely shook his head. "Sorry, Guv."

"And when was the call received?"

"Sometime within the last hour. At least that's what I was told."

Rose left the officer to go about his business and continued toward the house. When she reached the front door, nothing seemed particularly unusual. Apart from the presence of a few over-zealous police officers, there were no obvious signs of an intrusion. Nothing to indicate that anything out of the ordinary had occurred. She shot a glance at Stipes as details of the Sampson case replayed in her mind. If there was the slightest possibility that the murders were connected….

She shook the thought off and stepped into a narrow hallway. If the killer's tactics bore any resemblance to that of the Sampson case, the scene of the crime certainly didn't. The house was small and compact, with a series of tall oak doors that led off a narrow hallway. The first of these was open, and the sounds of voices resonated through its thin plasterboard walls.

For the second time, Rose stopped a passing officer. "Can you tell me how the killer got in?"

The young man, probably in his early twenties, turned to face her. "There was a loose pane of glass in the door out the back. It wouldn't have been hard for someone to slide it out and climb through."

Rose stepped back slightly. Something in his reply bothered her, but she wasn't quite sure what it was. She brushed it aside. "Had it been replaced when you got here?"

The officer shrugged. "If you could call it that. But whoever removed it didn't take the time to secure it back properly. It was virtually hanging off."

Rose considered the killer's mode of entry. Unlike the Sampson case, he or she had made their means of access clear. But how was that relevant? She returned her attention back to the officer. "Has it been secured now?"

"No, we thought you might want to see it. But we've positioned someone out there. There *is* something else though."

Rose felt her stomach tense. She nodded for him to continue.

"The fuse has been removed from the circuit breaker."

It was certainly more sophisticated than removing a light bulb. The officer turned to walk away, and Rose shouted after him. "Are there any signs of burglary?"

He turned his head but didn't stop. "There's nothing obvious. But that doesn't mean nothing was taken."

Rose nodded, and the officer passed. Stipes followed her through the open door to a modest sized lounge, decorated in an unflattering shade of green. It clashed vehemently with the dark red of the hallway, but she barely noticed, instead focusing her attention on the industrious Dr. Weller. As on their previous encounter, he was seated on the floor, crouched over the victim like a tiger stalking its prey. He looked up before she had a chance to surprise him.

"Good morning, detectives." It was his standard greeting line. "Who knew I'd be running into you again so soon?"

Rose stifled the smile that pushed against her lips. "Not meaning to sound rude, Doctor, but it's hardly through choice." She stepped further inside, surveying the sparse living area. It was clear to see that the victim had been a man living alone. Other than a couple of bowling trophies and a large framed photo of some footballer whose identity was unknown to her, there were virtually no adornments. The long window sill was empty, as was the narrow teak mantle above the fireplace. She turned back to Weller. "So what have you got for us?"

Again, Weller looked up from his endeavors. In the harsh morning light, she could see that the wrinkles on his forehead had advanced into deep, penetrating grooves, and dark red patches encircled the skin beneath his eyes. They were no doubt symptoms of his demanding vocation.

Weller cleared his throat, apparently oblivious to her train of thought. "Well, as you can see, the victim suffered a nasty blow to the head."

He pointed to a large laceration barely two inches from the base of the victim's skull. The blood around it had long since congealed, though not before it had spread to the thin beige carpet. A thick pool of blood had matted its fibers, coating it in a thick, sticky resin, which would probably never come out.

Rose stood back to examine the body in its entirety. The victim was lying face down, his arms tucked beneath his body as though he'd made no attempt to break his fall. Presumably the blow had rendered him unconscious. The similarity to the Sampson case was striking.

"And that was what killed him?"

The doctor waited a moment before answering. "I'd like to

say that was the case."

His response sent a shiver through Rose's body. "Excuse me?"

"Well, if it wasn't for this needle mark at the back of his neck...."

A sudden dull ache invaded the base of Rose's spine. It gradually ascended to her collar bone, causing the hairs at the back of her neck to prickle. Her eyes followed Weller's hand, which led her to a tiny indentation just above the victim's shirt collar. It was so small, if he hadn't pointed it out, she would never have noticed it.

"Shit." The obscenity slipped out before she had chance to sensor it. "Is this the same as the other one?"

The doctor eyed her with seemingly mild amusement. "Two bodies with needle marks to the back of the neck? It's not exactly common, is it? I'll have to run tests to know for sure, but I'd stake my career on it."

Rose shot a glance at Stipes, who was barely a foot away from her. He had the same banal expression he'd had at the pathology lab, when Weller had labelled cause of death of the first victim "unusual." Sometimes she wished he was easier to read. She asked the first question that entered her head. "How soon can you do the post mortem?"

Weller sighed. "I may not be able to do the full post until later today. I've got a couple of urgent cases already pending. But I'll run a test for potassium chloride ASAP and get back to you with my findings. It shouldn't take too long."

Rose stepped away. It was the best they were going to get. Besides, they had their first appointment with one of the women in the box of files in just over thirty minutes, and the address was a good twenty minute drive away. She reached the door, then turned back around.

"Anything on time of death?"

This time the doctor didn't look up. "I'd put it at somewhere between seven and nine yesterday evening."

For a moment, Rose stood rooted to the spot. A heavy weight clutched at her chest, restricting her airflow and preventing her from getting her words out. When it finally subsided, her voice sounded croaky. "Sorry?"

"Between seven and nine yesterday evening."

The doctor's words were deliberately slow and calculated. Rose digested them again. "Then how come a disturbance was reported this morning?"

"I've absolutely no idea. That's not within my remit, I'm afraid."

After a quick search of the rest of the house, Rose examined the loose pane of glass in Sampson's back door and headed outside. As she stepped onto the smooth concrete drive, a blast of wind struck her square in the face. Still, she'd never been so pleased to inhale the freezing December air. Beads of sweat were trickling from her forehead, and she felt as though her head were about to explode.

Stipes echoed the words that resounded inside of her. "What the hell's going on, Guv?"

She lifted the collar of her jacket, raising her face to the pale winter sky. "God knows. But if we don't get a handle on it soon, things are going to get difficult. Let's get to our appointment. It might give us something to work on. Besides, we have to wait for Weller to get back to us, and we both know how long that can take."

As they walked back up the narrow driveway, Rose's attention was drawn to the large black four by four hovering in front of them. She'd noticed it on her way in, but hadn't had time to stop and look, so now she stepped towards it. A member of the forensics team, who'd been carefully dusting for prints, moved aside as she tried to peer through the large, blacked out windows. "Do we know if this belonged to the victim?"

The blue clad woman continued spraying the driver's door handle for prints. "It does. We've run a check. It's registered to a Mr. Zack Finlay, the property's owner."

Rose stepped back. Even though she was still gloved, she was reluctant to contaminate anything. "Well, if you find anything in it, can you let us know ASAP?"

The woman merely nodded.

Rose turned back to Stipes, who was busy admiring the vehicle's immaculate black paintwork. "OK, let's go. We don't want to be late for our appointment."

CHAPTER ELEVEN

Although barely a stone's throw from the prestigious Dahlia development, Ivy Road seemed a million miles away from the palatial properties of Amber Court. Rose parked her car at the roadside and stared through the window at the rows of neatly lined terraced houses. The people who lived here probably worked hard, manual jobs, and they no doubt resented the likes of the Sampsons intruding on their hard-earned space. She removed the key from the ignition and, tucking it into her jacket pocket, stepped from the car. Stipes followed her out.

As their feet clipped noisily against the stony pavement, Rose thought of the woman they were about to meet, Mrs. Linda Frederickson. As might be expected after such a long period of time, hospital records on her were sparse. However, they'd established that Frederickson had one child, a boy, who, according to his birth records, would be twenty-eight now.

Together they headed toward number four and Rose continued through Frederickson's details in her mind. Frederickson had given birth at the same hospital Mrs. Sampson had been assigned to, so it seemed safe to assume that the obstetrician, formerly *Dr.* Sampson, had been her consultant at the time. It was the only scenario that made sense.

They ascended the property's narrow pathway and Rose knocked on the door. Mrs. Frederickson answered on the second knock. She was a small woman, in presence as well as in stature. She had short auburn hair infused with flecks of grey, and she wore a deep crimson blouse that matched the dark circles around her eyes. Rose stepped forward and both she and Stipes flashed their IDs. Rose placed hers back in her pocket, then held out her hand in greeting.

"Good morning, Mrs. Frederickson. I hope we're not putting you out."

The latter smiled, flashing an unusual set of crooked white dentures. Her hand was icy to the touch. She, too, stepped forward slightly. "Not at all, though I'm not sure how much help I'll be. I was told this was regarding an obstetrician I might have seen when I was pregnant with my son, and that was almost thirty years ago."

She stepped aside, signaling for the detectives to follow her into the narrow hallway. The moment they had, they found themselves veering left into a small, sparsely furnished lounge. The doorway was so low, Stipes had to duck his head so as not to hit it.

Walking inside gave Rose a sensation akin to that of stepping inside an ancient tomb. Aside from the light from a tiny lamp in the far right corner, the room was almost totally bathed in darkness, despite the fact that it was near on eight thirty and the curtains were fully open. She took a deep breath and forced her eyes to focus. Their host closed the door behind them and indicated a long beige sofa.

"Please...take a seat. Can I get you a cup of tea?"

Stipes opened his mouth to accept but Rose raised a hand to stop him. They couldn't afford to spend more time here than was necessary. They had two murders to investigate, and if her team didn't get an update from her soon, they'd begin to think she'd given up on them. She leaned forward in her chair. "That won't be necessary. We don't want to keep you any longer than we have to. We'd just like to ask you a few very quick questions."

Mrs. Frederickson sank into a small armchair opposite them. It had a head-sized dent in it...she clearly sat there a lot. Rose flashed her most empathic smile.

"I know all this must seem very strange to you, but we're investigating the death of a Mrs. Elise Sampson, a former obstetrician at St. Thomas's Hospital. The hospital I understand you were assigned to when you were pregnant with your son. You'd probably have known her as *Dr.* Sampson. She dropped the title upon retirement."

Mrs. Frederickson showed no reaction. Rose continued.

"Well, at Mrs. Sampson's home, we found a box of files containing brief details on a small number of individuals. Yours were amongst them. Have you any idea why that might be?"

Rose thought she detected a flicker of embarrassment cross the woman's face, but as soon as she'd noticed it, it was gone. Mrs. Frederickson raised a hand to her chin, furrowing her eyebrows in thought.

"No. I'm sorry. I have absolutely no idea. What kinds of details?"

"Oh, nothing personal. Name, date of birth, current address, that kind of thing; which is why we're here. You see, we're currently treating Mrs. Sampson's death as suspicious, and we're wondering if anyone in that box of files might've had contact with her in recent months."

It wasn't a lie, but it wasn't exactly true either. What she really wanted to establish was the significance of the files to Mrs. Sampson's death, if, indeed, there was any.

Mrs. Frederickson fiddled with the arm of the chair. She

looked edgy and nervous. Rose wondered why. "I see. But surely, if the people in the files were all previous patients, it's unlikely they'd have stayed in touch... Can I ask how this Dr. Sampson died?"

Rose looked her host in the eye. "I'm sorry, I'm afraid I'm not at liberty to divulge that information at present. All I can say is that it doesn't appear to have been natural causes. I don't suppose you've any idea why someone might've wanted her dead? Did you find any of her practices to be...unethical?"

Again, she thought she noticed a flicker of embarrassment cross Frederickson's face. But the latter masked it well. "To be honest, I don't even remember seeing a Dr. Sampson. Then again, it *was* a very long time ago. I suppose I wouldn't remember any of the doctors' names. I'd have no reason to. But I don't recall having felt awkward or uncomfortable with anyone, if that's what you're asking. Surely she'd have had more recent patients you could ask?"

Rose shook her head. "Mrs. Sampson's been retired for a long time. Besides, as I said, we're trying to establish why she kept the box of files."

Frederickson twisted in her chair, clawing at a small red patch on her forearm. Rose wondered if it was a nervous tic. She looked anxious and distracted, and when she spoke again, her voice was croaky. "Now, that really does seem odd. I presume we wouldn't have been her only patients?"

Rose retained eye contact. "Mrs. Sampson probably saw hundreds of patients throughout her career."

"I see."

Rose shot a glance at Stipes, who had his notebook at the ready but hadn't yet taken any notes. She pushed on. "Was there anything unusual about your pregnancy? There's not a great deal recorded on the system. Did you have any problems or complications? Anything at all that might've categorized your experience as unusual?"

Again, that hint of discomfort. "No, nothing. I'm sorry, I really don't think I can be of help. As I said, it was a very long time ago."

Rose shifted in her seat. All this to-ing and fro-ing was getting them nowhere. She decided to try a different tack. "Is your husband around? I wonder if he might remember anything."

Mrs. Frederickson looked visibly shaken. "My husband left early for work. But he wouldn't be able to tell you anything that I haven't told you. I usually went to my appointments alone. He probably never even saw...sorry, what did you say her name was?"

"Dr. Sampson."

"He probably never even saw Dr. Sampson." She pulled herself up from her armchair and smoothed out the creases in her long navy skirt. "I'm sorry, I'm actually in a bit of a hurry. So if there's nothing else...."

The detectives rose from the sofa. Suddenly Rose wondered if Mrs. Frederickson had intentionally picked this time slot, so that her husband wouldn't be around. She was definitely being cagey about something. Perhaps even her husband didn't know what it was. Whatever the case, she had the feeling there was more to be gained here than was currently being offered.

She reached the door, then turned back around. "I know it was a long time ago, but I don't suppose you have any paperwork relating to your pregnancy?"

Frederickson shot her a look that told her the answer would be no, even if she did have. "I'm afraid not. In those days, people didn't bother with sentimental keepsakes. You just had your baby and got on with it."

"And your son was your only pregnancy?"

"Yes. My husband and I weren't blessed with any other children."

"I see."

Rose entered the hallway, then stopped again. She was determined to have one last shot at uncovering what Frederickson was hiding. "You know, if there's something you're not telling us, and it turns out to be relevant, I could arrest you for withholding evidence."

This time her host didn't reply.

"Mrs. Frederickson?"

The latter seemed to shake herself back to reality. "I told you, there's nothing I can say that might help you."

"You can't, or you won't."

"I can't. Look, I really don't know what you want from me."

Rose decided to end the visit on an amicable note. At this stage of the investigation, she couldn't afford to be making enemies. "OK, well, thanks for your time. We appreciate it. And I'm sorry if it feels like we've been a bit hard on you today. But an old lady is dead, possibly murdered, and it's our job to follow every line of enquiry, however obscure. I'm sure you understand."

Mrs. Frederickson merely nodded before closing the door in her face.

When they were both back in the car, Rose turned to Stipes. "What do you think?"

Stipes fiddled with the buckle of his seat belt. "I think she's hiding something."

"Me too. What times our next appointment?"

"Not 'til two thirty."

"OK, let's get back to the station and see if anything's come in on the Finlay case yet. It's possible Sampson and Finlay were connected, and if that connection's not related to their mode of death, I'll eat my hat."

Stipes shot her a smile, flashing an immaculate set of straight white teeth. "You don't have a hat, Guv."

"Then I'll buy one."

CHAPTER TWELVE

While Rose and Stipes had been busy with Mrs. Frederickson, Banks, whom Stipes had spoken with on leaving Violet Crescent, had managed to trace one of Zack Finlay's estranged girlfriends; a former fashion model who now ran a column in Brackley's one and only gossip magazine, *The Brackley Voice*. She was fifty-three years old, and her name was Lucy Brannigan.

Seeing as Finlay had no living family, Brannigan appeared to be the closest thing he'd had to a relative, particularly as they'd engaged in brief periods of contact since their split almost five years ago. Uniform had been given Brannigan's name by one of Finlay's neighbors, who'd grown quite friendly with her, even remaining in touch with her after the split, if only sporadically. Banks was trying to arrange an informal interview with the former model.

Uniform still hadn't established what it was that Finlay had done for a living, though, according to his neighbors, he'd always left the house early in the morning, sometimes not returning for several days. Most had assumed he was some kind of salesman, due to the long hours he kept and the smart suits he wore. But none had ever broached the subject with him.

As for records, Finlay didn't appear to have an occupation

listed on any official documents. Being an only child, he'd inherited Three Violet Crescent from his deceased parents; and he had no credit cards or loans to his name. However, he appeared to possess a reasonably healthy bank balance. All of which was slowly leading Rose to one conclusion…Finlay was some kind of professional con-man.

When they finally got back to the incident room, most of Rose's team were in situ. Banks had even begun constructing a second murder board, and the gruesome photos of the deceased Zack Finlay already took pride of place at its center.

Rose poured herself a coffee from the drinks machine and took up her usual spot beside the board. It was fast becoming her default position. "OK, you've all heard the news by now." She cleared her throat and took a generous sip of the coffee. "We have a second murder victim with a severe head wound…and a tiny puncture wound to the back of his neck."

She hadn't divulged the last part of the sentence until now, for fear of a leak. One could never be sure that the phone lines weren't being tapped, or that there wasn't someone nearby listening in. There was an audible gasp, and she paused for a moment before continuing. "We're currently waiting on Weller to confirm whether or not this is another case of potassium chloride poisoning. But, seeing as though the circumstances are so similar, I think it's safe to assume that our two murder cases are very possibly connected." She cringed as she spoke the words aloud. The media was going to have a field day with this. "So we have to consider the possibility that Mrs. Sampson and Mr. Finlay may have crossed paths at some point." She turned to Banks. "Any luck with Finlay's ex-girlfriend?"

Banks fiddled with the papers on his desk. "She's coming in after work at four thirty. I don't think she liked the idea of us turning up at the mag."

Rose shook her head. She didn't give a damn what the woman liked or didn't like. If Brannigan had information pertaining to Zack Finlay's lifestyle, it was imperative that they attain it. *Now.* She shot Banks a thunderous look. "Four thirty? Have you forgotten this is a murder investigation? Why the hell didn't you threaten to pull her in? We need her here *now*!"

Banks flushed an unflattering shade of pink. It was the first time she'd seen him embarrassed, but she wasn't about to feel guilty. If he couldn't take the heat, he shouldn't be here.

Banks cleared his throat. "Sorry, Guv. But after everything you said about keeping things on the low, I didn't like to push it...after all, she *is* a journalist."

The portrayal made Rose smile. "A journalist? She's a gossip columnist, for heaven's sake! Get on that phone and get her here. *Now.*"

Banks picked up his mobile and left the room.

Rose turned to Reece. "What about Sampson's estranged sister? Any luck contacting her yet?"

After Banks's previous grilling, Reece looked nervous. "We're still trying to track her down. Records show she moved to Belgium over thirty years ago, but the trail goes cold after that."

Rose shook her head, frustration getting the better of her. "Well, keep pushing, will you? It's Belgium, not the other side of the world. For all we know, her reasons for moving *could've* been connected to what's going on now."

Reece nodded. "On it, Guv."

Rose turned back to face the rest of her team. "OK, in the meantime we need to keep reviewing the Sampson case, and follow any leads we get. If we actually *get* any. And we need to attain all the same information for the Finlay case. If it turns out they *are* connected, and I'd say the chances are pretty damn good, it could mean the killer will strike again. So we can't afford to leave any stone unturned." She took a moment to catch her breath. "Uniform has already begun house to house at Violet Crescent, and a full account of their findings should be here by lunchtime. But our inquiries don't end there. I want everyone with the slightest connection to Zack Finlay questioned. Friends, acquaintances...even the neighbors' fucking dogs if necessary. There has to be someone out there who can help us."

She thought back to the call that had alerted them to Violet Crescent. An anonymous tip-off reporting a disturbance. It had been made from a pay as you go phone, which had been disabled shortly after...meaning there was no way of tracking it. But why had the caller waited until morning to make the call? By that time any disturbance would have well and truly dissipated. So why not simply report a murder? This had led her to conclude that the caller was either the killer themselves or someone very close to them.

She voiced her concerns, adding, "So we need to find out who made that call, and why they waited until morning to do so. Whoever it was, they're probably in receipt of valuable information, and if they're not our killer, they *could* be in danger. Blake, can you take the lead on that?"

Blake acknowledged the task and she pressed on.

"Also, I'd like Mrs. Sampson's neighbors questioned again. Her murder was meticulous, so it's possible the killer did some research beforehand. If that *was* the case, the person we're looking for might not be a stranger to the area. But he or she might've shown an unhealthy interest in that particular property."

The briefing over, Rose retreated to her desk. Once there, she stretched out her legs and took a long, slow sip of her coffee. Thankfully it was still hot. Placing it down on the table in front of her, she thought back to the crime scene at Violet Crescent. There had to have been someone who'd heard or seen something. It was a quiet area, and it wasn't every day that a neighbor was brutally murdered just yards away.

She was about to look for Stipes when the door opened, and Willis's familiar face appeared around it. "Uniform has something they want you to see Guv. Its CCTV footage recovered from a camera at the rear of Violet Crescent."

Rose grabbed her coffee and followed him into the corridor.

Five minutes later, Rose sat staring at a large TV screen in a small back room of Brackley Police Station. The two officers who'd recovered the tapes sat on either side of her, with Willis and Stipes, who'd had the sense to follow her out of the incident room, taking up position at the rear.

After a few moments, a rear view of the properties in Violet Crescent appeared on the screen. Rose looked at the timeline in the bottom right corner…6:47 p.m. If the pathologist was right, it was almost within the time-frame of Finlay's death. One of the officers fast-forwarded the tape slightly and a small dark figure appeared in the garden of one of the houses.

"That's number three," the officer volunteered.

The five of them watched as the figure, as yet unidentifiable, skirted the property's boundary, finally winding up at the door with the loose panel.

Stipes leaned forward in his seat. "D'you think they're looking for a way in?"

Rose's eyes remained fixed on the screen. "Looks to me like they've already found it."

When it had reached its destination the figure crouched down, finally settling in a kneeling position. For a good few minutes it remained unmoving, until eventually it leaned forward and placed an object on the grass beside the door. Rose voiced her thoughts aloud.

"That has to be the glass panel."

The figure then stood up and walked back toward the property's boundary, bringing it closer to the camera. Rose squinted her eyes as though she were in the dimly lit garden herself. But the nearby streetlight was barely adequate to light the area in front of it, let alone add more detail to something a good nine or ten meters away.

After no more than ten seconds the figure turned again, and, for a few seconds, the individual stared directly into the camera.

Stipes audibly caught his breath. "Is that...?"

Rose was perched on the edge of her seat. "It looks like a woman. Does anyone else think it looks like a woman?"

The officer freeze-framed the shot. There was no denying the figure's petite frame and small stature. But dark, shapeless clothes and a lack of any facial definition made it impossible to determine gender with any certainty.

Willis cut in. "I don't know, Guv. I see some pretty skinny kids these days. Both male and female. I wouldn't like to hazard a guess without more to go on."

Rose had to agree. She stared more intently. A tight black hood fully encompassed the figure's head, making it impossible to determine hair style or color. She couldn't even establish skin tone. Again, she glanced at the timeline...six fifty-three. She wondered if Finlay had entered the street yet. According to the elderly couple across the street, his familiar four by four had ascended the driveway at around seven.

She nodded, and the officer continued the recording. The figure walked back towards the door, having undoubtedly checked the property's perimeter for potential witnesses. Once there, it crouched back down, and they watched as it gradually disappeared from sight, presumably through the hole made by the missing panel.

Rose leaned back in her seat. "That's the killer entering the property. It has to be. But how did they know when Finlay would return? According to the neighbors, he hadn't been around for a couple of days."

The question went unanswered and the officer began to slowly fast forward the recording. It wasn't until seven twenty-one that the figure re-emerged. No lights had been switched on within the property, indicating that the circuit breaker had probably been deactivated shortly after the killer's entry.

There was a moment of silence in the room, a shared recognition that they had probably just posthumously witnessed Finlay's time of death.

It was Stipes who broke it. "How come the killer didn't disable the security camera?"

Willis twisted in his seat. "Maybe they didn't know it was there. It *is* pretty well camouflaged by trees. Or maybe they thought it wasn't close enough to the property to be a threat."

A switch flicked on in Rose's head. "Could it be…a threat? Is there a chance you could get something from this?"

Willis stared intently at the screen. "I can give it a shot. Visual enhancement *is* pretty good these days. Then again, it's not good quality. Until I try, I really couldn't say."

Another thought struck Rose, and she turned in her seat. "If the killer *wasn't* aware of the camera, maybe Finlay's murder wasn't something they'd originally planned. Method of entry wasn't anywhere near as discreet as in the Sampson case, and his murder was nowhere near as brutal. Perhaps Finlay knew too much and wasn't about to keep quiet."

"In which case Finlay and Sampson might not have been connected," Willis was quick to add. "Finlay's connection *might've* been with the killer."

His words sent a chill along Rose's spine. If Finlay had no connection to Mrs. Sampson, finding the motive for the murders could be even harder than she'd anticipated. She let out a deep sigh. This case was growing more complicated by the second. Their only hope was to get something identifiable from the footage.

The officer controlling proceedings stood to switch off the TV. Willis followed suit, rising from his chair and stepping forward.

"I'll get to work on this ASAP. As I said, I can't promise anything. But I'll give it my best shot."

Rose nodded. That was all she could ask for. "Great. Even if we can't get a clear ID, we might get something good enough to release to the press. It's amazing how even the smallest of things can make a person recognizable to a close relative or partner." She had to be optimistic.

Willis left the room and Rose turned to Stipes.

"Get ahold of Forensics, will you? After yesterday's rain, there must at least be footprints. They might not give us much but, if we find a suspect, they could prove useful as secondary evidence." Stipes pulled out his mobile and headed for the door. Rose called out after him. "And while you're at it, see if they have anything else! They don't seem too quick at coming back to us lately!"

The uniformed officers left with the detectives and Rose was alone with her thoughts. She sank back into the hard plastic chair. Had the killer been in Finlay's garden before, perhaps to plan their mode of entry? Perhaps they'd even loosened the pane of glass, to make it easier when the time came. Finlay didn't appear to be home very often, so it could easily have gone unnoticed. And if the killer had been there in daylight, there *could* be a better image. A thorough search through the surveillance tape *had* to be their number one priority. Not that Willis wasn't doing his best.

She crossed one leg over the other, staring blankly into the dark TV screen, and the possibility that the killer was female returned to the fore. Her mind drifted back to the box of files and to her feeling that Mrs. Frederickson had been hiding something. If the killer really *was* a woman and these cases *were* connected, it made sense that it was someone Sampson had treated in her professional capacity. Perhaps even someone they were visiting today. Though, unfortunately, Frederickson herself didn't fit the profile.

As she sat quietly, an idea began to form in her head. If potassium chloride *had* been used to signify some sort of staged execution, perhaps Mrs. Sampson had made an error of judgement somewhere along the way, a mistake that had cost one of her patients dearly. But if that *was* the case, why had no formal complaint been logged? There was nothing in the doctor's records to suggest any wrong-doing. Unless the incident hadn't officially been considered an error of judgement. Or it was something outside of the radar…something above and beyond the call of duty, and not necessarily above board. But what would all that have to do with Finlay?

Still, the idea struck a chord and she pondered it further. If the former obstetrician *had* been adopting illegal practices, it might explain why she'd dropped her title on retirement. It might also explain the excessive security measures she'd opted for. Not that she could think of a reason why someone so well educated would need to manipulate the system. But then, why did anyone do it? People did the strangest things for the most obscure of reasons. If all behavioral patterns were logical, there'd be no over-crowded prisons, and she'd probably be out of a job.

She pulled herself up from the seat and stretched her arms out behind her neck. The theory still didn't explain why the killer had waited until now to exact revenge, unless something had happened recently to bring things to the fore. She decided to get Blake to trawl through recent media reports. If there was anything that could be remotely connected to either Sampson or Finlay, he'd be the person to find it.

As she picked up her bag and headed for the door, there was another thing that continued to trouble her. Even if her theory fell somewhere near to the truth, Sampson's patients would be middle-aged women by now, perhaps even older. Like Frederickson, they most likely wouldn't resemble the lithe figure they'd just witnessed in Finlay's back garden, unless the perpetrator was a friend or relative. And if that *were* the case, it would only serve to make her job harder.

CHAPTER THIRTEEN

It didn't take Willis long to work his magic on the surveillance recording, but, even with his considerable expertise, he was unable to attain the facial details of the figure in Finlay's garden. The image was too grainy, and the dark hood served a valuable purpose in sheltering such features from sight. Whoever it was, they'd been successful in concealing their identity.

Still, with the backing of the chief, Rose had enlisted two uniformed officers to help sift through the rest of the recording in detail. Any activity considered suspicious was to be reported to her immediately, however minor. If the killer *had* been to Finlay's house before, they might be easier to identify in daylight.

In the meantime, she intended to conduct an in-depth search of Finlay's property, *and* his background. No one was invisible. Finlay had a story somewhere, and she was determined to find out what it was.

She was just heading to her desk, when Stipes caught her unawares.

"I spoke to Forensics, Guv. There *were* footprints in Finlay's garden. But whoever made them wore boot covers. It'd be impossible to determine shoe size, let alone get an identifiable print."

Rose felt her heart sink. If the killer had been astute enough to wear boot covers, it was unlikely they'd left a trace anywhere. She shook her head. "Fantastic. This day just keeps getting better." She continued toward her desk, but Stipes was still hovering. She looked to him for enlightenment.

"There *was* something though."

The comment unnerved her. "Go on."

"They recovered a partial print from the glass panel. It's possible the killer ripped their gloves whilst removing it."

"And?"

"Even though it wasn't complete, it was enough for them to make a positive ID."

"The ident was in the system?"

"Yep, and you're gonna love this. It belongs to a Mr. Anthony Campbell. He's an employee of Holland and Carter. I checked out the company, and they've been delivering logs to Finlay for the last two winters. The last occasion was a week ago."

Rose felt a tingle at the back of her neck.

Stipes continued. "And there's more. They've also been delivering logs to the Sampson house for the last six years."

"Yes! A connection!"

Rose's words ripped through the modest incident room like a mini tornado, though subconsciously she was kicking herself. She'd meant to check if Sampson had used a log delivery company but hadn't gotten around to it yet. If she had, she might have prevented a second murder. She turned her attention back to Stipes.

"Why was he in the system?"

"A minor pub brawl a couple of years ago. The manager dropped all charges, and there's been nothing since."

Rose nodded. The fact that Campbell hadn't been apprehended for anything serious didn't mean he wasn't capable of murder.

Many of history's most notorious killers had operated beneath the radar for a while before being unmasked. The question was, could Campbell pass himself off as female? She shot her colleague a satisfied look.

"It's good enough for me. Bring him in."

CHAPTER FOURTEEN

When Campbell arrived at the station, he looked twitchy and nervous, though not unnaturally so. An impromptu visit to the police station tended to have that effect on people. Plus, Campbell had been picked up from his place of work, which was never conducive to putting someone in the best of moods.

Rose had requested he be taken to one of the larger interview suites, where members of her team could get a good view of the proceedings. That way, even if she missed something, one of her colleagues would be sure to pick up on it. Plus, there was the added benefit of a more comfortable environment.

She now stared through the large two-way mirror into the dimly lit room beyond. Campbell had refused the option of legal representation, presumably because he felt it was unwarranted. Either that, or he was astute enough not to want to appear guilty. Either way, there would be no unnecessary hold-ups. Which was good, considering this day was getting busier by the minute.

Rose entered the room alongside Stipes, dismissing the officers who'd accompanied Campbell in. As she closed the door behind her, she shivered involuntarily. The room was cold and bereft of atmosphere. It reminded her of a prison waiting room, the only departure being its one small window, which, at present, was devoid of sunlight. She folded her arms tightly across her chest, taking a seat directly opposite their guest. Stipes sat beside her.

Anthony Campbell was a small man in his early thirties. He had a slim, some might say athletic physique, and thick dark brown hair that fell intriguingly over one eye. He wore the tattered blue overalls of a manual laborer, which were smothered in wood shavings and dirt. No doubt he'd been out chopping logs at some point in the not too distant past. His odor was a combination of chemicals and sweat.

Rose's immediate impression of the man was that he looked too muscular to be the figure in Finlay's garden, even if he were clad in dark, baggy clothes. She switched on the tape recorder and took care of the formalities before finally addressing him.

"Good morning, Mr. Campbell. Do you have any idea why you're here?"

Campbell looked nervously around the room, like a rabbit caught in the headlights. He was clearly unused to being questioned. "I've no idea. I was pulled out of work with barely an explanation. All they said was they needed me to assist with something at the station. To be honest, it was embarrassing. I'll be lucky if I have a job to go back to."

Rose smiled empathetically. "I'm sure your employer will understand. You're only here to assist us with our inquiries. You can refer them to me if you have any problems."

Campbell smirked, as though the suggestion was incredulous. Even so, the dialogue seemed to relax him. Rose took advantage of his sudden change in demeanor.

"Would you like something to drink? Tea, coffee, water?"

For a few seconds Campbell considered the question, as though it were a deliberate ploy to unnerve him. Finally, he relented. "Coffee. White, two sugars."

Rose signaled to Stipes to get coffee, then registered his absence for the purposes of the recording. When she was done, she leaned forward and rested her elbows on the table in front of her. "So, you deliver logs for a living?"

Campbell fiddled with a button on his overalls. "That's right."

"How long have you been delivering to Three Violet Crescent?"

Campbell raised his eyes to the ceiling. He'd gone from nervous to cocky in less than a minute. Rose wondered what else he was capable of. When he finally answered the question, there was an edge to his voice.

"A while. A few years or so. Why? Has there been a complaint?"

Rose leaned back in her chair. "No. There hasn't been a complaint. But there *has* been an incident at the property and we're keen to rule out—"

Campbell reverted to looking nervous again. "What kind of incident?"

Rose sat up straight. He clearly didn't read the papers or watch the news. Still, she wasn't going to show her hand before she was ready. Besides, if he *had* had anything to do with the murders, he already knew. She retained her deadpan expression.

"We'll get to that later. How about Six Amber Court?"

"On the Dahlia development?"

"Yes."

"What is this, an itinerary of all my customers? Why do you want to know?"

Campbell was starting to look agitated now. Stipes arrived back with the coffee, providing a necessary break in proceedings. Rose announced his return for the tape, then continued her line of questioning. It was important to keep up the momentum.

"As I said, there's been an incident and we're keen to rule out...."

"At Violet Crescent or Amber Court?"

Campbell was starting to become obnoxious. He had so many sides, Rose wasn't sure quite how to handle him. She looked him in the eye. "Both."

Her reply seemed to temporarily appease him, most likely because it was so extraordinary. She pressed on while the going was good. "So, how long have you been delivering to Amber Court?"

"A few years. Maybe longer. Longer than Violet Crescent."

It fit with Stipes's research.

"And did you ever speak to the owner?"

"Only when she signed the delivery sheet."

Either he hadn't noticed her use of past tense, or he was deliberately being clever. She continued. "But you *did* speak to her?"

Campbell averted his eyes to the table. "I wouldn't really call it speaking to her. I said hello, she signed the sheet, I went on my way."

Rose smiled. "I see. Do you recall if she ever looked troubled? Or anxious perhaps?"

"No."

"No, you can't recall, or no she didn't look troubled?"

"Both...either...I don't know. I was only there a few seconds."

Campbell was fidgeting in his seat and Rose wondered if his defensiveness was more than just nerves. She glanced up at the mirror before continuing. Blake and Sherman were on the other side, and she wondered what their thoughts were. Again, she pressed on. "When you arrived at Amber Court, how did you get in? I mean, it's like Fort Knox there, isn't it?"

"I pressed the buzzer and she opened the gates."

"So you didn't have the security code?"

A flash of frustration crossed his face. "No. Why would she give me the security code?"

"So you already knew where to put the logs?"

"Yes. There's a container out back. I just leave them there."

Rose had already noticed the large wooden log holder. "And did you deliver there often?"

"Two or three times each winter."

Stipes shuffled the pile of papers in front of him and Rose took a moment's repose. It would give Campbell a chance to think. Perhaps even change his story if needed. When she looked back across the table, he was staring straight at her. She decided to revisit his earlier replies.

"So, after several years of delivering logs to the same person, there wasn't any kind of rapport between you? You didn't, say, share a joke or discuss the weather?"

"No. Never. People are keen to get back to their business."

"I see. And it was the same with Mr. Finlay?" Campbell seemed to draw a blank and she was forced to elaborate. "The owner of Three Violet Crescent."

"Yes. It was the same. I didn't deliver there often, but the order each time was quite large. So I guess he stocked up."

Rose leaned back in her chair. "I'll be honest with you, Mr. Campbell. There've been two suspicious deaths in Brackley in as many days, and you appear to have had access to both individuals."

Campbell audibly gasped. "You're kidding me, right?"

"I'm not kidding you. If I were, you wouldn't be here."

Campbell twisted in his chair, perhaps finally grasping the seriousness of his predicament. "But there must've been loads of people with access to them. Christ, I didn't even *know* them. I just delivered logs. It's my job."

91

Rose showed no emotion. "That's as may be. But we didn't find their fingerprint at one of the killer's points of entry."

Campbell's face instantly drained of all color. "Killer?"

"I did say the deaths were suspicious."

"But you didn't...I mean...." He raised a hand to his temple, then placed it back down at his side. "I don't believe this. You're telling me I'm a suspect in a murder investigation?"

"At this point we're just trying to rule people out."

Rose took in his shocked expression. He didn't look like a cold-blooded killer, despite his apparent mood swings. Then again, even Ted Bundy had the ability to fool people when necessary. She decided it was time to show her hand.

"What we're wondering, Mr. Campbell, is how your fingerprint came to be on a loose pane of glass on Mr. Finlay's back door."

A flash of recognition crossed Campbell's face, followed by the familiar flicker of relief. When he spoke again, it was as if a huge weight had been taken from him. "Is that what this is about?" The words were spoken almost playfully. "After I dropped off the logs last time, I noticed one of the panes of glass had come loose. Normally I'd just leave it, but it looked like we were in for a storm and I thought it might be dangerous...you know, if it came loose."

Rose made a note to check the weather report. "And when was this?"

"I don't know. A week ago...maybe two. You can check with my boss. Anyway, I just pushed it back in a bit...tore my glove in the process. I guess that'll teach me for trying to be helpful."

Stipes looked up from his note-making. "Do you still have the gloves?" Not that they would be of any great use.

"I threw them away. Not much point in keeping a ripped glove, is there?"

92

Rose lowered her gaze. The fact that Campbell had disposed of the gloves wasn't necessarily suspicious, but it bothered her. She watched him take a sip of his coffee. His hands were shaking, and a drop spilled onto his stained overalls. He put the cup down and wiped it with his hand. She waited a moment, then resumed her questioning.

"So you had no association with Mrs. Sampson or Mr. Finlay other than work?"

"No. None. Like I said, I didn't *know* them. I just delivered the logs."

"And if we make inquiries, we won't hear differently."

Campbell looked her in the eye, an air of defiance clouding his previously worried face. "No," he said simply.

After a few more questions, Rose requested Campbell's alibis for the nights of the murders. On the first, he'd apparently been out drinking with friends in Brackley Town Centre. And on the second, he claimed he'd been watching TV with his girlfriend in their apartment on South Street. Both would be checked out but, even if he hadn't been where he said he was, Rose had a feeling that his partner and friends would cover for him. These days it happened all too often, and it didn't make their job any easier.

She shot a glance at her colleague, deciding to call it a day. They already had Campbell's DNA and contact details. Besides, they couldn't take things further until they'd checked out his story with regard to the fingerprint. Not that it would be easy to corroborate, unless it was on the surveillance tape.

She ended the interview for the purposes of the recording. Her gut instinct was that Campbell wasn't their killer, and her instincts had never failed her yet. Campbell was slightly unpredictable...odd even. But a killer? She just wasn't seeing it. Nevertheless, she couldn't totally rule him out either. Instincts or not, Campbell had opportunity...*and* his fingerprint was at a crime scene.

After issuing him the usual warnings, Rose explained the purposes of the tape recordings and asked Stipes to walk him back to reception. Campbell exited the interview room without looking back. Either he was overwhelmed with relief or he couldn't believe his luck. Rose decided to put an informal tail on him. That way, if they discovered any contradictions to his story, they could pull him straight back in.

When the door closed, and she was finally alone, she glanced up into the two-way mirror. If they'd adhered to her instructions, her colleagues would be gone by now, having returned to the incident room to await instructions. Again, she wondered what they'd made of the interview. She fiddled with the pen in her hand. She'd find out soon enough.

Her eyes drifted to the table and to the scant few lines of scrawl that formed Stipes's notes. They held nothing that she didn't already know, and yet they'd form part of Finlay's case file...she never discarded anything, however insignificant it seemed. Sometimes even the smallest of details could evoke a thought or possibility that hadn't originally been considered.

A noise in the corridor fractured her thoughts, and she glanced at the clock...eleven fifty-five. Once again, the day was racing on without her. In a couple of hours they were due to meet with another of the women in Sampson's box of files, and she hadn't even checked out the Finlay property yet.

Suddenly she wondered if there'd been any news from Dr. Weller. The pathologist had promised to call as soon as he had any results, and that was a good four hours ago. She wondered how long the test for potassium chloride took. The sooner they had confirmation that the cases were linked, the sooner they could properly merge them and move things on. As if by fate, her mobile buzzed in her pocket. She pulled it out and stared at the display. Sure enough, it was the doctor.

"DI Rose."

The phone crackled. Weller was on the move. She waited until the line was clear, then tried again.

"DI Rose." Her words echoed shakily through the line.

"Hello again, Detective."

When Weller's voice finally broke through, it was distinctive and clear. She leaned her elbows on the table in front of her. "Dr. Weller. Do you have any news for me?"

He was still moving about on the other end. "Indeed, I do. Without saying too much, we have a positive connection. I'll email the details to you straight away."

Rose suppressed a smile. Like her, Weller was clearly skeptical of distributing information by mobile. Not that it mattered. She knew what he meant. Finlay, like Sampson, had been the victim of a potassium chloride overdose. She let out a deep breath, resigning herself to the mayhem that would follow.

"Thank you, Doctor. I'll be in touch."

CHAPTER FIFTEEN

The moment she was back in the corridor, Rose was aware of Banks heading towards her. He was accompanied by a small, smartly dressed woman, and he looked like a man on a mission. She closed the door behind her and stayed where she was. She was hoping his companion was Lucy Brannigan.

When Banks finally reached her, he seemed slightly out of breath. His face was flushed, and a few beads of sweat had formed on his forehead. Rose wondered if his anxiety was related to their earlier confrontation, then brushed the thought aside. Banks was a good detective. He was just overworked, that was all. He took a deep breath and seemed to calm himself.

"Guv. This is Lucy Brannigan."

Rose placed Stipes's notes into the groove beneath her arm and held out her hand. As Brannigan took it, Banks shifted attention from one woman to the other.

"Lucy, this is DI Rose. She's heading the investigation into Mr. Finlay's death."

His words seemed to strike a nerve, and Brannigan's expression visibly darkened. Rose pretended not to notice. Instead she stepped back, discreetly eyeing the woman's slender frame and naturally toned physique. For someone in her early fifties, she looked surprisingly agile. Was it possible she fit the profile of the woman in Finlay's garden?

She brushed the thought aside. Brannigan would've had ample access to Finlay over the years. Why would she need to break into his house? Still, the thought didn't quite placate her. People didn't always act rationally or logically, especially when they were under duress. Until they'd learned considerably more about the lives of the two murder victims, everyone was a potential suspect. She stepped forward, hiding her thoughts behind a thin smile.

"I'm very sorry for your loss, Miss Brannigan. I realize that you and Zack Finlay were close friends."

Brannigan merely nodded, and Rose turned to Banks.

"You can use interview room two. I'll catch up with you in a while."

Banks headed off and Rose made her way to the incident room. As much as she would've liked to sit in on their conversation, she had other things to do. If Brannigan had anything of relevance to impart, she'd learn of it soon enough. Besides, for the time being, the former model was only here to provide background information. If she appeared to be holding back, she could always be pulled in again later.

When she reached her destination, the first person Rose saw was Reece. The young detective was leaning over his desk, casually retrieving sheets of paper from the printer. As she passed him a thought struck her, and she immediately turned back, causing him to look up from his endeavor.

"Guv?"

She shot him a brief smile. "Banks is speaking with Finlay's ex-girlfriend in interview room two. Do me a favor will you, and sit in on it?"

Reece put down the papers he'd been holding. "Sure.

Anything in particular you want me to find out?"

"Yes. Find out what Finlay did for a living."

The mood in the incident room was quietly somber when Rose walked in. Her team was busy gathering all the information they could on the murder victims and searching for any leads that might materialize. In many ways, despite their industriousness, it reminded Rose of the calm before a storm. Once the leads started filtering in and the media realized that the deaths were connected, all hell would break loose. She just hoped they could get a handle on things before that happened.

She headed to the murder board to update the team on Campbell, allowing Blake and Sherman time to add their interpretations, which basically reflected her own. When they were done she relayed Weller's recent information, which came as no surprise to anyone. Then she turned back to Blake.

"Anything on the anonymous call yet?"

Blake settled himself into his chair. "Not a lot, except that the caller was a woman."

Something tingled in Rose's spine.

Oblivious to her response, Blake continued. "I've got a copy of the recording for you to listen to, but unfortunately it's short and sweet. As for the phone, there's nothing to trace. It was a standard pay as you go, and it hasn't been used since. The number wasn't registered."

Rose shook her head in frustration. Another dead end.

Willis looked up from his computer screen. "D'you think it was the killer, Guv?"

Rose shrugged her shoulders. "I really don't know. But if we get any female suspects, at least we can try voice recognition." She raised her eyebrows in an exaggerated show of exasperation. "At this rate, it might be all we have." Again, she shifted her attention to Blake.

"Can you trawl through local media reports for the last twelve months? If the murders were connected to something Mrs. Sampson did in her professional career, something could've triggered them."

Blake looked to her to elaborate.

"Sorry, I know it's vague. But if our killer was reacting to something that happened a long time ago, we need to ask why. Perhaps he or she has only recently become aware of it."

Blake nodded, retreating further into his seat.

Rose pressed on. "Just to let you know, there'll be another press release issued this afternoon, appealing for anyone who knew Mr. Finlay to come forward. Banks is talking to the ex-girlfriend as we speak. The sooner we can establish what sort of man he was and what he did for a living, the sooner we can begin piecing together his movements. In the meantime, Stipes and I will take another look at the property. If we can find something there to link Finlay to Mrs. Sampson, or her death, we *might* be able to establish a motive for these murders." She looked into the familiar faces that confronted her. "Does anyone have anything new to add?"

Blake raised a hand. "I've been looking up how easy it is to get ahold of potassium chloride, and I have to say, it's surprisingly simple, presumably because it's a natural substance. It's commonly used in medicines and supplements, so anyone can get ahold of it without leaving as much as a contact number. Not only that, but there's all sorts of info out there regarding safe and unsafe doses, different methods of ingestion, etc. Then there's other info on the lethal injection, detailing the chemical's ability to induce heart failure."

Rose shot him a knowing look. "I know. I've looked myself. So whatever else we can catch our killer on, it's not going to be his or her possession of an illegal chemical...though that might serve a useful addition to other incriminating evidence. Anything else?"

The team fell silent and Rose scanned the room for Stipes. It was already lunchtime the day after Finlay's murder, and she was growing increasingly concerned that they hadn't conducted a search of the property yet. Of course, SOCOs and Forensics had done their bit. But that in no way served as a substitute for a personal evaluation, without which she felt totally detached from the intricacies of what had taken place.

Stipes looked up from the mountain of paperwork on his desk. "Looking for me, Guv?"

Rose shot him a half smile. "I think it's time we checked out Three Violet Crescent, don't you?"

CHAPTER SIXTEEN

When they first entered Violet Crescent, Rose was surprised by the number of cars that littered the roadside. Since news of a suspicious death had been released, reporters seemed to have ascended in droves. They hovered in front of Finlay's house like vultures circling their prey. If it wasn't for the crime scene tape, they'd have stepped into the driveway and probably forced entry to the house by now.

She pulled the car to a halt, squeezing it into a tiny space halfway along the road. There she distributed gloves and boot covers before shooting her partner a satirical look. "Ready?"

Stipes was wearing an expression that told her he'd probably never be ready. Nevertheless, they stepped from the car into the busy street.

The minute they'd closed the car doors, a handful of reporters rushed towards them. Stipes stepped forward, holding out his hands in a "keep back" motion. His sheer size was generally enough to deter people from getting too close. The reporters, however, were not most people.

Rose did her best to shield herself behind Stipes's imposing frame. When she could hide no longer, she took a deep breath and adopted her most authoritative demeanor. "OK, OK, move aside please."

Not that her words had much of an effect. Still, the reporters kept at bay just long enough for them to get to Finlay's property. Once there, they ducked beneath the crime scene tape and hurried toward the house.

When they were finally inside, Rose was struck by how dark the property was, despite the fact that it was only lunchtime. It suddenly occurred to her that a house with so little natural light would be in total darkness come evening. She wondered how Finlay had propelled himself forward. OK, so he'd had an obvious familiarity with the property. But it would still have been difficult for him to move about without the aid of a flashlight.

She thought back to the original crime scene photos. There'd been no flashlight found in the vicinity of his body, or anywhere else for that matter. Her phone buzzed in her pocket and she reached her hand in to retrieve it.

"DI Rose." Seriously, how many times had she said that today?!

The call was from Dr. Weller, informing her that, aside from the head injury, the puncture wound, and the significantly increased levels of potassium chloride, nothing unexpected had arisen from Finlay's post mortem. Cause of death, as expected, was cardiac arrest brought on by the said levels of potassium chloride. He'd obviously made Finlay a priority.

Rose nodded her head as he spoke. "Have you any idea what caused the head injury?"

As always, the doctor paused for a moment. "All I can say is it was a blunt instrument, probably resembling a small hammer. I'll make some comparisons and see what I can come up with."

Rose paused. There'd been nothing like that found at the crime scene, so it was likely the killer had taken it with them. She thanked the doctor and placed the phone back in her pocket.

As she did so, she wondered if Finlay had possessed a mobile phone. If she'd been in his position, stranded in the darkness with no flashlight, it would've been the first thing she'd looked for. It might not have provided the best form of illumination, but it would certainly have been better than nothing.

The scenario played out in her mind. As Finlay had just returned home, it was likely he'd have had the phone on his person. The question was, if there'd been one, where was it now? There'd been no phone found on or near his body. And, if SOCOs had discovered one anywhere else on the property, they'd have already alerted her. She ran the theory past Stipes, who only stated what she already knew.

"If Finlay had known his killer and had been in contact with them at some point prior to his death, the phone could have contained incriminating evidence."

Rose could already see where this was going. "The killer took it."

She continued along the hallway, then veered off into the lounge. She'd chase up whether or not Finlay had possessed a mobile phone later. When she reached her destination, she was again confronted by the unflattering shade of green that dominated the walls. She squinted, as though its presence caused her actual physical pain.

"Seriously, why would anyone *choose* to have this color in their house?"

Stipes ran his eyes over the offending veneer. "People have varied tastes, Guv."

Rose deliberately shielded her eyes. "You can say that again."

Stipes stepped up alongside her and together they scanned the modest space. It didn't take long. There was unusually little in the form of furnishing. Rose lowered her gaze to the long chalk figure that dominated the room, and for a moment she was transported back to earlier that morning, when Finlay's lifeless corpse had lain there. The deep red blood stains that had seeped from his dying body still splattered the thin beige carpet. At some point in the future, the cleaners would be called to try to erase them. But for now, things had to remain as they were.

She stepped forward, carefully pulling open a narrow teak sideboard. As with the room itself, it was virtually empty, containing nothing more than a small pile of papers, a collection of glasses, and a boxed cutlery set. She flicked through the papers, which appeared to be flyers and pieces of junk mail, as opposed to the financial records she'd been hoping for. She shifted her thoughts to Finlay's actions in the minutes prior to his murder.

"So, what do you think made him come into the lounge, since the lights were off, and the fuse box was further along the hallway?"

Stipes was glancing through the window into the small gravel driveway. "Perhaps he heard something."

"But if he could barely see, why wouldn't he wait until he'd checked out the fuse box?"

Stipes shrugged his shoulders, but otherwise didn't move. "Perhaps the killer spoke to him. Said something to make him change course."

Rose let out a deep sigh. As with the Sampson case, something wasn't quite adding up.

Having checked out the other items, she closed the sideboard, the papers still in her hand.

"Must've seemed a bit odd though. That they were waiting here in the dark."

Her statement went unanswered, and Stipes moved away from the window, stepping back to examine a bowling trophy. He had a knack of flicking from one thing to another at the drop of a hat. When he spoke again, his voice seemed lighter. "There doesn't seem to be much in the way of personal possessions."

Rose did a 360 degree turn of the room. It did nothing but make her feel nauseous. If there was something she was missing, it wasn't in plain sight. She replied belatedly, "I guess if, as the neighbors said, Finlay was only here sporadically, there would've been no reason for him to harbor personal possessions. He wouldn't have been around much to enjoy them. Seems a pretty sad way to live. Then again, who are we to judge?"

She turned her attention back to the papers in her hand. It seemed odd that someone would keep flyers and other forms of promotional material. Particularly when they didn't seem the type to collect much else. She wondered if they might be related to Finlay's vocation, or if they reflected particular interests or hobbies. She pulled an evidence bag from her pocket and carefully slotted them inside.

Once again, her eyes swept the impersonal space. If this was where the killer had lain in wait, why had the curtains been left open? Like Stipes before her, she looked out into the quiet driveway. Despite the property's modest size, it wasn't overlooked.

She thought back to the house's lack of light. Even without the curtains drawn, it would've been dark enough to shield a person. Particularly if that person was wearing dark clothes. The killer had probably found no need to draw the curtains. Even so, it seemed haphazard, if not downright sloppy. She was beginning to think that whoever had killed Mrs. Sampson and Zack Finlay wasn't a natural killer.

The thought sent her mind back to the figure squeezing through the pane of glass in Finlay's back door. Natural killer or not, they'd had their entrance carefully planned, and they were frustratingly capable of disguising their identity. Plus, they'd left nothing behind to reveal the motive behind their crimes...at least nothing that had been recovered so far. And they were clearly forensically aware.

For no apparent reason, she suddenly recalled their two-thirty appointment with the second of the women from the box of files. She glanced at her watch…five past one. With any luck, they just had time to search the rest of the property. Raising her head, she took one last look around the dismal room. What she desperately needed was some thinking time; a few minutes of solitude to get her head together and get a handle on recent developments. So far, nothing about this case seemed straightforward. But there had to be a pattern somewhere. She just needed time to draw it out.

A search of the other rooms revealed little of the man Finlay had been. Other than the usual necessities, there was nothing that could tell them what he had liked to do or how he had spent his time. This had clearly been a house rather than a home. Four walls to offer protection from the elements and from the harsh world outside. Ironically, they hadn't protected him when he'd most needed it.

Rose descended the staircase into the hallway from which she had come. Apart from the obvious signs of neglect that one would expect from a property that was rarely lived in, there was nothing to indicate that a brutal murder had recently taken place here. She pulled open the front door and hovered on the threshold. For a few moments she just stood there, staring out into the dreary day. Then she pulled out her phone and dialed Banks. He answered on the second ring. "Did you get anything helpful from Brannigan?"

Banks coughed to clear his throat. "Not a great deal, Guv. She insisted she never knew what Finlay did for a living. Said he told her he was a business man, but he would never elaborate. She was concerned he was up to something illegal due to the odd hours he kept, and the fact that he wouldn't tell her where he was going. Plus, he seemed to live a fairly extravagant lifestyle. When he was around they ate out most nights, and he was always forking out for posh weekends away. In the end, she said she just couldn't be with a man who kept so many secrets. She said it was the main reason they split up."

Rose shook her head in disbelief. "So she was with him for five years and she had no idea what he did on a daily basis?"

"That's what she claims."

Stipes stepped into the doorway and Rose moved aside. "Did you show her the photo of Mrs. Sampson?"

Banks coughed again and the phone line crackled. "She said she didn't recognize her, and I believed her on that. But I *did* feel there was something she was holding back."

"What made you think that?"

There was a moment's pause while Banks considered the question. "I can't quite put my finger on it, but there was something about her reactions. She was clearly grieving, but it was as if she wasn't giving me the whole story…I can't explain it. It was just the way she acted when she spoke of him. As if she were appropriating a mask. Pretending things were a certain way when they clearly weren't. D'you know what I mean?"

Rose let out a deep sigh. "I know what you mean. Maybe we'll pull her in again later. In the meantime, I want a search team out here to look for a murder weapon. A blunt instrument, possibly a small hammer. But I want it done on a small scale. There's enough mayhem out here already. Besides, the killer probably took it with them. I just want to cover all bases."

She ended the call and turned to Stipes. "We got nothing from Lucy Brannigan. But that doesn't mean she doesn't know anything. Banks thinks she might've been holding back."

She glanced at her watch again…one fifty-five. "If we're

lucky, we can get to our appointment early. I need to get back to the station and get my head around all this. If we don't start making some progress soon, we'll have a media riot on our hands."

As soon as she'd said it, she took a deep breath and stepped out into the busy street.

CHAPTER SEVENTEEN

Twelve Empress Road was a few miles to the North of Brackley, where the streets were more crowded and the houses more compact. Rose drove there in a little under twenty minutes, giving them fifteen minutes to spare before they were due to meet with the second of the women in Mrs. Sampson's box of files...Mrs. Irene Broom.

Mrs. Broom had two children, now aged thirty-three and thirty-four. As with Mrs. Frederickson, her hospital records from the time Mrs. Sampson was consulting were sparse. But since she, too, had been a patient at St. Thomas' Hospital, Rose assumed she'd been under the care of the obstetrician during one or both of her pregnancies.

She shot a glance at Stipes and they both exited the car. She was hoping that their early arrival wouldn't be a problem. Time, at present, was in short supply. They had a lot to discuss when they got back to the station. Not only would the team need updating on recent developments but, now that the cases had officially merged into one, they'd need to fully synchronize their inquiries. If they weren't all singing from the same hymn sheet, what chance did they have of catching their killer?

When the first knock on the door went unanswered, Rose felt

her heart sink. Either Mrs. Broom was out and hadn't returned home yet, or she was too preoccupied to answer the door. She leaned back on her heels. She didn't even want to consider the third option…that Sampson's former patient had changed her mind and no longer wanted to talk to them.

Stipes stepped forward and knocked again. When that, too, went unanswered, they shared a concerned look. Rose checked the time…two-twenty.

She took a deep breath and walked back up the pathway. The streets were surprisingly quiet. She supposed that was only natural, considering the time of day. Most people would be at work, and it wasn't time for the school run yet. Her eyes scanned the empty pavements, in search of an approaching figure, but none materialized.

By two thirty-five, Rose felt any hope she'd previously had slowly ebbing away. She tried the phone number Banks had used to make the appointment. When she lifted the letterbox, she could hear it ringing inside the house. But there appeared to be no one at home to answer it.

Frustrated, she looked to her partner. "What the hell's going on here? This is a murder investigation, for heaven's sake. Don't people realize it's a criminal offense to obstruct the course of justice?"

Stipes threw her a banal look. "I doubt Mrs. Broom realizes that's what she's doing, Guv."

"Like that makes a difference."

She indicated for him to try the side gate, but it was padlocked and there was no point in pursuing unlawful entry. They didn't even know if Broom had anything to offer them yet, and even if she *was* hiding out in the house, what right did they have to force their way in?

Frustration prickled her, and she raised her eyes to the steely grey sky. It wasn't so much that the woman had misled them that was irking her, although Broom *could* possess information crucial to the investigation. It was more the fact that they'd wasted valuable time. Time that could've been better spent hunting for their killer.

Again, she turned to Stipes. "How long shall we give her? Another five minutes?"

Stipes nodded.

At two forty they headed back to the car. The minute they were inside, Rose was on the phone to Banks. "Mrs. Broom didn't show. You haven't heard from her, have you?"

It was the first time she'd considered the possibility, though she knew it was a long shot. Banks would've called her if he'd heard anything. The latter was quick to reply.

"I'm afraid not, Guv. But I was just about to call you. We've had a witness come forward. A Miss Leah Fawcett. Reckon she might've seen Finlay's killer. I was just heading out to pick her up."

Rose felt goosebumps ascend her spine. "I'll let you go then. We'll be back at the station in thirty minutes."

CHAPTER EIGHTEEN

When they arrived at the station, Banks hadn't gotten back yet, so Rose began updating the team on his meeting with Lucy Brannigan, and on their recent visit to the Finlay house. Not that a great deal of progress seemed to have been made during either of those events.

When she was done, she looked to her colleagues to inform her of any headway they'd made. As it turned out, they were still no closer to discovering what Finlay had done for a living, and Reece hadn't yet succeeded in tracing Mrs. Sampson's estranged sister, Mrs. Joy Turner. Facts that would only make their job harder.

Rose felt the muscles in her neck tense. She continued regardless. "Finlay didn't have a landline, but he must've had a mobile. Especially if he was some kind of 'business man.'"

She raised her fingers in the air to emphasize the phrase. "I'll get Banks to check it out with Brannigan. But in the meantime, Sherman, can you look into it?"

Sherman nodded, and Rose raised a hand to her aching neck.

"And there are no further updates? Nothing that's come up on either Sampson or Finlay that we haven't discussed yet?"

For once her team fell silent.

"Great. Let's hope Banks's witness can enlighten us then."

When everyone had gone back to their tasks and Banks still hadn't arrived, Rose began to wonder if he was having problems. People often claimed to have witnessed something, when really, they were just seeking attention...or worse, having a laugh at the department's expense. She was about to call him when his familiar face appeared around the door.

"The witness is here, Guv. She's currently sitting in room three with a uniform. I'm off to get her a coffee."

Rose signaled for him to enter the room. "Have you spoken with her yet? D'you know what she saw?"

"Not really. I didn't like to ask, in case she claimed I put the words in her mouth."

Rose nodded. She knew he was right. They couldn't dispense with protocol, even if they *were* in the middle of a murder investigation. If the witness later claimed that Banks had encouraged her, it would make any statement they got inadmissible.

She leaned back in her chair and let out a loud, resounding sigh. "OK, go ahead and get the coffee. Stipes and I will meet you there in five minutes."

Leah Fawcett was a small woman in her early twenties. She had long, bleached blonde hair and a series of piercings and tattoos that gave her the look of someone much older. When Rose entered the room, she was slouched in the chair, clearly not nervous of the conversation to come.

Rose took in her worn clothes and stained jacket. She'd need a total makeover before any jury would believe her. That was, if her testimony was even valid. In this day and age, witnesses were on trial as much as the suspects. And this wasn't a respectable-looking, educated young woman from one of the more reputable areas of Brackley. This was someone whose very appearance bore the scars of a harsh, possibly unlawful existence.

Rose leaned across the table and held out her hand, cursing Banks for not having prepared her. "Good afternoon, Miss Fawcett. I'm DI Rose, and this is DS Stipes." Stipes stepped up alongside her. "We're heading this investigation."

Fawcett reached forward to shake their hands. At least she was well mannered. They took a seat opposite her and the uniformed officer took his leave. A few seconds later, Banks entered the room, coffee in hand. He placed the cup on the table and promptly left the room.

Rose listed the room's attendees for the purposes of the recording. When she was done, she leaned her elbows on the table and formally addressed their guest. "So Miss Fawcett, my colleague tells me that you witnessed some suspicious activity outside Three Violet Crescent yesterday evening...that's the evening of December 10."

Fawcett shifted slightly in her seat, but if she was uncomfortable, it didn't show. "That's right. I was walking through Violet Crescent on my way back home. I do some volunteer work on Main Street most days...a small charity shop there. At the end of Violet Crescent, there's a walkway that takes me to where I live."

Her response surprised Rose. Perhaps this young woman was a more reliable witness than she'd given her credit for. "So it's a route you take often?"

"Most days."

"And why was yesterday evening different from the other days you make this journey?"

Fawcett took a sip of her coffee, and Rose noticed a tiny stud resting on the tip of her tongue. As a trial witness she would *definitely* need work. Fawcett placed the coffee cup back on the table.

"When I first entered the crescent, I didn't notice anything unusual. Mind you, it *was* pretty dark, and I was keen to get home."

"And what time was this?" Rose hated to interrupt, but such details were crucial.

"Six-fortyish."

"That's pretty late, isn't it? What time do you finish work?"

Fawcett took another sip of her coffee. "Usually about six-thirty." Seeming to realize where Rose was coming from, she added, "I don't work behind the counter. I just help sort stock. I usually start around noon and finish around six-thirty. Most stock doesn't come in 'til the afternoon."

Rose nodded in understanding. "I see. So, when you first got to Violet Crescent, there was nothing that seemed unusual?"

"No. But then, just as I was walking past this house—I've realized since that it was number three—I saw something climbing over the side gate."

Rose felt her pulse quicken. After watching the earlier video, she'd assumed the killer had used the rear entrance. Perhaps, if he or she had entered via the side gate, they simply hadn't noticed the security camera.

Fawcett continued. "At first I thought it was an animal. I dunno, a cat or something. It was pretty dark, and all I could make out were shadows. But when I walked a bit further on, it suddenly got a bit clearer. There's a street light on the other side of the road, so I guess it was because of that. Anyway, it was then that I realized it was a person."

Rose shot a glance at Stipes. Despite her initial reservations, this could be their first real break. She took a deep breath. "Did you see what they looked like?"

Fawcett raised her eyes to the ceiling, seemingly in thought. "They were wearing dark clothes and they must've had some

115

kind of hat or hood on, 'cos I couldn't see their hair. But it looked like a woman."

Rose felt the hairs at the back of her neck tingle. She recalled the figure in the garden and how she, too, had gotten the impression that it was a woman. Then there was the anonymous caller …. She leaned forward in her seat, her heart beating at a hundred miles an hour. "What makes you say that? I mean, if they were wearing dark clothes and you couldn't see them clearly."

Again, Fawcett raised her eyes to the ceiling. "I dunno. I must've got a glance of their face or something. Or maybe it was just the way they moved. It all happened so quickly, I can't really remember. I just remember thinking how odd it was that a woman would be climbing over the gate. Especially in the dark."

Again, Fawcett picked up her coffee cup, and Rose thought she noticed a flicker of satisfaction cross her face. It seemed odd considering the circumstances. She pushed it aside.

"What made you come forward with this now?"

"I saw something on TV. A picture of the house, and someone saying that a man had been murdered there. I realized that the person I saw could've been the murderer."

She raised a hand to her eyes, but something about the way she did it made Rose uneasy. It didn't look natural. She continued regardless. "Is there anything else you can tell us about this person? Were they tall, short…were they heavily built?"

Fawcett paused for a moment. "They weren't big. I mean, that's probably one of the reasons I thought they were a woman. But they looked quite fit…athletic, I mean. They didn't have any trouble climbing the gate."

"Did you manage to see any of their features? Or their skin color?"

"No. Sorry. It was too dark, and I was too far away."

"What about their shoes? Did you happen to notice what

kind they were wearing? Trainers, boots...."

Fawcett reached for the coffee cup again, then, on realizing it was empty, leaned back in her chair. "I really don't know. Like I said, it was dark. I'm sorry, there's not a lot I can tell you. I just thought you should know what I saw." She was fidgeting more now. The situation was no longer a novelty.

Rose decided to throw something different into the mix. "Y'know, sometimes our mind plays tricks on us and only recalls what it finds most relevant. It could be that you saw something more, but you don't remember. Maybe because you didn't pay much attention to it at the time." For the first time Fawcett looked nervous, unsure of where this was going. Rose continued. "Would you have any objection to hypnosis? We have a colleague who's a specialist in retrieving details that might otherwise have remained forgotten." Still Fawcett looked uncertain. Rose pressed on. "It really is a very painless process...you won't even realize you're being hypnotized. But it *could* give us valuable information. Assuming the person you saw was our killer."

There was a long pause before Fawcett offered a response. "Can I think about it? I'm really not sure."

Rose nodded, even though frustration was gnawing away at her. "Sure. But there really is nothing to it. And it *could* be an enormous help." She signaled to Stipes, who pushed a piece of paper and a pen in Fawcett's direction. "DS Stipes is providing Miss Fawcett with a paper and pen." Every detail had to be logged for the recording. She stared back across the table. "Before you go, could you provide us with your contact details, both at home and at work?"

Fawcett picked up the pen and started writing. Rose hoped the details she provided would be accurate, for she had a feeling this young woman wasn't all she purported to be.

When Fawcett had finished writing, Rose took the details

from her and handed them to Stipes, who had one last question of his own.

"You said you didn't realize the house was number three until later, after you'd seen the news report. Does that mean you're not that familiar with Violet Crescent?"

Fawcett shrugged her shoulders. "Like I said, I just use it as a shortcut."

"So you've never noticed anyone entering or leaving that property before?"

"Not that I remember."

"Are you sure?"

Fawcett let out a deep sigh, indicating her readiness to leave. "Like I said, I don't remember. I don't make a point of looking at every house as I go by."

Rose shot a glance at her partner and ended the interview. They'd gotten all they could from Banks's supposed witness. Whether it was relevant or not had yet to be revealed.

CHAPTER NINETEEN

By the time Rose got back to the incident room, it was near on four o'clock. She skirted past the members of her team and headed straight to her desk. She'd barely spent any time there in the last two days, and she desperately needed to collate the information that was coming in. Besides, the chief was a stickler for paperwork, and she'd barely even started writing up the details for this case yet.

She sank into her familiar chair and glared at her answering machine. The LED informed her that there were forty-two new messages. She reached for a pen and paper, reminded of the sometimes banal nature of police work. It made her appreciate the fact that she wasn't office bound. She might face danger on a daily basis, but if she were forced to sit behind a desk for eight hours a day, she'd probably go insane.

For a few moments she just sat there, silently digesting the events of the day. So much had happened, and yet they seemed to have achieved so little. It was as if fate itself was deliberately keeping them from uncovering the truth. Still, she couldn't hold off on the formal side of things for long. She took a deep breath, reached for the answering machine, and pressed play.

Five minutes later, having gleaned nothing of real value from

119

the messages, Rose sank back into her seat and glanced back at the murder board. The photos of the victims glared out at her like ghostly apparitions. These were two people who seemed to have had very little contact with the outside world. People who'd kept their secrets close to their chests, not even confiding in their closest allies. Was there a reason they'd chosen such solitary existences? More importantly, had they been connected? And, if so, how?

She wondered how much they'd be missed, if they'd even be missed at all. And although the thought saddened her, it also struck her how much easier that would've made it for their killer. The victims were relative loners, or at least that was how it appeared. They had no one watching out for them. No one to come home to at the end of the day. They were private individuals, isolated from society's protective gaze.

Rose lowered her eyes to the list of individuals they'd spoken with so far, and it struck her that, potentially, any one of them could've been involved in the murders. In one way or another they had all given her cause for concern, despite the fact that most of them had only been questioned for background information.

Her eyes slowly scanned the list. The first name that leapt out at her was Mrs. Frederickson. The woman had clearly been hiding something. But could that something have had anything to do with Sampson's and Finlay's deaths? If not, why had she been so keen to get them out of the house? Perhaps it was time they questioned Frederickson again, this time on a more formal basis.

The next name to catch her eye was Anthony Campbell. Although she hadn't initially considered Campbell guilty, his alibis were shaky, and his version of how his fingerprint came to be on Finlay's back door was pretty much unverifiable. Sure enough, Willis had found the incident he'd described on the

120

surveillance tape. But it'd been impossible to tell whether or not Campbell had ripped his glove on that occasion, or whether that had occurred later, on the night of Finlay's murder.

She pondered the thought further. She'd checked the weather report on the day of Campbell's last professional visit and, as he'd stated, they'd been in for strong winds. So in that way at least, his alibi checked out. But that didn't detract from the fact that Campbell was the only person known to them who'd had a connection with both Sampson and Finlay. She balanced the tip of the pen against the ridge of her chin. It wouldn't hurt to delve a bit deeper into the man's personal life. She'd already authorized a discreet tail, albeit on a casual basis. But a more in-depth analysis *might* help implicate him or eliminate him from their inquiries.

She pulled a fresh sheet of paper from a pile on her desk and began constructing a spider-gram. At the center were the two murder victims, and on the long spindly legs were each of the individuals they'd tried contacting as a result.

When she'd listed Frederickson and Campbell, she added Mrs. Irene Broom. The fact that Broom hadn't been home for their appointment and there'd been no call to explain why was odd to say the least. Blake had already been tasked with chasing her up. But the incident itself had created suspicion. Again, she thought back to Mrs. Sampson's files and their potential relevance. Whatever their purpose, it was seeming more and more likely that it was something that people didn't want uncovered. But was it in some way connected to her death?

After Mrs. Broom, Rose added Leah Fawcett. Fawcett had seemed an unlikely candidate for a witness from the start. Even after she'd redeemed herself slightly, there was something not quite right in the way she'd composed her narrative. There'd been a definite disparity between her words and her actions, something that generally only occurred when someone wasn't telling the truth. Plus, her evidence was shaky to say the least, and her reluctance to try hypnosis only added to Rose's concern that her statement might not be valid.

Rose sank further into her seat. Like Lucy Brannigan, Fawcett was slim-framed and athletic, just like the figure on the surveillance tape. Was it possible that she could be their killer? It was a well-known fact that murderers often involved themselves in the investigation. Could that have been the real reason Fawcett had come forward? It was a huge leap to make, but one that *had* to be considered.

She pushed thoughts of Fawcett aside and turned her attention to Lucy Brannigan. As she hadn't actually spoken with Finlay's ex-girlfriend, it was impossible for her to make any kind of judgement on the woman's character. But Banks had gotten the impression that she was holding something back, something perhaps connected to Finlay.

The thought irked her, and she ran her hand along the arch of her brow. What *was* it that Finlay had been involved in? It had to have been something shady, or there would have been a record of it. And was it possible that Brannigan really *did* have no idea? It seemed unlikely.

She shook her head, her eyes fixing on the name Andrew Dyer. They'd recently discovered that Dyer had had two modes of association with Mrs. Sampson. Firstly, as her gardener, and secondly, as a relation to one of the women in the box of files…a woman they were scheduled to meet tomorrow. Dyer hadn't been questioned yet, due to the fact that his visits to the house had been infrequent and had not been considered suspicious. But perhaps it was time they paid him a visit, if only to establish his alibis for the nights in question.

An idea struck her, and she sat up straight in her seat. They hadn't checked out whether or not Zack Finlay had ever hired a gardener. She recalled the modest two-story house in Violet Crescent. Although it was relatively compact, it possessed its own driveway and a small rear garden which, despite Finlay's frequent absence, was relatively well maintained. Had Dyer been the one who'd taken care of it? The team assigned with viewing the Finlay tapes hadn't mentioned it. But then, they'd been focusing on "suspicious activity."

She made a note of the anomaly, then turned her thoughts to Mrs. Sampson's estranged sister, Mrs. Joy Turner. Despite repeated attempts to trace her, including the use of covert contacts, there hadn't been as much as a lead. She seemed to have vanished from the face of the earth. And when that happened, it generally followed that the person concerned was either dead or in hiding. If either were true, there could definitely be a connection to the case.

She raised her hand to the back of her neck, stretching her head up until it clicked. As if things weren't complicated enough, they were fast becoming more so. There *had* to be a pattern here. Something that, if it hadn't actually been said, had deliberately been alluded to. Something that held secrets terrible enough to justify two brutal murders…possibly executions.

A phone rang out in the background and she turned her attention back to the murder board. There was one person she'd been forgetting in all of this. Sampson's neighbor, Ms. Mills, who'd discovered Sampson's body and had since been uncontactable. She'd left no details with the station, other than her mobile phone number, which seemed to be permanently without a signal, and, according to Banks, she hadn't returned home yet. If they didn't make contact with her soon, they'd have to put out a call for her return.

Having finished her spider-gram, Rose put down the pen

and examined her creation. On first glance it was a mish-mash of unkempt scrawls; a shapeless web of names, thoughts, and question marks. She cleared her head, viewing its contents as though considering them for the first time. It sent her to the one thing that *could* potentially connect at least six of the people in her drawing. The box of files.

Tired and frustrated, she drummed her fingers against the dusty table. If the box of files *did* hold any relevance to the murders, Mrs. Frederickson and Mrs. Broom had to be suspects. Then there was Andrew Dyer and his mother. Plus, if the purpose of the files was what connected the two victims, that was two more names to add to the list.

A sudden burst of laughter erupted in the room behind her, but she refused to be distracted. Even if the files had nothing whatsoever to do with the case, it was imperative that their purpose be established, and the sooner the better.

As Rose prepared to issue her team instructions, something else occurred to her, a thought that was both fascinating *and* disturbing. If the box of files *was* the connection, was it possible that they could they be looking for more than one killer? Even though the method of murder was the same, the killings *could* have been carried out by different individuals. She closed her eyes, then opened them again. They certainly seemed to be experiencing a wall of silence. Perhaps there was good reason for that.

The headache that had been lingering behind her eyes intensified. She reached for the box of pain killers in the drawer beneath her desk and swallowed two without bothering to wash them down. If the theory was correct, there *could* be more murders to come. It all depended upon how deep the conspiracy went, and how many people were involved.

She stroked her aching temples, her attention shifting to the small pile of flyers she'd found in Finlay's sideboard. Slowly she flicked through them. The first thought that hit her was how old they looked, not as much in condition as in style. They seemed dated, as if they weren't a part of the modern world.

Laying them on the table, she took a closer look. The first two were from take-out restaurants in Finlay's local area. She made a note of their names and addresses, in case he'd used them as meeting places. At the very least, the staff might remember him. They might even recall if he'd come in alone or if he was ever accompanied by another or "others."

Putting the take-out flyers to one side, she turned her attention to the rest of the pile. There were a few flimsy hotel brochures, perhaps places Finlay had visited with Brannigan. It was something they could establish when they called her back in.

She was about to brush the hotel flyers aside when another thought struck her. Hotels held conventions. Was it possible that Sampson and Finlay had attended such an event, and that *that* was where they'd made contact? Again, it was a long shot. But one definitely worth chasing up.

A brief flick through the other flyers yielded nothing of relevance. There were a couple of dry cleaning brochures and a timetable for the local launderette, items she guessed might have proved useful if Finlay had been engaged in illegal activity. Still, as with the fast food flyers, a visit to the places might, at the very least, yield some insight into Finlay's endeavors.

She rose from her chair and headed for the murder board, clearing her throat as she got there. The action achieved the required response. Her colleagues stopped what they were doing and turned to face her. "OK, so there are a few things that have come to my attention, and I'd like to run them past you."

Rose's words came out quicker than she'd anticipated, and she took a deep breath to slow herself. Having explained the anomalies she'd uncovered through her recent research, including the need to bring Brannigan back in, do more research on Campbell, and keep a close eye on Fawcett, she handed the fast food flyers and cleaning brochures to Banks, who was tasked with visiting the addresses and making the relevant enquiries. When the more mundane of points had been covered, she explained her theory with regard to the box of files.

"I want Frederickson, Broom, and Dyer brought in first thing tomorrow. No excuses. And that's *Mrs*. Dyer. We can question the son separately." She looked each of her colleagues in the eye. "When they get here, I want them all interviewed simultaneously. I want to know, conclusively, why their details were in that box of files, and I want alibis for each of them for the nights of the murders. I also want them to look at photos of the two victims. It might be harder to disguise any knowledge they have when faced with actual images."

She paused for a moment, turning her attention to Blake. "Blake, I want you to contact the hotels contained in these flyers." She handed over the rest of the sheets. "Find out if they hold or have held any conventions in the last thirty-five years." She hoped she was going far enough back. Blake shot her a look that reflected the challenge of the task. She met it with an expressionless stare. "I realize it's a long way to go back. But do your best. If it's necessary to contact previous managers or members of staff, do so. Whatever it takes. We need that information. If this was how the victims met, it *could* go some way to explaining why they were murdered."

Having done with Blake, she turned back to Banks. "Did you get hold of Brannigan regarding Finlay's phone?"

Banks looked up from the mobile he'd been holding in his hand. "Yes, Guv. I literally just put the phone down. She said he didn't believe in contracts, so he used a pay as you go, and he was always changing it. She gave me his last two numbers, so I'll see if I can get them checked out now. Plus, I've told her we'll need to take a look at her phone. If there are any messages from Finlay on it, deleted or otherwise, we should be able to recover them."

Sherman held out a hand to interrupt. "I couldn't find any phone contract in Finlay's name either Guv."

Rose leaned her arm across the murder board. "I guess there's been nothing on the murder weapon?"

Again, Banks looked up. "There's been nothing found yet. Did you want us to extend the search?"

"No, I doubt we'll find it anyway. The killer's too thorough. But can you find out if Finlay hired a gardener? His garden was pretty tidy, and if he used the same company Mrs. Sampson did, we *could* have another connection."

Banks nodded, and Rose turned away, signaling the end of the update. It was beginning to feel like Finlay had been an invisible man. If it weren't for the fact that there was a body lying in the morgue, she might have even started to believe that.

When everyone had gone back to their business, she returned to her desk and glanced at the clock...four forty-five. She decided to give the pathologist a call. He'd undoubtedly still be at the lab, and she wanted to check whether or not her theory regarding more than one killer might be credible.

Weller answered the call on the second ring. Perhaps he wasn't as busy as she'd anticipated. "Good afternoon, Dr. Weller speaking."

His voice was so distinct, Rose felt as though she were in the room with him. She explained her theory, and there was a moment's silence before the doctor responded.

"I guess it's possible. I mean, the assumption that this was one killer was primarily based on the circumstances surrounding

127

the crime…and the method of murder. But since there's been no forensic evidence, there's nothing to suggest that this couldn't have been the work of two people. If both were forensically aware and singing from the same hymn sheet, so to speak."

Rose ended the call and looked back down at her spider-gram. The more she thought about it, the more likely it seemed that the box of files was somehow connected to the murders. Mrs. Sampson had kept it for good reason. And since the individuals it represented were clearly reluctant to elaborate, that reason was undoubtedly controversial.

She was so deep in thought she was totally unaware of Stipes's presence behind her. When he spoke, she almost jumped clean out of her chair.

"D'you really think the files could be the connection, Guv?"

She pulled herself up straight again. Stipes seemed to have the uncanny ability of reading her mind. At the best of times, it unnerved her. At the worst, it made her seriously question her reactions. She turned to face him. "At the moment it's the best we have. Let's just see what happens tomorrow."

As she spoke the words aloud, she felt a dull churning in the pit of her stomach. If it turned out that the files had no relevance to the murders at all, they'd be right back to square one…a situation almost too grim to comprehend. Instinctively she turned back to her partner.

"We need to get hold of the other women in those files. They might live abroad, but that doesn't mean they're incapable of organizing a killing…or two."

CHAPTER TWENTY

That night, Rose slept even more restlessly than usual. Her nightmares were interrupted only by brief periods of conscious panic, when she awoke in a cold sweat and had to convince herself she'd been dreaming. When she finally gave up and pulled herself out of bed, it was 5:55 and her alarm hadn't yet sounded. She switched it off and headed to the kitchen to make herself a coffee. She still hadn't managed to shake the churning in her stomach. Today would be the day they learned more about the women in the files, and even if she didn't get the answers she was hoping for, they'd be one step closer to discerning the motivations that had driven the former Dr. Sampson.

Once the coffee had brewed, Rose poured herself a steaming mug and curled up on the end of the sofa. There she began subconsciously going through the day's itinerary. With any luck, they might get access to some of Finlay's latest phone messages. Perhaps even a few of his contacts. The thought prompted her first and possibly only smile of the day. But it was quickly replaced by notions of the mayhem to come.

She finished her coffee and placed the mug on the floor beside her. Late yesterday, Stipes had begun trying to contact the other individuals in Sampson's files. The problem was, when they finally *did* make contact, she wasn't sure she could spare the resources to fly them over. Unless she could demonstrate the relevance, and that depended on what happened today.

Still dreary from lack of sleep, she leaned her head against the soft peach cushion. The first hints of daylight were already seeping through the thin beige curtains, filling her with the false promise of warmth. She snuggled into her faded pink dressing gown. In a couple of weeks, it would be Christmas, and she had absolutely no idea how she would spend her two days off. As usual, she'd been invited to the Southampton family home. But, as always, the idea filled her with a cold sense of dread. As far as her family was concerned, Christmases left a lot to be desired. Family in general left a lot to be desired. She rose from the sofa and headed for the shower, the forthcoming dilemma still on her mind.

When she finally arrived at the incident room, Rose felt as though she'd been up for hours, though, in reality, it was still only a little after seven. She headed to her desk to check the answering machine. For once she'd made it in before Stipes, and she hoped to make the extra minutes count.

Having settled herself in her chair, she glanced at the LED. There were twelve messages in total, which, considering the circumstances, was surprising. She listened to each, neither of which were particularly enlightening. Then she took another look at her spider-gram. She'd just begun jotting down notes for the forthcoming interviews when Stipes arrived.

"You're early, Guv."

She knew the words had been meant to elicit a reaction, but she didn't have the inclination. She turned back to her endeavor and Stipes headed for his desk.

It wasn't until several minutes later, when the rest of her team had arrived, that Rose finally finished her note-making.

Instinctively she made her way to the murder board. Two uniformed officers had already left to pick up the first of the day's interviewees, Mrs. Linda Frederickson, and she wanted to make sure that everyone was doing what they should be before she arrived.

As usual, she turned to her team for any updates. As it turned out, there'd been no sightings of Dyer Junior on the Violet Crescent surveillance tape, and Reece was *still* getting nowhere with Mrs. Sampson's sister, Mrs. Turner, a fact that almost made her want to give up. Plus, they had no further information on Zack Finlay.

She turned to Banks. "Any luck with Brannigan's or Finlay's mobiles?"

Banks shifted uneasily in his seat. "Still no luck with Finlay's. As Brannigan said, both numbers were pay as you go, and both have since been disabled. If there was any information on either of them, it was eradicated with the SIMs. Sorry." He paused. "There were a couple of messages on Brannigan's, but nothing particularly interesting. Just mundane stuff. I guess, since she was no longer dating Finlay, they didn't have a great deal to talk about. Either that, or he was careful what he sent. One did refer to a B&B he was visiting, so I'll check it out. See if he met up with anyone while he was there."

Rose tried to hide her frustration, nodding before switching her attention to Blake. "I take it you've found nothing in the media reports?"

"Nothing as yet. But I'm only a couple of months in, and there're a lot of publications. If I find anything, I'll let you know ASAP."

She forced a half smile, becoming more deflated by the minute. Nothing appeared to be working out as she planned. Her reply was instinctive. "In that case, prioritize checking out those hotels today, will you? If you haven't found anything in the media yet, there's nothing obvious. We can look into it as we go."

Blake nodded, and she turned back to Banks. "I know you've got other things to do, but can you also prioritize those flyers? Anything that might provide some background on Finlay *has* to come first."

The briefing nearly over, Rose turned to Willis. "I take it you've found nothing useful on the surveillance tapes?"

Willis shifted in his seat. "Not yet. But that doesn't mean there's nothing there. There's a lot to look through, and some of it's pretty blurred. But if there's anything useful, we'll find it."

He sounded like Blake and Rose quickly shifted her attention to Reece.

"We really need to find Mrs. Turner. She's the one person who could provide us with the key to all this. Are we really no closer to obtaining her address?"

Reece merely looked sheepish, which did nothing to quell her frustration

"Well, get everyone you can on it, will you? How hard can it be? For heavens' sake, find her."

Reece flushed an unflattering shade of pink. "Yes, Guv."

"Did you get anything more from the neighbors?"

"Not as yet."

"Great. It's beginning to look like our victims lived under an invisibility cloak."

Rose pinned back her fringe and looked to the final member of her team, DC Sherman. Sherman had been tasked with organizing an informal tail on Campbell, which had so far proven fruitless. Nonetheless, Rose wasn't ready to call it off yet. They needed time to assess his routines and behavioral patterns. He *could* still be lying about the leaving of his fingerprint. Plus, his alibis weren't concrete enough for them to rule him out completely.

As Campbell's financial records were already being accessed, Rose assigned Sherman with a search of his more personal information. Details such as how he got on at school, what he did in his spare time, and who his close friends were. Such data could yield valuable insight into a person's character, not to mention their proclivities. If anything out of the ordinary came up, they might have justification to bring him back in.

As her colleagues drifted off, Rose glanced at the clock... eight-ten. Mrs. Frederickson would be there soon, and then the fun would really begin. She thought back to the woman's behavior yesterday. She'd certainly believed she could pull the wool over their eyes. Rose envisaged her face when two uniformed officers had appeared at her door, and the image gave her an odd sense of satisfaction. No one had the right to interfere with a murder investigation. A fact that Mrs. Frederickson was soon to discover.

CHAPTER TWENTY-ONE

When Mrs. Frederickson was finally brought in, she looked tired and slightly disheveled. Rose wondered if their recent visit had had an adverse effect on her. The dark semi-circles beneath her eyes looked even more pronounced, and she looked shaky and pale. Was it possible her husband had been at home when the officers had come to call? In a perverse way, Rose hoped that he had. Pressure at home might be enough to prompt her into revealing what she knew. At the very least, it would make it more difficult for her to keep her secret.

After little deliberation, Rose decided to use the same interview room they'd used for Campbell. Again, Blake and Sherman would oversee proceedings, taking up positions behind the large two-way mirror. If nothing else, it would allow her a different take on her guest's reactions...something that, at this point in the investigation, could prove enormously beneficial.

As always, Rose entered the room alongside Stipes. Despite the fact that it was still relatively early, it was surprisingly warm when she walked in, and she was glad of the opportunity to remove her jacket and place it on the chair behind her. Mrs. Frederickson had already been furnished with a coffee, in order that there need be no interruptions. Strangely, like Campbell

134

she hadn't requested legal representation. Perhaps because the questioning was still of an informal nature, and she hoped to keep it that way.

Frederickson didn't look up as the detectives entered. Instead she remained hunched over in her seat, staring into her lap as though it held the answers to her problems. Rose thought she detected an air of defiance in her demeanor, but she instantly dismissed it. One way or another, she was going to get the truth from this woman.

Rose switched on the tape recorder and reeled off the formalities. When she was done, she formally addressed her subject. "Good morning, Mrs. Frederickson. I hope our officers didn't disturb you too much today."

Frederickson shot her a look that suggested they had, whining, "I really don't know why I'm here. As far as I can make out, you're looking for information on a doctor I may or may not have visited thirty odd years ago. Surely you've got better things to do with your time."

Rose bit her lip to hide her frustration. The time for playing games was over. If Frederickson wanted to continue her charade, she was going to find it a lot harder than she had done yesterday. She leaned forward in her seat. "Perhaps we should explain the purpose of this interview again, since you clearly seem to have missed the point."

She shot a glance at Stipes, who was watching her reactions through the corner of his eye. Whatever he thought, she was determined to keep her cool. She waited a moment before continuing.

"So, Mrs. Frederickson, the reason we've brought you here today is because we discovered a box of files in Mrs. Sampson's — formerly *Dr.* Sampson's — home. A box of files containing information on a few specific individuals, including yourself." She

135

paused for a moment to let the words sink in. "As my colleague and I explained to you yesterday, Mrs. Sampson was recently found dead in her home under suspicious circumstances. What we're trying to ascertain is whether or not that box of files *might've* had any relevance to her death." Frederickson shifted in her seat, but made no attempt to respond, forcing Rose to elaborate. "So we're wondering why you might have been of interest to the former obstetrician."

Frederickson shivered, despite the warmth of the room. Rose wondered if it was her nerves or if she was genuinely feeling the cold. When she spoke, her voice quivered too. "As I've already told you, I don't know anything about a box of files. I don't even remember seeing a doctor of that name. It was a very long time ago. Surely you can just look up my medical records."

Rose smiled to herself. Whatever it was that Frederickson was hiding, she clearly knew that it wasn't going to be discovered on any hospital database. She reached for the large brown envelope she'd placed on the table in front of her, and slowly pulled out two A4 photos. They were copies of images found in Mrs. Sampson's house, depicting the former doctor in her professional capacity. She separated them and slid them across the table, describing her actions for the tape recorder. When she was done, she looked back to Frederickson.

"You say you don't recall anyone by the name of Dr. Sampson, but perhaps you might recognize these. Images can be far more memorable than names."

Frederickson glanced at the photos then slid them back, far too quickly for Rose's liking. "No. I'm sorry. I don't recall ever having seen this woman. Though, as I said before, we *are* referring to a very long time ago. It's possible I saw her, and I just don't remember."

Rose bit her lip again. Frederickson was really starting to

get to her. "Are you sure? You don't want to look at them a bit longer?"

Frederickson maintained her composure. "I'm sure."

Rose slid the photos back in the envelope and decided to try something different. "When we met yesterday, you told me that you and your husband had only been blessed with one child. Is that correct?"

Frederickson looked nervous, as though she wasn't sure where this was headed. "Yes, that's correct."

"Have you ever had any other children? Say, before you met your husband?"

If Frederickson had conceived a child out of wedlock, she might have wanted help getting rid of it, and if that was the case, perhaps Mrs. Sampson had dabbled in the illegal adoption of babies. It would explain the method of her "execution." It might also explain her association with Finlay. Again, it was a long shot. But long shots were all she had right now.

For a moment Frederickson seemed lost for words. Then her face took on a deep shade of crimson, and Rose thought she was about to explode. When she finally responded, there was an edge to her voice.

"I don't know what you're trying to imply here, but I have never had any other children, with or without my husband. We have one child, and we consider ourselves very fortunate."

Rose responded with an even stare. "I'm not trying to imply anything, Mrs. Frederickson. I'm merely trying to establish why Mrs. Sampson might've considered you important enough to keep a file on you. You've already told us that there were no complications with the pregnancy and birth of your son." She leaned back in her chair. She was growing tired of pussy footing around. If Frederickson wasn't going to give them what they wanted, she was going to make damn sure she knew the consequences of her actions. She took a long, deep breath. "Mrs. Frederickson, I believe you know exactly why Mrs. Sampson kept that file on you. And, as I explained before, withholding information in a murder investigation is a criminal offense. If you persist in doing so and we later prove that you were lying, you *will* be prosecuted."

If her words struck a chord, it didn't show.

She glanced up into the two-way mirror. Was she being too hard on the woman? Every instinct in her body told her that Frederickson was deliberately keeping something from them. Was it possible she was wrong? She didn't think so. She turned back to the envelope on the table in front of her and carefully removed a photo of Finlay. She slid it across the table, again describing her actions for the tape. "Do you recognize the man in this photo?"

Frederickson took a fleeting glance, then slid it back. "No. I've never seen him before."

Rose took another deep breath before leaning back in her seat again. "Before we conclude this interview, I'd like to inform you that we're also interviewing the other individuals from that box of files. Presumably their details were kept for the same reason yours were. If they give us information that contradicts what you've told us, it will put you on very shaky ground."

Frederickson seemed to consider the statement, and, for a brief moment, Rose thought she was about to come clean. She opened her mouth to speak, and Rose braced herself for the revelation. Then came the two words all detectives dreaded.

"No comment."

Unwilling to pursue the pretense any longer, Rose requested Frederickson's alibis for the nights of the murders, which were far from rock solid, and ended the interview. If Frederickson chose to play games, let her. They'd get what they wanted one way or another and, when they did, she'd wish she'd cooperated. Besides, her colleagues would have left to collect Mrs. Broom by now.

CHAPTER TWENTY-TWO

Mrs. Irene Broom wasn't at all what Rose had expected. Not that she'd built up a particularly detailed profile of the woman. But Broom's appearance was so strikingly unusual, it would be difficult to understand how she might be what anyone had expected. Still, Rose welcomed her into the station with a warm smile and the promise of a coffee. If there was a chance the woman could help them, she'd probably walk barefoot over hot coals to make her feel welcome.

Once Broom was settled in the interview room, Rose viewed her through the two-way mirror. She was a small woman, with piercing blue eyes and eyebrows that appeared to meet in the middle. She had thin mousey hair that rested in a tight bun atop her head, making her look ten years older than she actually was. And she wore baggy clothes that hung loosely over her slender frame. What gave her a sense of uniqueness was the thin, almost birdlike quality of her face. It was so extraordinary and so breathtakingly striking, it endowed its bearer with an almost alien quality.

Rose shot a glance at Stipes, who'd stepped up alongside her. He was clearly digesting the woman's appearance himself; but whatever he was thinking, he didn't choose to share it. Rose forced herself to focus. Broom *could* be the one to enlighten them as to the nature of Sampson's files. Someone had to. Blake and Sherman took up position behind the mirror and she stepped into the familiar room.

Twenty minutes later, having spoken with Broom at length, Rose left the interview room empty handed and frustrated. Like Frederickson before her, Broom had seemed uncomfortable even discussing the former Dr. Sampson. Plus, she had alibis for the nights of the murders, even if they weren't water tight.

Rose drifted into the corridor, wondering if the women were involved in some sort of conspiracy...a contract of silence that prevented each of them from ratting out the others. If that *was* the case, who knew what they might unearth? If only they could open the Pandora's box and unravel the puzzle inside.

Stipes walked Broom back to reception then met Rose back at the incident room, where she was sitting with her head in her hands. As he approached, she lowered her hands, shooting him an inquiring look. "What the hell's going on here, Stipes? Am I wrong? Am I wasting ours and everybody else's time? Have I totally fucking lost it?"

Stipes pulled up a chair and sat opposite her. "I'm sorry, Guv. I really don't know." He paused for a moment, finally leaning forward in his seat. "What I do know is that you've always been right to follow your instincts. If you believe something's not right, you have to follow it up. Even if it *might* turn out to be a waste of time."

Rose forced a half smile. Stipes was always the voice of wisdom. He knew exactly what to say when she most needed it. "Thanks, Stipes." She didn't exactly feel better, but she *did* feel she wasn't going entirely insane.

Stipes made to stand, then stopped in his tracks as Banks came dashing towards them. "I've got some good news and some bad news, Guv."

Rose raised her hands to her aching temples. "What's the bad news?"

"It's Mrs. Dyer. She got rushed to the hospital with severe abdominal pain late last night. Doctors are still trying to find out what's wrong with her. But it's unlikely she'll be in a position to talk to us for a couple of days."

Rose banged a fist on the table, causing a thunderous echo that burst through the room like a tsunami through water. When the noise subsided, she took a deep breath. "What's the good news?"

Banks leaned back on his heels. "You might want to brace yourself for this, 'cos it's pretty damn good."

Rose closed her eyes, then opened them again. "Just get on with it Banks."

"Well, I just had a phone call from a lady in Germany. A lady who's in your box of files. She'd returned from a few days away to find a message from Stipes on her answering machine."

"And?"

"And she's catching the next flight over to talk to us."

Rose leaned back in her chair, instantly skeptical. "Wait a minute. You're saying she got Stipes's message and, on the basis of that, she's flying straight over here?" She turned to Stipes. "What the hell did you say?"

"Only that we found a box of files in the deceased Mrs. Sampson's home, and we're trying to establish its relevance."

Rose looked uncertain. She turned back to Banks. "Did she say anything else?"

"I'm afraid not. She was reluctant to talk over the phone. But she seemed to think she had information that could help us."

"And she's flying all the way here, on her own accord, without as much as a formal request...just to help us?"

"That's right."

For a minute or so they all reflected on the strange development. If the woman was so keen to talk to them, she had to know something, and it had to be something pretty significant. The question was, would it help them solve the case?

Rose turned back to Banks. "When will she get here?"

"Late tomorrow morning."

"I thought you said she was catching the next flight?"

Stipes was quick to cut in. "I guess we have to give her chance to prepare herself, Guv."

Rose leaned back in her chair. "That's all well and good under normal circumstances. But these aren't normal circumstances. This is a fucking murder enquiry, and it's about time people started realizing that." She shook her head, again raising her hands to her aching temples. "I'm sorry. We're lucky she's coming here at all. It's just been a frustrating morning, that's all. And the fact that someone might actually be prepared to divulge something and she's not coming in 'til tomorrow...."

Stipes shot her a knowing look. "I know."

Banks was about to drift off when Rose looked up, realizing she wasn't done with him yet. "What's her name? The woman from Germany?"

Banks turned back to face her. "Mrs. Andrea Simmons. She's a fifty-five year old widow with two adult children who no longer live with her. She moved to Germany with her husband twenty odd years ago, and he died eighteen months ago. She teaches in a local secondary school."

Rose recognized the name and had already established most of the other details. "At least you've done your research. Thanks, Banks. I appreciate it." She was about to excuse him when something else occurred to her. "What about the B&B Finlay visited? Have you had chance to check it out yet?"

"No one recognized his photo, but his name was in the register. If it comes to it, we could put a poster in reception to see if anyone-else recognizes him."

"Don't worry about it. If he wasn't a regular, I doubt if anyone would remember him anyway. And the flyers?"

"No one seems to recognize Finlay's photo. But I haven't spoken to all the employees yet. They work shifts."

"OK, well keep me updated." Before Banks could leave, she added, "What about Brannigan? Have you made arrangements to get her back in yet?"

"It was the next thing on my list. I thought you might want to get the other interviews out the way first."

Rose nodded, and Banks wandered off. She was slightly peeved that he had anticipated her wishes without asking again, but for now she let it slide. It had been a long couple of days, and she knew her team was doing everything they could to bring Sampson and Finlay's killer to justice. So instead she focused her attention on Stipes. "I just hope, whatever it is Mrs. Simmons has to tell us, it helps us solve our murders. Because there's no guarantee of that. That box of files might hold sensitive information that Sampson's ex-patients would rather remain hidden. But it may have nothing at all to do with why Sampson and Finlay were killed."

Stipes shrugged his shoulders. "I know, Guv. But we've got to get lucky some time."

Rose glanced at the clock…five past eleven. "OK, since Mrs. Dyer's not coming in, let's move on to her son." She picked up a piece of paper containing the profile of Mrs. Sampson's gardener. "It's time we found out if he has alibis for the times of the murders."

Stipes nodded, and Rose's attention drifted to a copy of the *Brackley Herald* on the desk in front of her. Even from a few feet away she could read its headline. "Two Brutal Murders in Brackley in 24 Hours." It made her cringe.

"Shit. Go get Dyer, will you? I'll check in with the rest of the team."

Once she'd finished with the briefing, Rose decided to call Forensics. Even though Sherman had already spoken with them, there could've been a development. She knew how long it took to run tests and obtain results.

A doctor from the forensics lab answered the phone on the third ring. But, unfortunately for Rose, there'd been nothing useful recovered from either crime scene. As if feeling guilty for delivering such negative news, the doctor elaborated.

"Whoever committed these crimes was clearly very forensically aware. And that's reiterated by the fact that we've found nothing at either of the properties that seemed like it shouldn't have been there. Not a single fiber."

Rose nodded silently. "And that's unusual, right?"

"It's not totally unheard of in this day and age. Due to programs like *CSI*, people *are* becoming more forensically aware. That said, total lack of transference *is* hard to achieve. Even if the killer wore gloves and boot covers, the slightest tear in the fabric could yield a fiber without them realizing it."

The statement made Rose think of Campbell and his torn glove, and of the person in Finlay's garden. They hadn't gotten a good look at the intruder's feet, but subsequent prints had suggested they'd worn boot covers.

The doctor continued. "And of course, there's always the risk of transferring saliva. A cough or a sneeze could be enough to reveal blood type for approximately eighty five percent of the population, and even that could be of help."

Rose already knew that eighty five percent of the population were defined as "secreters," meaning that their blood type could

be revealed through their bodily fluids. Not that the knowledge
was of any use to her right now. Nothing had been recovered,
even if they *did* have a suspect to test it against.

She thanked the doctor and ended the call. Stipes would be
back soon with their next interview of the day. Not that she had
particularly high hopes of getting much from Dyer. She folded
her arms, then unfolded them again. At the moment, it seemed
like the only way they were going to break this case was through
sheer luck.

CHAPTER TWENTY-THREE

Andrew Dyer was a short, stocky man, with broad shoulders and a body that looked slightly too long for his legs. He had short ginger hair that was prematurely greying around the temples and sides, and a belly that overlapped the waist of his trousers. Somehow he looked different in the flesh than he had in his work photo.

Rose viewed him through the two-way mirror. He looked tense and anxious. His face was almost as red as his jacket, and he was holding his hands together as though he didn't know what to do with them. She watched him as he crossed his legs and uncrossed them again. Normally she wouldn't have bothered pulling in someone with such a tenuous connection to the victims. A brief home visit would have sufficed. But under the circumstances, they needed to cover all bases. Besides, Dyer's connection with Mrs. Sampson *was* double edged. He could well have spoken with his mother regarding the clients he visited, and, if she'd recognized Sampson's name, she could've convinced him to act on her behalf. Presuming she had some sort of score to settle with the former doctor.

Rose pondered the thought further. There was just one problem. Dyer didn't fit the profile of the figure in Finlay's garden. Even in baggy clothes, he'd be far too stocky. But that didn't mean he didn't know anything. She signaled to Stipes, and together they entered the room.

Once she'd initiated proceedings, Rose leaned forward across the table. "Good morning Mr. Dyer. I'm sorry for any inconvenience we might've caused you by calling you in at such short notice. Particularly at such a difficult time." She was referring to Dyer's mother, though the statement seemed to go over his head. "Do you have any idea why you're here?"

Dyer shook his head vehemently. He looked like he was about to cry, and Rose wondered if he had some kind of impediment that prevented him from communicating properly. She considered offering him legal representation, but the front desk had already informed him of his rights. Besides, at the moment all they wanted was an informal chat. She decided to just go easy.

"Well, I don't know if you've seen it on the news, but there've been two suspicious deaths in Brackley over the last few days. One of which involved a lady you gardened for…an elderly lady who lived at Six Amber Court."

If Dyer knew what she was talking about, he didn't react.

"Do you recall the last time you visited Six Amber Court?"

He leaned forward and, for the first time, looked responsive. "No. I'm sorry. You'd have to speak with my employer." His voice was deep and soft. Rose smiled. At least he was polite.

"OK, we'll do that. In the meantime, is there anything you can tell us about the lady who lived there? Mrs. Sampson? She was a former doctor at St. Thomas' Hospital." She wanted to know if the name meant anything to him, but if it did, it didn't show.

Dyer fiddled with a small knot of wood on the table, then finally looked up to meet her gaze. "Not really. I just knocked on the door to let her know I was there and knocked again when I left."

Again, Rose smiled. She wanted this discussion to remain relaxed. "She didn't offer you a drink or anything?"

Dyer looked back down. "No. I always bring my own. People like to keep to themselves, so I always bring my own stuff."

He was echoing Campbell's words, though Rose could see why people wouldn't want to engage him in conversation.

She nodded, and Stipes leaned forward in his chair. "What about electricity? Didn't you need access to plug sockets?"

Dyer stopped fiddling with the table. "The lady ran an extension cord outside. It was all ready when I got there."

Rose recalled Sampson's obsession with security, and guessed it wasn't surprising that she'd prepared things before Dyer got there.

Stipes continued. "D'you get that a lot?"

"Yes." Dyer ran a hand along his nose and Rose offered him a tissue. He took one but didn't use it. "People know what we need, so they generally have it ready when we get there."

There was a moment of silence, during which Rose shuffled the papers on her desk. When she looked up again, Dyer was staring at the window. She tried to keep her voice even.

"But you *do* recall the old lady at Six Amber Court?"

Dyer maintained his focus on the window. "Yes. I've been going there a long time. But I don't go there often. Some people let their gardens get overgrown before they want them done again."

Rose waited a moment before responding. "I see. And did you ever see her outside of work? Say, at the shops, or just walking along the street? Or in any social capacity?"

Again, Dyer shook his head. "No. Never. I don't live near there."

"And did you know she was a doctor?"

149

"No."

As with the previous interviewees, Rose picked up a large brown envelope and pulled out a photo. "I'm showing Mr. Dyer exhibit 2a." She slid the photo across the table. "Do you recognize this man?"

She knew Dyer had never gardened at Three Violet Crescent, at least not for his current employer, but that didn't mean there wasn't some other connection to Finlay. Dyer stared at the image for a long time, though his expression remained blank.

"No," he said finally.

Rose took the photo back and returned it to the envelope. If Dyer was in any way implicated in the murders, she'd be extremely surprised, unless he'd been implicated without his knowing. He didn't seem clever enough to orchestrate such seamless executions, let alone leave no forensics.

She placed the envelope back down on the table. "Did you ever do any of the other gardens in Violet Crescent?"

He thought for a moment. "I don't think so."

"But you *do* know Violet Crescent?"

"I know where it is. But I don't go there. I've got no reason to."

Rose inhaled a deep breath and let it out slowly. Like the other interviews today, this was getting them nowhere. She glanced into the two-way mirror, knowing her colleagues would be thinking the same thing. She felt like a broken record, continually asking the same questions. Still, it had to be done, however frustrating it was.

After a few more questions, Rose asked Dyer for his whereabouts on the nights of the murders. He told her he'd been at home with his parents, alibis she knew weren't totally verifiable. Parents were often prepared to lie to protect their offspring. Still, she'd check it out. If the Dyers offered any contradictions, she might rethink their son's capabilities.

She glanced at the tape recorder. "OK, Mr. Dyer, that's it for now. But if you think of anything unusual you witnessed at Six Amber Court, anything at all, give me a call." She passed him her card and ended the interview. "And I do hope your mother is better soon."

Once Dyer had left the room with Stipes, Rose collected the paperwork from the table. She was just about to rise when Blake popped his head around the door.

"Just to let you know, Guv, Sampson's neighbor, Ms. Mills, has just returned home."

Rose stopped what she was doing and looked up. "Thank God for that. Did she say where she's been?"

"Apparently at her sister's. Would you like me to get her in?"

"That won't be necessary. Not at the moment. At least we know where she is if we need her."

Blake disappeared back the way he'd come and, for the third time that day, Rose headed out of the interview room.

CHAPTER TWENTY-FOUR

Rose had barely gotten back to her desk when she looked up to find Reece hovering over her. He looked flushed and excited, as though all his Christmases had just come at once. When he finally caught his breath, his words came out in one continuous string.

"I've finally managed to trace Mrs. Sampson's sister, Guv. She's living alone in a remote part of Belgium. Apparently, she's too fragile to travel, but the officer who located her, an Officer Crane, reckons he might be able to set up a Skype interview… that's if she agrees to it."

Rose let out a sigh of relief. First Mrs. Simmons, now Mrs. Sampson's sister. Perhaps they were finally starting to get somewhere. Then the skepticism flooded in. "So this Officer Crane hasn't spoken with her yet?"

Reece looked slightly deflated. "He's spoken with her, but only briefly. She's pretty old and not in great health, so he has to tread carefully. But with a little persuasion, he thinks he might get her to cooperate."

Rose raised her eyebrows. "I guess that depends on whether or not she's happy with the topic of discussion."

"We can only hope."

Reece walked back the way he'd come, and Rose sank back into her chair. Suddenly she felt lightheaded. She gripped the edge of the desk, realizing that she hadn't eaten since yesterday evening. It was beginning to become a habit, one she really had to address if she was to continue to function at the best of her ability. She stretched out her legs beneath the table and closed her eyes, wondering if she had the strength to make it downstairs for a sandwich. If there was one thing she didn't need right now, it was for her own body to fail her.

When Stipes returned, she practically dragged him to the cafeteria. Not that he put up much of a protest. The last couple of days had taken their toll on both of them. If they continued to operate at such a pace, they both knew something would eventually have to give, and neither they nor the department could afford for that to happen.

When they reached their destination, Rose was pleasantly surprised. Since her last visit, the cafeteria had been completely refurbished. Old metal chairs had been replaced with new white plastic ones that matched the smooth white tables. And the fresh white walls held modern black and white images that detracted attention from the otherwise utilitarian space. It looked vaguely pleasant, a word she didn't use often when describing her place of work.

Stipes insisted on getting lunch, so she took a seat at a table beside the window and stared out into the dreary day. The sky had darkened since that morning, changing from a hazy blue to a dark, leaden grey. It looked like it was about to rain, but the ice she'd scraped from her car that morning suggested it was more likely to be sleet. The thought made her shudder, and she reached for the radiator beneath the window. Despite the time of year, it was cold to the touch. Apparently, heating wasn't something the department was willing to waste money on.

She fastened the buttons on her jacket and pulled out her mobile to check the display. She'd switched it to silent during the interview, but there were no recent messages. She turned up the volume and placed it back in her pocket. It felt good to be out of the fray for a while, even if it was just to get a sandwich. It gave her a chance to clear her head, and to mull over the days' events so far.

When Stipes returned with the sandwiches, Rose was busy poring over her spider-gram. She'd taken to carrying it around with her, so she could update it should the need arise. He glanced at it from across the table. It was the first time he'd seen it, and he was clearly surprised by the amount of information it contained.

He put down the tray and leaned forward. "It's surprising how much info we've collected when you look at it like that."

Rose shrugged her shoulders but didn't look up. "The problem is, how much of it's relevant?" She took a good long look at the tangled web of words. "Still, I guess things *do* look clearer when the facts are in front of you in black and white." She took a bite of her sandwich, which tasted surprisingly good, then quickly took another.

Stipes shot her a doubtful look. "Do you still believe the box of files is the connection?"

His comment unnerved her. "Don't you?"

"I don't know. I mean, I wouldn't rule it out. But I worry we might be missing something else while we're so busy pursuing its relevance."

Rose put down her sandwich and shot him a concerned look. "Like what?"

"I don't know. Maybe we're not looking objectively enough. Maybe, if I hadn't found those files, we might have worked harder to find something else, and we might be closer to catching our killer." He added sugar to his coffee and stirred it. "I'm sorry.

I know I told you to follow your gut. I guess I'm just feeling a little deflated today."

"You and me both."

After the days' disappointing start, it was hardly surprising. Rose had hoped this would be the day things finally began to fall into place. Instead, they just seemed to be going around in circles. And the media attention was doing nothing to ease the pressure. She could already feel the chief breathing down her neck. She had a briefing with him later this afternoon, and at this rate, it wasn't going to be pleasant.

She shrugged her shoulders, taking a mouthful of coffee to wash down the sandwich. It was natural for Stipes to have doubts. Everyone had them. Doubts about whether or not they'd missed anything, doubts regarding if they'd looked in the right places or asked the right questions, even doubts concerning their own abilities. At the end of the day, that was the nature of police work. If you didn't have doubts, you weren't doing your job properly. At least that was what she told herself.

She pushed the spider-gram to the center of the table. "Our problem is, there's almost too much information. Willis and his team have been going over those surveillance tapes for hours, but so far we've had nothing of significance from them. Then there's the missing details. We still don't know for sure how Mrs. Sampson's killer got in, and we have absolutely no idea what Finlay did for a living. How can anyone be that invisible? Then there's his missing phone."

Stipes raised his eyebrows. "It *could* still turn up."

"So could Lord Lucan, but I don't think it's likely. And, as well as all that, there's the hours Reece has spent tracing Mrs. Sampson's estranged sister. Thank God she's finally been found. But we still don't know if she'll be able to offer us any insight into her sister's death. Or much of her life, since she's been abroad for the last thirty years. And that's if she even agrees to talk to us." She took another bite of her sandwich, then swallowed quickly. "And I keep coming back to Fawcett's statement. Did she really see the killer climbing over the side gate, when there's perfectly good access to Finlay's garden from the rear?" The recording hadn't panned wide enough to show exactly where the figure had emerged from. Rose raised her eyebrows. "But why would she lie?" The question prompted a thought. "Has anyone checked out her address yet?"

Stipes took a large gulp of his coffee. "I'm not sure. I'll get on it as soon as we get back."

Rose nodded, returning her focus to the spider-gram. "Also, should we accept Campbell's version of how his fingerprint came to be on that pane of glass? Or believe Brannigan's statement that she didn't know what Finlay did for a living? At the moment I'm finding it impossible to tell the truth from the lies, and there are definitely lies here."

Stipes bit into his sandwich, sending a spurt of ketchup straight into the corner of his mouth. Rose barely noticed. "What we need is motive. Unfortunately, if Sampson was engaging in illegal activities, any number of people might've had reason to want her dead. As for Finlay, hell, someone as dubious as him could've dug himself into all sorts of holes. Again, too much information."

She raised her hands in the air as if to reiterate the fact, and Stipes leaned his elbows on the table. "We'll get there, Guv. It may not seem like it, but somewhere in all that information there's something that can help us. There has to be."

"You really think so?" She was beginning to wonder if they hadn't been on the wrong track from the outset.

"If I didn't, would I still be smiling?" He lifted the corners of his mouth with his fingers.

"Anyway, we'll know more tomorrow, when we've spoken with Mrs. Simmons."

Again, Rose returned her focus to the spider-gram. There had to be something she was missing. Something vital. Something that, if she could draw it out, would lead them one step closer to the killer. But what in God's name was it? She focused on its' center, adding, "We don't even know for sure if Sampson and Finlay shared a connection…if we knew that, at least we'd have something definite to focus on."

She was about to pursue the subject further when her phone sounded in her pocket. She pulled it out.

"DI Rose."

Blake's distinctive drawl filled the line. "I just spoke with the manager of the Benton Hotel in Kent, Guv. Until ten years ago, they held a few conventions. Mostly in the '80s and '90s. A lot of them were one-offs. But there was one in particular that kept returning. A convention entitled 'The Myths Surrounding Abortion'"

Something clicked in Rose's brain. "Go on."

"Well, Mrs. Sampson, or *Dr.* Sampson as she was known then, attended a few."

"What about Finlay?"

"There's no one on record by that name. But that doesn't mean he wasn't there."

"Thanks, Blake. Good work."

Rose put the phone back in her pocket and turned to Stipes. "We might have just found the connection. Mrs. Sampson attended a series of conferences entitled 'The Myths Surrounding Abortion' in the '80s and '90s. It's possible Finlay did too, since the hotel's flyers were in his sideboard."

She folded the spider-gram and placed it back in her pocket, struggling to make sense of the new information. "What we need to know is whether or not potassium chloride is used in abortion. Weller told us it's been linked to suicide, and we know it's present in the lethal injection."

She pulled out her phone for the third time and dialed Weller's number. When he didn't answer, frustration prickled her.

Stipes leaned forward, deliberately lowering his voice. "So you're thinking Mrs. Sampson could've been involved in helping women have abortions?"

Rose looked at him evenly. "It wouldn't be *that* surprising. She *was* in the profession of caring for pregnant women. And abortions would've been perfectly legal then." She drained her coffee cup and drummed her fingers on the table in front of her. "The question is, were those abortions conducted through official channels."

Stipes put down the remains of his sandwich. "If Finlay was somehow involved, it *could* provide a motive for both of their deaths. Particularly if Sampson was operating under the radar, and possibly gaining financially from her endeavors."

Rose was about to resort to the Internet to answer her question on potassium chloride when her phone sounded again. She pulled it out to see Weller's name printed across its screen. Weller issued his standard polite greeting, which she barely had the patience to listen to. When he'd finished, she launched straight in:

"Thank you for returning my call, Doctor. I just have a quick question for you. Potassium chloride...is it used in abortion?"

Weller hesitated, but only for a moment. "It's not used in standard abortions that take place in the first trimester...that's the first three months of pregnancy. But in abortions that take place in the second or third trimester, it's sometimes injected to stop the fetus's heart, so that the mother doesn't suffer the trauma of delivering a live but not fully formed baby."

Rose couldn't hide the shock that tainted her voice. "So you're telling me that women can still have abortions in the mid to late stages of pregnancy?" A young officer from a few tables away shot her a horrified look, and she quickly lowered her voice.

The doctor continued. "It's rare. But in cases where an acute medical complication is discovered, it *can* happen."

Rose felt her stomach turn. There'd been no record of any acute medical conditions in the women featured in Sampson's files.

She ended the call and turned back to Stipes. "It seems potassium chloride is used when women have abortions later in their pregnancy." Even saying the words aloud felt unnatural. "So maybe we've found Sampson and Finlay's niche. It's just a shame there were no dates on those files. Then again, perhaps that was intentional. We have no way of knowing if the pregnancies they depicted achieved the usual outcome."

A thought occurred to her and she dialed Blake. He answered before she heard it ring. "Blake. That hotel...The Benton. Find out if they still have the contact details for the organizer of those conventions, will you? There's a chance, albeit slim, that they might recognize a photo of Sampson or Finlay."

She put down the phone and placed her head in her hands. If it turned out that the motive underlying the murders had something to do with abortion, it wouldn't be good for team morale, let alone social politics. Particularly if those abortions had occurred during the mid to late stages of pregnancy. The thought made her feel physically sick, and she pushed her plate away.

Once again, she stared out into the dreary day. A pattern was finally starting to emerge. It just wasn't the pattern she'd anticipated...if it was even the pattern they were looking for. She turned back to the table and drew in a heavy breath. "I guess we should head back upstairs. This could be the breakthrough we've been looking for. If one of the women in those files had an abortion that went wrong, or even regretted their decision after the event, they'd definitely have had motive for murder."

Stipes finished his coffee and rose from his seat. "Should we call Frederickson and Broom back in, Guv? See if we can't get to the bottom of this?"

Rose considered the question. As much as she wanted to confront the women with her newfound knowledge, she knew she had to tread carefully. She *could* still be totally off track. Against every instinct in her body, she replied, "No, let's wait 'til we've spoken with Mrs. Simmons. We need hard facts before we take things any further. The media will be watching our every move, and we can't afford to make an issue of something unless we're absolutely sure it's relevant. Not when it's taken us so long to get this far." She stared back out into the cold December sky. "In the meantime, let's see if Reece can lean on that officer in Belgium. If we can get something from Sampson's sister, we might be able to piece things together better."

Stipes nodded. "On it."

As he turned to leave, she added, "Anyway, Banks should be arriving soon with Brannigan...and this time I'd really like to sit in."

CHAPTER TWENTY-FIVE

When Rose met Brannigan for the second time, she was surprised by how frail the woman looked. She seemed to have aged almost overnight, and Rose wondered if the news of Finlay's death had hit her harder than they'd realized. She and Finlay had clearly been close, or they'd never have remained in contact after their break-up. But had that closeness been deep enough for him to have revealed his secrets to her? Or for her to risk a prison sentence to protect his reputation?

Rose led the way to the interview room, accompanied by Stipes. Banks and Brannigan followed behind. They paused for Stipes to grab four cups of coffee on the way. If Brannigan finally started to talk, the last thing Rose wanted was to halt proceedings for something as insignificant as a drink.

When they were all seated and furnished with refreshments, Rose switched on the tape recorder and reeled off the usual spiel. For the time being, like the previous interviewees, Brannigan was refusing legal representation., A move that made Rose wonder if she really *was* as in the dark as she purported to be.

Rose cleared her throat and pulled herself up straight in her chair. Brannigan was staring down into her lap. Like Frederickson earlier, she had deep red semi-circles beneath her eyes: and her long black hair looked lank and greasy. Rose shot a glance at Stipes, then directed one at Banks. Due to his history with Brannigan, she'd decided to let him sit in on the interview, in the hope that he might provide some much-needed stability. Or at the very least, a friendly face.

She leaned forward. "So, Miss Brannigan, I take it you know why you're here?"

Brannigan nodded but didn't speak.

"If you could state your response clearly for the tape recorder."

Brannigan murmured a yes, without moving her lips, and Rose pressed on.

"For the purposes of the recording, I'd like to reiterate that you're here to hopefully provide us with some background information on the recently deceased Zack Finlay."

The mention of his name fueled a stifled groan. Rose ignored it.

"So how long have you known Mr. Finlay?" She decided to stick to the present tense, to make the questioning easier. From her experience, the newly bereaved found it difficult to refer to their loved ones in the past tense so soon after their expiration.

Brannigan rolled her eyes. "Nine…nine and a half years."

"Wow. That's a long time. You obviously knew him very well."

"As well as anyone could have."

Rose shuffled the papers in front of her. It was a tactic she used to make people think she had more information than she actually did. Plus, it gave her something to do. "Can I ask what you mean by that?"

Brannigan made eye contact for the first time. "Zack was a very private individual. He had hidden depths. Places he retreated to when he found a topic of conversation uncomfortable or not to his liking. It was probably why he didn't have friends. He didn't find it easy to confide in people."

Rose managed a brief smile. "Did he ever confide in you? About anything?"

Brannigan was silent for a moment. "He confided in me about the problems he had in his childhood. He wasn't planned, you see. His parents had been professional people who hadn't wanted children from the outset. When Zack came along, I guess they just couldn't cope. He remembers — *remembered* — being raised by a succession of nannies and babysitters, some of whom weren't particularly patient. One in particular took pleasure in torturing him."

"And his parents never knew?"

"I think he was too scared to tell them. They weren't close, and I don't think they were particularly patient with him either."

Rose merely nodded. The dialogue was flowing easier than she'd expected. Brannigan had even reverted to past tense herself. Perhaps she was coping better than she appeared to be.

Rose leaned her elbows on the table in front of her. "That's very sad. It must've had a huge impact on Zack's life." Her statement went unanswered, but she continued regardless. "I don't suppose he gave you the name of the nanny...the one he claims tortured him?"

Brannigan looked like she was about to cry, and Rose passed her a tissue which she subsequently used to dab her eyes. "No. He never went into detail. I think the memories were too painful."

Again, Rose nodded, shooting a discreet glance at Stipes. Finlay's disjointed upbringing *could* explain why he'd led such a solitary existence, and perhaps gotten involved in things he shouldn't have. His treatment at the hands of his nannies could also give him motive for becoming pro-abortion. She decided to pursue the matter further. "Did Zack tell you *how* he was tortured?" If he'd later exacted revenge on his tormentor, it *could've* provided a motive for his "execution."

Brannigan's response was simple. "No."

Rose decided to change tack. "Did Zack ever tell you anything about his daily life? Anything at all? Even something that might've seemed insignificant at the time."

Brannigan lowered her eyes to her lap again. "Sometimes he'd call me from a hotel or a B&B and tell me what he was eating or which movie he was watching on TV. But he would never tell me why he was there. He just said it was business and he didn't want to talk about it. When I pressed him, he just clammed up and ended the conversation. So I learned not to ask. It created such a rift between us, I couldn't be with him anymore. It's impossible to be intimate with someone when you know hardly anything about them." She seemed to consider the implications of what she'd just said. "Not that I thought Zack could ever do anything bad. He just liked to keep things to himself. Maybe because, when he was growing up, that was what he had to do. But I think, in many ways, he preferred it when we were just friends. He didn't have to deflect any uncomfortable questions."

The mention of hotels made Rose think back to the flyers. She pulled them out from beneath the pile of papers and pushed them across the table. "Do you recognize any of the hotels in these flyers?"

Brannigan picked them up and studied them closely. Despite her appearance, she was holding up remarkably well. Again, Rose considered her potential to pull the wool over their eyes. If she *had* known something worth killing Finlay for, how would they know?

When Brannigan finally put the flyers back down, she had a deflated look about her. "No. Sorry. But these seem really old. It's possible we visited one of them, but it doesn't look the same

164

anymore."

She picked up her coffee cup, and Rose noticed that her hands were trembling. Either it was the grief kicking in again or she was nervous. But nervous of what? Rose reached for the envelope she'd been fumbling with and pulled out two A4 photos. They were the same ones she'd shown Frederickson and Broom, images of Mrs. Sampson when she'd still been functioning in a professional capacity. She pushed them to across Brannigan, explaining her actions for the recording.

"Can you tell me if you recognize this woman? Her name's Mrs. Elise Sampson, and she was a qualified obstetrician."

Brannigan pulled the photo closer.

"Take your time."

Again, Rose shot a glance at Stipes. Brannigan was deliberating over the photo, even though Banks had shown it to her before. Perhaps she was having second thoughts about revealing what she knew. She crossed her fingers beneath the table.

When Brannigan finally looked up again, she looked confused. "I'm not sure. I know I've been shown this photo before but, to be honest, I wasn't really sure then either."

Rose forced a reassuring smile. "That's OK. You don't have to be one hundred percent. We won't hold you to it. Do you recall where you might recognize the woman *from*?"

Brannigan looked at the photo again. "I think I might've seen her at one of the hotels we visited, but it wasn't one of these." She glanced back at the flyers. "Or was it? Sorry. It would've been a while ago. I'm really not sure."

She unfolded the tissue and blew her nose. After a few seconds of silence, something seemed to click in her brain. "Hang on a minute. It wasn't a hotel. I think we were on some kind of trip. I can't remember where, but it was somewhere I hadn't been before, because I remember keeping close to Zack so I wouldn't

165

get lost." She visibly relaxed a little while reminiscing. "And it was kind of weird, because I felt as though Zack knew this woman. But they deliberately bypassed each other. Like people who are embarrassed to be acquainted. It made me feel slightly awkward."

Rose sighed, wondering why Brannigan hadn't told Banks this before. She fiddled with the pen in front of her. "You didn't confront him about it?"

"No. I guess I didn't want to make an issue of it and spoil the day."

Rose leaned further forward across the table. "When you say it was a long time ago, are you referring to months? Or years?" If Finlay had been in contact with Sampson recently, it *could* explain the timing of their deaths.

Brannigan scrunched up the tissue again. "Definitely years. Zack and I were together at the time, and it was probably in the early days, because the trip thing fizzled out quite early on. But this lady, if it was her, looked older. Quite a lot older."

Rose nodded. "That would make sense." She pressed on while the going was good. "So Mrs. Sampson, if that was who you saw, made no attempt to speak to Zack? Or vice versa?"

Brannigan shook her head. "No. It was just a slightly awkward moment. Like I said, it was as if they didn't want people knowing they knew each other. But the moment passed, and I never saw her again."

Again, Brannigan took a sip of her coffee, and Rose looked first to Banks, then to Stipes. They hadn't expected to get so much from her. If it *had* been Sampson she'd seen, it proved that not only had Sampson and Finlay shared a connection, but their business together had been dubious in nature.

She decided to backtrack a little. It was imperative they attain as much information on the deceased Zack Finlay as possible. "Is

166

there anything else you can tell us about Zack? Did he have any hobbies or interests?

Brannigan put down her empty coffee cup and placed it to one side. "He liked fishing."

"I see. Do you know if he was a member of a club? Or if there were any particular spots where he regularly fished?"

The former model looked close to tears again. Rose offered her a fresh tissue. "I don't even know that. It's as if I shared those years of my life with a total stranger."

There was a moment of silence while Rose considered Brannigan's responses. If the woman *had* known what Finlay was up to, she was doing a damn fine job of acting like she hadn't, and she was certainly convincing. But that didn't detract from the fact that she'd lied to Banks about the photo. Still, Rose adopted her most sympathetic demeanor.

"I'm very sorry to have to ask all these questions, but we're almost done. Did you ever know Zack to have any health problems?"

Brannigan composed herself again. "No. None at all. He was fit and well. At least as far as I knew."

Rose nodded. "OK. Well, did you ever know him to go by a different name?"

Brannigan frowned. "No, I didn't. Why? Did he ever go by a different name?"

Rose simply shrugged. "I've no idea. That's what we're trying to find out."

She looked to Stipes again. It was clear that the questioning was taking its toll on Brannigan, and she didn't know how much longer she could keep it up. Treading as carefully as she could, she requested the woman's alibis for the nights of the murders, quick to emphasize that it was merely for the purpose of ruling her out. Brannigan's responses, however, were less than satisfactory.

She'd apparently been at home alone on both occasions, which would do nothing to prove her innocence.

Rose asked a few more questions, from which she gleaned very little, and ended the interview. She watched as Stipes accompanied the columnist out through the narrow doorway. She still hadn't formed a judgement as to the woman's character, which was odd considering she was generally quite good at such things. Perhaps the reason for her uncertainty was Brannigan's ability to morph herself to suit the circumstances. Or perhaps it was just the woman's overall disposition.

She was about to leave the room herself when her phone sounded in her pocket. For what seemed like the hundredth time that day, she pulled it out. Again, it was Blake.

"The hotel located the organizer of those events, Guv, Mrs. Eileen Sharp. As luck would have it, she still lives at the same address. She's even got the same phone number. I've spoken to her, and she's happy for us to go around. As it happens, she's home all afternoon."

Rose smiled silently to herself. Things were finally starting to unravel.

CHAPTER TWENTY-SIX

Mrs. Eileen Sharp answered the door before Rose even had a chance to knock. She was a short, vivacious woman in her late fifties. She had spiky blonde hair and wore bold, vibrant clothes that had probably been out of date twenty years ago. Nevertheless, she was friendly and welcoming, and she had a liveliness about her that was almost contagious.

Sharp ushered Rose and Stipes into a brightly decorated lounge that smelled like fresh flowers and vanilla. There were an assortment of ornamental angels occupying every available surface. It looked more like the quiet room of a chapel than an actual living space. They seated themselves on a soft, dark red sofa, and Rose pulled out the brown padded envelope she'd brought with her. There was no point in delaying things. They all knew why they were there.

Sharp offered refreshments, probably more out of politeness than anything else, and they graciously refused. It was already close to three-thirty in the afternoon, and Reece's officer in Belgium could call at any time. If they missed their window of opportunity, another might not arise.

Sharp reached for the photos Rose had removed from the envelope and perched herself on a small armchair opposite.

She took her time examining each image before finally looking back up. "So, you say these people were at the conferences I organized?"

Rose leaned forward slightly. "We know that at least one of them was. The other one could've been. What we don't know is how big a role they might've played."

Sharp looked at the images again. Rose couldn't tell if there was recognition in her eyes or not. She'd have made a good poker player. After a few long seconds, she turned the photos around, facing them back towards Rose. "I think I recognize this one." She had her finger on the image of Mrs. Sampson. "The other one I'm not so sure about. We had a lot of attendees. Conferences like that stir up a lot of emotion. It's possible he was a delegate, but he didn't particularly stand out."

It made sense. Finlay seemed to have liked blending into the background.

Rose managed a thin smile. "The one you think you recognize. Do you recall if she played a significant role at any of the conferences? She might have given a talk, or offered some kind of counselling or advice session? She was a qualified obstetrician."

Sharp shook her head. "If she did, I don't recall it. Then again, a lot of people gave talks. Or offered sessions. We didn't record them, and it *was* a very long time ago."

Rose had heard that excuse so many times today.

Sharp shifted from the chair's arm to its actual seat, and Rose finally got to the question she'd been waiting to ask. "So, what inspired you to arrange these conferences?"

Sharp handed back the photos and, for the first time, there was sadness in her eyes. "I had a bad experience when I was younger. I wanted an abortion, but I was too scared to go through the official channels for fear that someone might find out. In the end, I found a back-street practitioner who was willing to help without asking too many questions. Needless to say, there were complications. I almost died; and the surgery put pay to me ever having children. I guess I just wanted to demonstrate that there can be positive aspects to abortion, not just negative ones. Not all people that have abortions are evil; some of them are just in a bad place. I thought it was time to clarify things...highlight both sides, so to speak, and hopefully quash some of the bad press."

Rose almost wished she hadn't asked. "I'm so sorry. That's terrible. I totally understand why you would want to help prevent other women from suffering the same misfortune." She wondered if Sampson had experienced something similar, since she'd never had children, then ruled it out. It would've come up in the post mortem. But that didn't mean that someone close to her hadn't experienced it. Someone like, perhaps, her sister. She tried to lighten the mood. "When you organized the conferences, did you produce itineraries, lists of attendees, that sort of thing?"

Sharp regained her previous cheerful demeanor. "I can see why you would ask that, and, in different circumstances, we would have. But due to the conferences' sensitive nature, we thought it better not to. As you can imagine, we had a lot of opposition. Producing official documents, especially a list of attendees, could've been downright dangerous. Besides, your man and woman wouldn't necessarily be on it. A lot of people turned up on an ad hoc basis. In fact, we actively encouraged that. We didn't want people to feel pressured in any way."

Rose nodded in understanding. "When you say 'we,' can I ask who you're referring to?"

Sharp smiled. "Well, I *did* have people who helped me. I didn't do it all on my own. But for obvious reasons, they preferred to remain anonymous."

Rose considered asking for their details, then decided against it. If they'd requested anonymity, it was unlikely they'd be very cooperative. Besides, if it turned out to be relevant, they could always request them at a later date. A clock chimed somewhere, and she replied belatedly. "I see."

Rose took a brief pause and Stipes leaned forward. "You mentioned the sensitive nature of the conferences, and the fact that you had a lot of opposition to them. Did you ever receive any direct threats as a result?"

Again, Sharp smiled. "I received a few, but nothing I took seriously. Just the usual vicious slander that tends to be associated with the subject matter."

"So you didn't inform the police?"

"I think they'd have laughed me out of the station."

Rose placed the photos back in the envelope. "Well, thank you for your time, Mrs. Sharp. You've been very helpful. If you *do* happen to recall anything about the people in the photos, you can call me anytime."

She held out her card and Sharp accepted it, immediately leading them back into the hallway. When they reached the front door, she paused. "I don't suppose you could tell me why the people in the photos are significant?"

Rose turned to face her. "They're both dead, and we're wondering if their deaths were in any way connected to what went on at those conferences." She took in Sharp's appalled expression and backtracked slightly. "It's just a line of inquiry. I wouldn't read too much into it."

Sharp pulled open the door and they stepped out into the freezing air.

As soon as they were back in the driveway, Stipes took a call. It informed them that Reece's attempts at leaning on the Belgian officer had only succeeded in arranging an interview for that following morning, which Rose wasn't best pleased about.

172

Still, the fact that the elderly lady, Mrs. Joy Turner, had agreed to speak to them at all meant a great deal.

They climbed into their respective cars and headed back to the station. Blake still hadn't found anything in the media reports, and no news on Finlay had come in since the press release. So there was an urgent need for further research. Plus, there were still lines of inquiry Rose intended to pursue with regard to the women in the files.

The rest of that afternoon passed by in a blur. Rose had ended up spending the majority of her time compiling all the questions she wanted to ask tomorrow and justifying their lack of concrete evidence to the chief, who was under pressure to announce details of a suspect. When she finally got back to her desk, it was almost seven-thirty, and most of her team had already drifted off.

She sank into her chair and stared out through the tiny window. The street outside was in total darkness, just like the darkness that consumed her soul. Two brutal deaths had occurred in Brackley in as many days, and they were still no closer to finding the killer. But he or she was out there somewhere, drifting among the shadows. Possibly preparing to do it again.

She stretched out her legs and reached for the headache tablets in her drawer. The pressure in her head was so intense, it felt like it was about to explode, like the storm that was about to erupt in Brackley if they didn't make progress soon. The thought sent her mind back to tomorrow's meetings with Simmons and Turner. Hopefully they'd be able to put her on the road to finding their killer.

She swallowed the tablets and pulled herself up from the desk. It'd been a long day, and tomorrow promised to be even longer. A good night's sleep was just what the doctor ordered. Not that she was likely to get one.

CHAPTER TWENTY-SEVEN

When Rose awoke to the sound of the telephone ringing, she was almost too afraid to move. A call at such a late hour couldn't possibly be good news. She shuffled onto her side and picked up the receiver. The moment she had it in her hand, Stipes's distinctive voice sounded in her ear.

"You're not gonna wanna hear this, Guv, but there's been another murder."

His words pierced her skull like a bullet through flesh. "What? Where?" Her voice was so croaky, it didn't sound like her own.

"On South Street."

For a moment Rose struggled to digest what Stipes was telling her. Another murder? On South Street? The address struck a chord, but, in her dazed state, she couldn't recall where she'd heard it before.

Stipes drew in an audible breath. "It was called in a few minutes ago by the victim's girlfriend, so we already have an ID. You're not gonna believe who the victim is."

Rose slammed her hand down on the bed. "For Christ's sake, Stipes. Just tell me."

"It's Anthony Campbell. The guy who delivered the logs."

174

Rose was so surprised she almost dropped the receiver. "The guy with the fingerprint."

An icy chill ascended her spine. She'd still had Campbell pegged as a potential suspect, and perhaps rightly so. The fact that he'd been murdered didn't rule out the possibility that he'd killed Sampson and Finlay. He could've simply outlived his usefulness. Or become too much of a liability, especially since his fingerprint had been found. She wished she'd put more of a formal tail on him, as opposed to one that hadn't specified round the clock surveillance. If she hadn't had such a tight budget to adhere to, he *could* still be alive.

She recalled his reactions during their interview. He'd seemed genuinely shocked on hearing of the murders, *and* on becoming a suspect. Not that a person's reactions could necessarily be relied upon. Nevertheless, there'd been something about him that had struck a chord with her. Something she couldn't quite put her finger on. He hadn't struck her as their killer.

She put down the phone's receiver and leapt from the bed to get changed. She was jumping to conclusions. Campbell's murder wasn't necessarily connected to the case. But even as she thought it, she didn't believe it. Campbell had had associations with both Sampson and Finlay, and now he was dead. The coincidence was too startling.

She reached for the familiar black trouser suit on the chair in front of her, and as she did so, she glanced at the clock...three-fifteen. If Campbell's girlfriend had just called the incident in, where the hell had she been until three in the morning? More importantly, how had Campbell's killer known she'd be out?

When she reached South Street, Stipes had just pulled up. She parked her car at the roadside and together they headed for the property. It had already been cordoned off by the officers who'd initially attended, the speed of their actions emphasizing

175

the high priority of the case. However, the benefit of their haste was double-edged. On the flip side, it would attract unwanted media attention, and that was something they *didn't* need right now.

As they ducked beneath the crime scene tape, Rose noticed how overlooked the apartment was. Not only was it situated in a block, surrounded by at least half a dozen other apartments, but it was flanked on either side by two similar buildings. If someone hadn't seen Campbell's killer, it would be a miracle. Then again, if the incident had occurred in the early hours....

When they got to Campbell's first floor apartment, it was surprisingly quiet. For once Weller hadn't arrived yet, and Campbell's girlfriend had been removed and taken to the station for questioning. Not that they'd get a lot out of her in her apparently distressed state. So now all that remained were a few uniformed officers, who were busying themselves with securing the property.

Rose stepped inside. The apartment was bigger than it had looked from the outside. It had a spacious open plan kitchen/lounge area, with comfortable sofas and a large flat screen TV. She guessed the log delivery company must've paid pretty decent money. Unless the girlfriend was the one with the good job, or Campbell had been engaged in a profitable little sideline.

Campbell's body was in the bedroom. Like Sampson and Finlay before him, he was lying face down on the floor, a huge bloody gash clearly evident at the base of his skull. The similarity to the other two victims was so striking, Rose physically felt her heart skip a beat.

"Looks the same as the others, Guv," Stipes chipped in.

Rose shot him a look. She didn't want the other officers discovering the connection before it had been confirmed. Not that they weren't capable of figuring it out for themselves.

Rose leaned over the body, examining it for any sign of a needle mark. But the head injury seemed to have been more severe this time, and thick streaks of blood coated the entire neck area. She shook her head, her eyes drifting to the vicinity surrounding her. There were further streaks of blood on the soft beige carpet, and a large splatter tainted the surface of a nearby wall...no doubt a result of the impact.

She took a few steps back, until she was standing directly in the doorway. It seemed likely that Campbell had just entered the room when the killer had struck from behind. They'd probably been hiding out in the bathroom, which was situated directly opposite. Perhaps they'd expected to strike him as he walked in, but he'd opted for the bedroom instead, which had probably made their task easier.

She moved slowly forward. As with the other properties, there was no outward sign of a disturbance. The pale lilac bed coverings were still intact, as was the pile of clothes that rested tidily on a nearby chair. She instinctively looked to the light fitting. The lights were still on. The killer, if it hadn't been Campbell who'd murdered Sampson and Finlay, was growing more confident.

The sound of voices erupted from the living room, and Weller's distinctive face appeared in the doorway. "Good morning, detectives."

He entered the room accompanied by an assistant, and the confined space instantly felt crowded. Rose cursed beneath her breath. She'd been hoping for a few minutes to herself. A little tranquility to analyze her surroundings and conduct a preliminary search. She shot a glance at Weller, then, without responding, headed to a small bedside cabinet. Stipes moved towards its counterpart.

Opening the cabinet was more difficult than Rose had

anticipated. It clearly hadn't been used a lot, and its drawers were surprisingly stiff. When she *did* eventually open it, its contents were disappointing. It contained a couple of books, a notepad and pen, and a few other miscellaneous items. There was nothing that could be described as overtly personal. Nothing to indicate what its owner's preferences or tastes had been. Rose glanced across at Stipes, who merely shook his head. Its counterpart had proved similarly unrewarding.

They drifted to the other items of furniture, leaving Weller time to examine the body. When Rose finally turned to him, he was just in the process of turning it. She winced as Campbell's lifeless face sprang into view, then cursed herself for her over-sensitive nature. After all her years on the police force, she'd have thought it would've been beaten out of her by now. She took a deep breath. "So, what can you tell us?"

The doctor didn't look up. "On initial inspection, it looks the same as the others."

"So there's a needle mark?"

"There's a needle mark. But I have to get him back to the lab before I can confirm cause of death."

His response was unusually abrupt, and Rose wondered if she'd offended him in some way. She brushed the thought aside. No one was at their best at this time of the morning. She pressed on. "And time of death?"

This time Weller raised his head. "He hasn't been dead long. I'd say between midnight and two."

Rose nodded, more to herself than the doctor. "What about the head injury? Was it the same weapon as that used on Finlay?"

Weller let out a deep sigh, then glanced up again. The bags under his eyes seemed to be growing by the minute, and his skin had an unhealthy pallor. If he wasn't careful, he'd end up on one of those cold metal slabs he was so familiar with. Rose scolded herself for the thought.

"On first glance, it appears it could be. Though again, I'll have to get him back to the lab to be sure. There's more blood, but that's simply a result of the amount of force used."

"So, would you say this one was more frenzied?"

The doctor shook his head, turning back to his work. "Not at all. There was one blow to the back of the head as before. The killer probably just got lucky this time."

While Weller continued his examination, Rose ushered Stipes through to a small, pale peach bathroom. If this was where the killer had lain in wait, there was a serious shortage of hiding places. She pulled the shower curtain to one side. There were no muddy footprints in the bath it had shielded. Nor were there any obvious signs of intrusion. The killer was so adept at hiding his or her tracks, they were proving more elusive than the indefinable Zack Finlay.

They left the bathroom and headed for the living room, where, after a brief preliminary search, they gave up and decided to return to the station. SOCOs were busy conducting their own investigation, as was Forensics, and the competition was just too stifling. Rose concluded that more would be achieved if they returned later.

As they exited the apartment a uniformed officer walked by, presumably on the way to his car. Rose shook herself from her daze, tapping him on the shoulder and causing him to drop the set of keys he'd been carrying. He leaned forward to pick them up, shielding his face to hide his embarrassment. As it turned out, he needn't have bothered. Rose was too engrossed in her thoughts to notice.

"Do we know how the killer got in?" In all the confusion, it was the one thing she hadn't asked.

The officer placed the keys in his pocket and turned to

face her. "Bathroom window. There's a drainpipe positioned alongside it, and we found signs of activity there."

"Signs of activity?"

"Mud from the garden. And scuff marks. Recent ones."

"Any prints?"

"It hasn't been dusted yet."

Rose glanced across at Stipes. Scaling a drainpipe was a risky business. Not only would the killer have needed to be athletic, but the pipe would've needed to be secure enough to hold their weight. It was certainly taking a chance. The killer had definitely been confident. Either that, or they weren't averse to taking chances, which didn't fit with the lack of forensic evidence. The possibility that they were looking for different killers struck her again.

She nodded to the officer and they headed back out into the dark street. It was time to question the girlfriend, and to establish her whereabouts during the time of Campbell's murder. With any luck, it *could* yield some insight into why Campbell had been targeted.

As she headed to her car, Rose reflected on the property's lack of surveillance cameras. For a communal building, it was a distinct failing. Whoever was responsible had a lot to answer for. She wondered if Campbell's death would change things, then decided it probably wouldn't. There were those who had a conscience and those who didn't. She turned away, cursing herself for her cynicism.

When she reached the car, she pulled out her phone and dialed Banks's number. Despite the early hour, it was imperative that Campbell's family was notified before the media got wind of what had happened. Banks answered the phone after several rings, his voice throaty and disjointed. Like most people at this early hour, he'd clearly been asleep. Nevertheless, he accepted the task without question.

Rose was about to end the call when another thought struck her. "Take the photos of Sampson and Finlay with you, will you? See if they recognize them. But whatever you do, don't let them know the significance. Just tell them it's something else you've been looking into."

She rang off and climbed into the car. It was unlikely Campbell's family would prove any use. She'd already had them checked out. But then, who knew what people got involved in behind closed doors?

CHAPTER TWENTY-EIGHT

To Rose's disappointment, their brief chat with Campbell's girlfriend yielded little in the way of new information. She'd been so distraught when she'd been brought in, she'd had to be sedated. So the dialogue they'd eventually managed to have with her had been oddly surreal and fragmented.

What they *had* established was that she'd been out with close friends that previous night, all of whom could be called upon to verify her alibi. Not that she'd ever been a serious suspect. To Rose, she'd seemed far too fragile to have inflicted the serious wound at the back of Campbell's head. Then again, it was amazing what a person could do once their blood was up.

What Rose *had* been hoping to ascertain was how the killer had known she'd be out, and Campbell would be alone. But, after several attempts at questioning, they were none the wiser. As they headed back to the incident room, she guessed there could be any number of explanations. If the killer had been someone Campbell had known, Campbell could've inadvertently informed them himself. Or the girlfriend could've mentioned it while going about her daily business as an estate agent. Sadly, it was a question they might never get an answer to.

One anomaly that *was* concerning her was the fact that they hadn't found Campbell's mobile phone. It hadn't been on his person, nor had they managed to find it in the apartment, and his girlfriend was in no state to recall where it might be. When they'd gotten her to ring it, it had gone straight to voice mail, leaving Rose to wonder if, as with Finlay's phone, the killer had most likely taken it.

When they got back to the incident room it was almost five-thirty in the morning. Rose had been hoping to start the day fresh. There was a lot riding on her next two interviews, and she didn't want to lose her focus. She grabbed herself a coffee and joined Stipes beside the murder board, which was now an amalgamation of two boards joined together...a reminder of the complexity of the case.

Once again, her eyes scanned the list of those they'd encountered so far. Was there someone they were missing? Someone they'd totally overlooked in their quest to find the purpose of the files? If there was, their identity eluded her.

She headed to her desk and began trawling through all the statements again. Frederickson, Campbell, Dyer, Broom, Mills, Brannigan, Fawcett.... There had been so many. Yet none had provided them with the answers they were looking for.

At eight-twenty they headed to a private room, along with Reece, to begin the Skype interview with Mrs. Joy Turner. Rose brought along her notepad and pen. She'd already scrawled down various questions she hoped might be resolved by the former doctor's last living relative. She just hoped that Turner was lucid enough and cooperative enough to answer them.

At eight-thirty, Reece's contact in Belgium appeared on the screen. He was a slim, middle aged man, sporting a smart police uniform and donning a neatly trimmed goatee. His expression was overtly serious, and Rose assumed he was recording this for his superior. They all put on their headsets, and she left it to Reece to make the introductions. The officer spoke perfect English, despite his thick Belgian accent.

When the formalities were over, she finally cut in. "Is it possible to speak with Mrs. Turner this morning?"

The officer smiled for the first time, and Rose thought she noticed a flicker of relief cross his face. "Of course. She's sitting right next to me."

Crane shifted in his seat, and an image of the elderly Mrs. Turner came into view. She looked even frailer than Rose had imagined. Her skin was so shriveled her eyes had virtually sunken into it, and her thin white hair had receded to a sparse patch of white that clung to her head like cotton candy. She reminded Rose of one of the Egyptian mummies she'd seen at the museum, and she subconsciously pinched herself for the thought.

Rose pulled herself up straight in her chair. "Good morning, Mrs. Turner. I hope you're well today."

Mrs. Turner merely nodded, an indication that this probably wasn't going to be easy. Rose continued regardless.

"I understand that Officer Crane has briefed you on the reasons for this conversation?"

"He has." Her lips quivered as she spoke. "It's to do with my sister."

Rose nodded. "That's right. We're the detectives investigating the death of your sister, Mrs. Elise Sampson. I understand the two of you hadn't been in contact for several years?"

Turner took a sip from a glass of water before she replied. "I haven't spoken to my sister in over thirty years."

"I see. And can I ask what the reasons were for that?"

There was a moment of silence while the old lady seemed to consider her response to the question. When she was ready to speak again, she cleared her throat. "My sister and I had different opinions on what was right and wrong. Although I admired her

184

for her work as a doctor, I didn't agree with her beliefs. Or some of her actions."

Rose smiled. "You must've felt pretty strongly about them if it prevented you from having contact with her for so many years."

"I did."

Turner hesitated, as though there was something she wanted to say but she wasn't sure whether or not to say it. Rose adopted her most empathetic smile. "You can be totally honest with us, Mrs. Turner. I can assure you that anything you tell us will remain strictly confidential."

The old lady took a deep breath. "Well, my sister was an obstetrician, as I'm sure you know. She helped women during their pregnancies. However, later in her career, she found different ways to help them...at least some of them."

She glanced across at Crane, and Rose decided to get straight to the point. "Mrs. Turner, are you trying to tell us that your sister helped women get off the record abortions?"

Turner seemed surprised by the bluntness of the question. For a moment she looked nervous, as though unsure as to whether or not she should continue. Rose wondered if she'd gotten it wrong. She repeated her earlier assurance. "You really don't have to worry, Mrs. Turner. We have no interest in what your sister did or didn't do, other than its potential relevance to our case."

She wondered if Crane had informed her of the three suspicious deaths, then guessed not. News that her sister's death had been suspicious would've been background enough.

Finally, the old lady looked up. "Do you think what she did might've had something to do with her death?"

Rose let the question hang in the air.

Finally, Turner continued. "She thought it was her duty to help them. She'd been going to these...." She hesitated, as if

185

struggling to find the right word.

Rose decided to give her a nudge. "Conferences?"

"Yes. She'd been going to these conferences. Listening to some of the most horrendous stories of backstreet abortions gone wrong."

Rose shot a glance at Stipes, then instantly turned back to the computer screen. "Do you know if she met anyone at these events? Perhaps someone who put her in touch with women requiring her assistance?"

Again, Turner paused. She looked even more tired than she had a few minutes ago. Rose hoped this wasn't proving too much for her. The elderly lady stared down at her wrinkled fingers, and when she looked up again there was an anger in her eyes that portrayed her depth of feeling for the subject.

"She met someone, all right, though she never told me his name. Not that I'd have wanted to know it. Apparently, he was some kind of counsellor. He put her in touch with desperate women, and she referred them to someone she knew. For a fee."

Rose smiled inwardly. If Turner was referring to Finlay, he'd clearly been no counsellor. Another thought struck her. "But if she was charging a fee, why didn't they just pay for a private clinic?"

Turner coughed and her whole upper body shook from its aftermath. "I gathered some of the women were in the later stages of pregnancy when they decided on terminations. No private clinic would've accepted them. Not unless they had serious medical problems."

Rose's mind shot to the killer's use of potassium chloride. If they weren't certain of its relevance before, they definitely were now. She tapped her pen on the table in front of her. "Do you have any idea who the friend was? The person she referred the women to?"

Turner shook her head so hard, Rose could envisage her teeth rattling. "No. I'm sorry, I have no idea." She took another sip of water, and Rose was reminded of the need to speed things up. Their time was coming to an end.

When she'd put down the glass, Turner continued. "Anyway, that was when we stopped talking. I mean, what kind of person does a thing like that for profit?"

Rose searched for an answer but found none.

Eventually Stipes cut in. "But she *was* helping people, wasn't she?"

Turner managed a sarcastic smile. "Was she? It's my belief that the act of pregnancy and birth is sacred. Who, but God, has the right to take a life?" She virtually spat the words. "And we're not talking about fetuses here. We're talking about almost fully formed babies."

Rose balked at the thought. If Sampson and Finlay *had* been in the business of helping abort babies of mid to late term pregnancies, what the hell had propelled them to do it? Surely it couldn't have just been about the money. She put this to Turner who, as expected, had no idea. She decided to alter the course of her questioning.

"Do you know if there were ever any complications? If any of the abortions went wrong?"

The old lady visibly shuddered. "I never got involved. I didn't even want to hear about it. It was one of the reasons I moved to Belgium. I couldn't have anything to do with it."

Rose leaned forward. "But you *didn't* have anything to do with it. Did you?"

"I didn't contact the police, did I? I could've put a stop to it, and I didn't. For that my soul will always be tainted."

Now Rose understood her agreeing to speak to them. She was hoping for forgiveness. Some kind of holy absolution. Perhaps

Sampson had been seeking the same thing in her final years, and that was why she'd bequeathed her estate to the NSPCC. She offered what she could. "You can't blame yourself for that. She was your sister."

The old lady seemed to physically crumble. "I just wanted to block out all knowledge. To pretend it wasn't happening. So you see, I couldn't have any more to do with her."

Turner looked close to tears. Rose cut in before she could end the interview. "I just have one more question for you, Mrs. Turner."

The old lady had started to shake.

"Do you know if anyone besides you found out about your sister's sideline? Or if she ever received any threats as a result of what she did?"

Turner shrugged. "No. But I guess it's possible that one of the women spilled the beans. Everyone needs to confide in someone, don't they?" She furrowed her eyebrows as though consumed by thought.

Rose changed tack slightly. "But you didn't confide in anyone...did you?"

"*I* didn't terminate my baby, did I?"

Rose nodded, and the old lady turned away. She was about to end the interview when Turner turned back, as though remembering something. "Do you think this had something to do with her death? Elise's death?"

Rose owed her an answer to the question. "At the moment, we're really not sure. But we haven't ruled it out." It was the best she could offer.

She thanked Turner and left Reece to tie up any loose ends with Officer Crane. The old lady had been more help than she'd realized. Not only had she confirmed their theory as to Sampson's box of files, she'd also confirmed a motive for Samson's, and possibly Finlay's murders. And finally, they had something concrete they could give to the chief.

As they stepped into the corridor, Rose turned to Stipes. "Once we're done with Simmons, I want Frederickson and Broom back in here ASAP. I want to know exactly what their business was with Mrs. Sampson. Any more lies and I'll have them arrested for withholding evidence and perverting the course of justice."

Stipes nodded.

"And the women in the files who've moved abroad. They're not getting out of this either. The ones you've already called, call them again; and do what you can to get hold of the others."

CHAPTER TWENTY-NINE

The wait for the arrival of Mrs. Andrea Simmons seemed almost unbearable, especially in light of the Turner interview. Rose used the time in the interim to pay another visit to Campbell's apartment. Not that it was particularly enlightening. Other than the usual items you might expect to find in the home of a young, modern couple, there was little of any interest, including no mobile phone. Needless to say, there was nothing there to link Campbell to Sampson and Finlay, other than his work commitments.

Rose did, however, receive a call from Dr. Weller, informing her that Campbell's body had contained extremely high levels of potassium. So, if there'd been any doubt, they now knew that Campbell had succumbed to the same mode of death as the others. She just couldn't fathom why.

Once she was back at her desk, she flipped through the information that had so far been compiled on Campbell, but there was nothing of great significance. His bank balance regularly hovered a few pounds short of his overdraft, and none of his previous acquaintances recalled him ever getting into serious trouble. Added to that, he didn't seem to have much of a social life, other than the pub. Overall, he appeared to have lived a fairly dull existence.

She pushed the file aside and reached for her fourth cup of coffee of the day. If Sampson's private endeavors had been the reason she and Finlay were killed, what possible role could Campbell have had? He wouldn't have even been born at the time. Her mind drifted to the fact that he'd visited both of their houses. Could he have discovered something and perhaps tried to blackmail them? She shook her head. Even that didn't make sense, for how could they kill him if they were already dead?

When Simmons' plane finally touched down at London's Gatwick Airport, Rose ensured that Stipes was there to collect her. This served two purposes. Firstly, it ensured that Simmons arrived as punctually and in as good a shape as possible; and secondly, it got Stipes out of her hair for an hour or so. Since their interview with Turner, he'd been almost as tetchy as she had, and his impatience for the forthcoming meeting was beginning to drive her insane.

It was a little after two-thirty when Simmons finally arrived at the station, and she looked surprisingly fresh for a person who'd just travelled almost six hundred miles to meet them. Rose's first impression was that she was younger than Frederickson and Broom; though, following a cursory check, records showed that there was little difference between them.

Simmons had thick auburn hair, which had been styled into a fashionable bob. She wore a pale blue trouser suit, accompanied by a padded pale blue jacket, and black wedged shoes that matched her handbag. On first impressions she appeared confident and self-assured, which for some reason wasn't at all what Rose had imagined. Nevertheless, it fitted with the women's willingness to travel so many miles without as much as a companion.

Once they were all settled in the interview room, Rose wasted no time in whizzing through the formalities. When she was done, she looked Simmons in the eye. "Mrs. Simmons, I understand you have some information for us concerning the late Dr. Sampson."

Simmons sat up straight in her chair. The skin on her face looked surprisingly taut, and Rose wondered if she'd had surgery. If she had, it looked good on her.

Sampson's former acquaintance inhaled a deep breath, replying, "Before we begin, can I just explain that it's been a good thirty years since I met Doctor Sampson, and that any information I supply is purely from personal experience?"

Her voice sounded clipped and practiced. She'd no doubt rehearsed that little speech in the hours leading up to this interview.

Rose flashed her most casual smile. "We completely understand. We're just very grateful that you travelled so far to speak to us."

There was a moment's pause, which Rose deliberately instigated to set the mood. When she spoke again, she'd adopted her most professional persona. "If you don't mind, I'd like to begin by asking you how you became acquainted with Dr. Sampson."

Simmons fiddled with her polished pink fingernails. "I wouldn't exactly say we were acquainted...well, I guess we were, but only in the loosest sense." She placed her hands down on the table. "I was referred to her through a young man I met at a clinic. I had a very specific problem at the time, and I was told she could help me."

Rose felt a tingle of excitement. "This young man. Do you recall his name?"

"He never gave it."

"I see. And how did he know you had this problem? Did you get to talking to him? Did he advertise his services?"

Simmons shook her head. "Now, that really *was* the strange part. You see, he just seemed to know. I don't know how, but he

192

did. He said he knew of a doctor I should speak to, and he gave me Dr. Sampson's card."

Her comments concerned Rose. If Finlay had sought *her* out, perhaps the net spread wider than they'd thought. Any number of healthcare professionals could've been involved. The possibility sent a chill along her spine. She viewed Stipes through the corner of her eye. He was perched on the edge of his seat, clearly as keen to find out what Simmons knew as she was.

She reached for the familiar brown envelope and pulled out two photos of Finlay, as always explaining her actions for the recording. She pushed the photos across to Simmons. "Is this the man you're referring to?"

Simmons barely looked at the photos. "Yes, that's him." She pushed them back in Rose's direction.

"Are you sure?" Rose pushed them to one side, surprised by the speed of Simmons's response.

"I'm sure. I've seen his face in my worst nightmares."

Rose glanced up into the two-way mirror. As before, Blake and Sherman were behind it. She wondered what they were making of things so far.

She turned her attention back across the table. "Mrs. Simmons, do you think you could explain what happened following your contact with this man?"

Simmons took a long sip of coffee. She seemed to be having trouble finding the courage to begin. But at the end of the day, that *was* what she was here for. Finally, she put down her cup and stared down into her lap.

She explained that she hadn't realized she was pregnant until the second trimester, when she was already four and a half months gone. By that time, she knew that any reputable clinic would reject her request for a termination. She gave no insight as to the motivations behind her actions, nor did she attempt to justify them. Rose guessed she'd simply been too young and unprepared, particularly as she'd gone on to later have children.

Simmons went on to explain her meeting with Dr. Sampson, recalling a slightly awkward conversation that had eventually led to the reason for her visit. After that, she'd had no contact with the doctor. Instead, she'd been directed to a young woman known only as "Samantha," who had subsequently performed the procedure. A teardrop fell from her eye as she recalled the moments directly after. "I wasn't prepared. They didn't prepare me. I saw it being taken away, and...." She took a deep breath but maintained her composure. "They should've at least told me what it would be like. I might've changed my mind. I didn't realize...."

She didn't finish the sentence, and Rose guessed she hadn't realized they'd be removing an actual baby. She could see why such an experience might've been traumatic.

Stipes leaned forward to offer a tissue, which Simmons accepted. Rose pressed on. "Did you speak to anyone about this? Perhaps a friend, or a member of your family?"

"I never told anyone. How could I? Later I moved abroad and began a new life. I never even told my husband." She lifted the tissue to the brink of her nose. "You try to forget it. As though by pushing it to the furthest corner of your mind, you can somehow pretend it never happened. But it always comes back to haunt you."

Rose noticed that she'd finished her coffee and offered her another, which she declined. She was clearly keen to get this over with, so Rose continued. "Did you feel Dr. Sampson was responsible for causing you this trauma? I mean, she should've explained what would happen. Shouldn't she?"

Simmons was fiddling with her fingernails again. It was clearly a calming mechanism. "You're right. She should've explained what would happen. At the very least, she should've tried to talk me out of it. But at the end of the day, the decision rested with me. It was me who opted for the termination. I could've changed my mind at any time. But I didn't have the courage."

Rose felt genuinely sympathetic. "You shouldn't be so hard on yourself. You were clearly very young and lacking in support."

Her statement seemed to appease Simmons slightly. She took another deep breath and leaned back in her seat, mumbling more to herself than the detectives. "Still, that was no excuse."

Rose waited a few moments before continuing. "Do you believe that this man referred other young women to Dr. Sampson?"

Simmons looked up from her lap. "I'd be surprised if I was the only one...he seemed very keen to help me. And as I said, he sought me out, not the other way around."

Rose shot a glance at Stipes. "Can I ask if you paid a fee for this service?"

Simmons managed a thin smile. "I paid six hundred pounds. It doesn't sound a lot of money now, but thirty years ago it was worth a lot more. At the time, it was more than a whole month's wages."

Rose nodded. For Finlay, a cut of six hundred pounds might've been enough. But for a qualified obstetrician like Sampson.... The doctor had obviously been driven by other motivations.

There was a brief pause while Rose digested Simmons's information. Then she reached for the envelope again and pulled out a photo of Campbell. "I'm showing Mrs. Simmons exhibit 3a." She slid the photo across the table and Simmons picked it up. "Have you ever seen this man before?"

Stipes shot her a quizzical look and she could understand why. Campbell was not only of a different age group to Simmons, he lived in a different country. Nevertheless, in a day and age

195

defined by the Internet, it had to be worth asking the question.

Simmons looked at the photo, then slid it back. "No. I'm sorry. I've never seen him before."

Rose asked a few more questions, then ended the interview and switched off the tape recorder. The fact that Simmons had identified Finlay helped them a great deal. Sampson and Finlay had *definitely* been connected, and their modes of death were almost certainly related to their means of association. But what about Campbell's involvement? They were still no closer to establishing a motive for Campbell's murder, nor were they any closer to catching their killer.

They also had another problem. Simmons was reluctant to put herself forward as a trial witness. Of course, she could always be subpoenaed. But the testimony of a subpoenaed witness was never as beneficial as the testimony of a willing one. Rose let out a deep sigh. She supposed nothing was perfect. At least things were moving forward.

She asked Stipes to escort Simmons back to the airport and headed out to inform the team. If nothing else, the case was progressing. Now all they needed was a lucky break.

CHAPTER THIRTY

By the time uniform had pulled Frederickson and Broom back in, it was nearing 4 p.m. Nevertheless, Rose felt a surge of excitement as they escorted the first to be interviewed, the obstinate Mrs. Frederickson, to the interview room. After the woman's previous attempts at misleading them, she was looking forward to watching her squirm.

What surprised Rose was Frederickson's continued refusal for legal representation. She guessed the woman was probably under some misguided illusion that, if she didn't opt for a solicitor, her actions wouldn't become public knowledge. What she didn't realize was that, whether she took advice or not, it would make no difference. If she was considered a suspect in a murder investigation, her entire world would fall under scrutiny.

As with her first interview, Frederickson appeared distant. Rose began by explaining their discussion with Sampson's sister and their meeting with Mrs. Simmons, outlining all the intricate details with considerable satisfaction. When she'd finished, Frederickson looked significantly less smug.

Rose took a deep breath and launched straight in. "So, I'd like to ask you again, Mrs. Frederickson. Under what circumstances did you have contact with Dr. Sampson?" Without waiting for a response, Rose reached for the envelope, pulling out the same images of Mrs. Sampson as before. "I'm showing Mrs. Frederickson exhibits 1a and 1b."

Again, Frederickson barely looked at them. Then a solitary tear fell from her eye and she lowered her gaze to her lap. It was the first time Rose had seen her vulnerable side, and she wasn't quite sure how to deal with it. So she merely pushed on. "I apologize if the question upsets you, Mrs. Frederickson, but we really do need an answer."

Eventually Frederickson admitted that, many years ago, in what seemed another life, she *had* undergone an abortion. Like Simmons before her, she'd been four months pregnant at the time, and no reputable clinic would've entertained her request. Particularly since she was a married woman living a stable life, and there were no foreseeable complications. Apparently, the reason for the termination resided in the fact that Frederickson's husband had been away for the last six months on a Royal Navy expedition, and therefore couldn't possibly have been the father.

When she'd finished, Rose showed her the same photos of Finlay she'd shown Simmons and got the same reaction. Finlay had undoubtedly been the middle man. Unfortunately, like Simmons before her, Frederickson had been given no name or number. Finlay had approached her, and, after that initial interaction, she'd had no contact with him.

Rose shot a glance at Stipes, who was clearly on the verge of tearing his hair out. If one of the women in the box of files wasn't responsible for at least orchestrating Sampson and Finlay's deaths, it would be a miracle. They'd clearly suffered considerable long-term effects as a result of the former's actions. Perhaps they *did* need to fly the other women over after all.

By the time Rose decided to call it a day, it was near on 8 p.m. and they were still no closer to catching their killer. Despite establishing a rock-solid motive for numerous individuals to want Sampson and Finlay dead, pinning down a suspect was proving more difficult than she'd anticipated.

She was just pulling on her black leather jacket when Stipes appeared in front of her. "Fancy a drink, Guv?"

His words caught her by surprise, and her first instinct was to refuse. She was overwhelmingly tired, which wasn't surprising considering she'd been up since just after three that morning. Nevertheless, her head was still buzzing from the developments of the day. A drink might help her sleep.

Finally, she relented. "Go on then. Just one."

The Nags Head on the corner of Duke Street was a hive of activity by the time they arrived. Rose had forgotten it was a Saturday, and she instantly regretted her decision not to go straight home. It wasn't until they'd found a quiet corner that she finally began to relax. She ordered the drinks, along with two packets of potato chips, then took a seat opposite Stipes.

He sipped his beer, then leaned forward in his seat. "You OK?"

She lifted the double vodka and coke to her lips. "I will be once I've got this down my neck and had a good night's sleep."

She took a sip, her mind drifting instinctively to the day's events. Comments from the numerous interviews were swimming around her head like tadpoles in a pond. But none gave her the insight she was looking for. What she wanted was to find the woman whose abortion had gone wrong...or, at the very least, someone who might have had recent contact with the deceased Mrs. Sampson. But so far, no such evidence was forthcoming.

She lifted the glass to her lips again. Of course, the killer could've been any one of the women, regardless of what had happened during their abortion, for all seemed to have been scarred in some way by the procedure.

When she was done thinking, she turned to Stipes. "Well, at least we have a motive for two of the murders, and an explanation for the unusual mode of death."

Stipes took a sip of his pint. "I agree. But we need to be careful. Things aren't always as they seem."

Rose wrapped her hands around the icy glass. "Oh, come on Stipes. Two people, whose only connection appears to be their covert activities, were murdered in a way that reflected those activities. It's a bit of a coincidence, don't you think?"

Stipes raised his eyebrows. "I'm not saying the evidence isn't mitigating. What concerns me is Campbell's role in all of this. If he even had one."

A minor brawl broke out behind them, which was quickly diffused by a burly security guard. Rose waited for it to subside before responding. "We already know that Campbell had a connection with both victims."

"Only through delivering their logs."

"True. But perhaps he discovered something. Or perhaps he was hired to kill Sampson and Finlay…then, when he'd outlived his usefulness…."

Stipes smiled again. "Campbell? A hired hitman? Sorry, I'm not buying it."

Rose wasn't giving up. "He had a pretty nice apartment for someone who delivered logs for a living."

"And he and his girlfriend held down stable jobs."

She let out a deep sigh. "I know, I know. But there has to be a connection somewhere. For all we know, he could've been blackmailing Sampson and Finlay."

"Then who killed him?"

Rose tried to keep up the momentum. If she looked hard enough, there was a chance she might find something. "He could've had an accomplice." She was clutching at straws now

200

and she knew it. She leaned back in her seat, tired of the constant back and forth. "What's scary is that our list of suspects isn't reducing. In fact, the more we speak to people, the more it seems to grow. But there's nothing concrete ruling them in or out. Why the hell is that?"

Stipes merely shrugged before turning back to his pint. Rose stroked her forehead with the palm of her hand. Was it the pain in her head that was stopping her from thinking straight? Or was it just that a fog seemed to have infiltrated her mind over the last few days? No matter how much information they gained, they never seemed any closer to catching their killer.

She took rather too large a gulp of her drink, and her throat burned from its after effects. She swallowed hard, staring through the window into the hazy darkness, and wondered, not for the first time, if Sampson or Finlay, or even Campbell, had known their killer. If they had, it could be someone they'd already questioned; perhaps even someone they'd subconsciously ruled out. Like a neighbor or some other seemingly banal acquaintance.

Stipes drained his pint glass and shot her an enquiring look. "Another one, Guv?"

She considered calling it a night; then, for the second time in the space of an hour, succumbed to the voice inside of her. "Go on then. But if my head feels fuzzy in the morning, I'll blame you."

CHAPTER THIRTY-ONE

When Rose woke the following morning, the pain in her head had been replaced by a dull, numbing ache that seemed to invade every cell in her body. She crawled from her bed and dressed almost mechanically. The stresses of the last few days had taken their toll. She felt like shit and looked even worse. Still, she knew there'd be no reprieve until their killer was safely behind bars. And that wasn't going to happen unless she got her finger out and started tying this case together.

When she got to the station, she was surprised to see Banks already there. Even Stipes hadn't arrived yet.

As though sensing her curiosity, Banks stepped forward. "I think I've found something, Guv. There was a number in one of Campbell's notepads. I've been gradually going through it. Anyway, I dialed the number and it put me through to a psychiatrist's office."

Rose put down her bag. "Now that *is* interesting." She recalled the state Campbell's girlfriend had been in after discovering him dead. "But we can't be certain the psychiatrist was for him. I take it you haven't managed to speak to them yet?"

Banks shook his head. "Not yet. It's still too early. But I've left a couple of messages. If they don't call me back by nine, I'll try

202

again. Failing that, I'll find the address and drive round there."

Rose smiled, impressed by his tenacity. If there was one thing she had on her side, it was the sheer dedication of her team. She brought the conversation around to Banks's meeting with Campbell's family. He'd already told her they hadn't recognized the photos of Sampson and Finlay. But she needed to know if there might be anything else of relevance. There wasn't.

Banks wondered off and she headed to her desk to check the never-ending influx of messages. Since her last meeting with the chief, she'd been warned against neglecting the more mundane aspects of her job. Besides, miracles could happen. There *could* be something there that could help her break this case.

Forty minutes later, Rose had found nothing of use in the messages, and the rest of her team had arrived. She was about to check in with them when her mobile buzzed in her pocket. She pulled it out and looked at the screen. It was Weller. She shrugged. No doubt he'd finished Campbell's post mortem and was keen to dispense with his responsibilities on that one.

She reluctantly took the call. "DI Rose."

Weller's distinctive voice shot through the line. "Good morning, DI Rose. I've found something that I think will interest you."

Rose pressed the phone closer to her ear. "Go on."

"Well, I found a hair on Campbell's neck, and it doesn't belong to the victim. Or his girlfriend."

He'd clearly been supplied with Campbell's girlfriend's DNA in order that he could rule her out. Rose asked the first question that came into her head. "Has it been tested against the database?"

"One of our guys has just finished doing it, but there's no match." The excitement inside of her retreated. Weller seemed to sense this and continued. "So the good news is, when you find your killer, you'll have something to test him — or her — against. Of course, it's not a lot of good without a suspect."

Rose smiled sarcastically to herself. "Oh, don't worry, we have plenty of those."

As she returned the phone to her pocket, she pondered the possibility of her previous interviewees supplying a sample of their DNA. At this stage, with lack of any concrete evidence, it could only be voluntary. Still, anyone who refused the request would immediately arouse suspicion, so one way or another, they might finally succeed in reducing their list.

She rose from her seat and headed to the murder board, but she was interceded by Sherman before she got there. "I just found something in Campbell's records Guv. Something we didn't see before. Campbell was adopted by his mother when he was five."

Rose stopped in her tracks, ingesting the implications of Sherman's words. Suddenly developments were occurring so fast, she was having trouble keeping up with them. When she'd had a chance to clear her head, she asked, "Why in God's name didn't this come up earlier?"

Sherman fiddled with the papers in her hand. "Initially all checks were surface ones, Guv. We only recently started looking at Campbell in more depth; we were focusing more on his financial and social activities. We literally just got to it."

Rose's mind drifted to the tenth woman in Sampson's box of files…the one they'd been unable to trace. Was it possible Campbell *had* possessed a reason to kill Sampson and Finlay? She held onto that thought. "What was the name of Campbell's real mother?"

"Mrs. Judith Carr."

It didn't fit with any of the names in the files. But then, they weren't necessarily the only women who'd been "helped."

Rose leaned back on her heels. "Was that the only name she

204

went by? Did she ever remarry? Or change her name for any other reason?"

Sherman looked despondent. "Not as far as I can see. But I'll check again."

"Do that, will you? If there's any connection between Campbell and Sampson or Finlay, besides his work, it's imperative we find it. Before any more dead bodies turn up." Sherman drifted off and Rose called behind out her, "And get more info on Mrs. Carr, would you? A photo would be good. That way we can see if any of our previous interviewees recognize her."

Sherman spoke without turning her head. "Will do, Guv. But just to let you know, she died a few years ago."

Sherman headed back to her desk and Rose let out a heavy sigh. Inside every silver lining there was a negative to equal its positive. It was about time they broke the cycle.

She shook her head, resuming her walk to the murder board. When she got there, she didn't need to clear her throat. Her team was so desperate for developments, all eyes were instantly on her. She decided to launch straight in. "I've just had a call from the pathologist, and it looks like we may have been blessed with a fragment of the killer's DNA. Weller found a stray hair clinging to the back of Campbell's neck and it doesn't belong to him *or* his girlfriend."

There was a collective sigh of relief. Banks was first to cut in. "Has it been checked against the database yet?"

"Unfortunately, it has, and the results came up negative. So we need to collect samples from all the people we've spoken with so far."

Stipes leaned forward in his seat. "What if they refuse?"

"If they refuse, we start asking ourselves why. And if there *are* any refusals, let me know straight away. Blake, Reece, can you deal with that?"

The two detectives nodded, and Reece instinctively raised a hand. "Sure, Guv."

Rose took a deep breath. She wasn't finished yet. "It's just come to light that Campbell was adopted when he was five. So Sherman's looking closer at his family tree. If it turns out his real mother had any connection with Sampson or Finlay, we may have a clearer idea of why he was murdered." She paused for a moment. "Also, we've been taking it that the women in the files are the only ones we need to be looking at, when, in reality, there are most likely others who were associated with Sampson and Finlay for the same reason. I'm not sure how we go about finding them yet, but it's something we need to keep in mind." She shot a glimpse at the murder board. "I take it there's still no news on Campbell's mobile?"

Blake looked up from his own mobile phone. "Not yet. But it was a contract phone, so we've been able to access the call log. I'm trawling through it as we speak."

Rose breathed a sigh of relief. "At least that's something. Let's just hope our killer's on it."

CHAPTER THIRTY-TWO

After a long morning of contemplation, during which Rose referred to her spider-gram many times, there were no further developments. She was about to rise from her desk when Sherman appeared in front of her.

"Campbell's mother.... I can't find anything to suggest a connection with the people we've spoken with, *or* with Sampson or Finlay. Though that doesn't necessarily mean they never met."

Rose exhaled a heavy breath. She'd had a feeling that would be the case. "I take it the rest of his family's been thoroughly researched?"

"We're on it now, Guv."

Sherman walked back to her desk and Rose headed off to find Stipes. There was a crucial piece of the puzzle they were still missing, and it wasn't going to find itself.

He found her before she found him. "Looking for me?"

Rose stepped back slightly, astounded by his uncanny ability to sense her approach. "I think we should take another look at Sampson's house. Everything seems to have started with her, so maybe there's something there we missed."

By the time they got to Amber Court, it was snowing. Thick puffs of white hurled from the sky like confetti from a streamer,

207

and the roofs of stationary cars had succumbed to a soft white blanket that seemed to mystify their appearance. Rose unclasped her seat belt and reached for the glove compartment.

As she pulled out the usual gloves and boot covers, thoughts of Christmas again invaded her thoughts. It was descending on Brackley like a rapidly approaching freight train, and there was nothing she could do to stop it. She brushed the thought aside and, alongside her partner, stepped out into the icy street.

Once they'd reached the property and ducked beneath the crime scene tape, Rose punched in the four-digit security code to open the gates. She still hadn't figured out the relevance of the numbers. They didn't reflect Sampson's birth date, or the date that she and her husband had married. But she'd be surprised if the old lady had selected them randomly. Even the most cautious of individuals generally picked a number that was significant, even if not consciously.

When they entered the driveway, she scanned the property's exterior once again. They still hadn't established the killer's mode of entry, and, as she scrutinized the formidable facade, she wondered if Sampson had been expecting her visitor. Perhaps not on that particular night, or even in that particular month, but at some point in the not too distant future. It would explain the lack of disruption to the property's interior, and, despite the level of violence that had occurred, the uncanny sense of calm that had subsequently prevailed.

When she was satisfied there was nothing she'd missed, she joined Stipes at the front door, and together they entered the house. As before, the sickly-sweet stench of chemicals invaded her nostrils, and she raised a hand to stem it. Even though it wasn't as strong as before, it was pungent enough to remind her of the brutality that had recently taken place, and that in itself unsettled her.

Once inside, they inspected the hallway again before continuing on to the kitchen. The white chalk figure still took pride of place at its center, like a specter awaiting exorcism. Rose eyed it with her usual respect. It was the one thing they had that truly reflected what had happened that night, and, even in its stillness, it commanded a certain reverence.

She stepped forward, taking a quick glance at the kitchen units, though deliberately skimming over the one with the bloodstain. Then she made her way through to the living room. Stipes hung back, presumably to check on something he felt he'd missed. Still, that was the way they worked. Independently and yet inexplicably related.

When she reached the living room, Rose paused for a moment. Despite the devastation SOCOs had left behind, it was evident that, like the other rooms, it had been immaculately cared for, despite its owner's age. A tall mahogany sideboard stood ornately at its far end, beside the window, and a small beige sofa and an oval shaped coffee table took pride of place in its center. Opposite the sofa stood a large armchair which, judging by its wear and tear, had been the victim's preferred resting place. Other than that, and the largest wood-burner she'd ever seen, there was little in the way of furniture.

She scanned the room for any hiding places she might not have noticed the first time around but found none. So instead she resorted to searching the places she'd already searched, starting with the sideboard. All relevant paperwork had already been removed, so now its polished interior looked surprisingly empty. She ran her hand along its shiny surface. There were no hidden compartments or secret pockets.

She pulled out the first of the three drawers. As with the rest of the sideboard, there was little to be found. She was about to close it again when the corners of a photograph that had been trapped in one of the cracks suddenly caught her eye. She pulled it out, holding it carefully between her thumb and forefinger. It appeared to depict Mrs. Sampson at some sort of non-formal gathering, and it didn't look to be more than a few years old. Sampson was wearing a blue flowery dress and a matching bolero jacket. Rose leaned in for a closer look. The young woman standing a few feet away from her looked familiar. She strained her eyes against the dim light. Was that...?

The sound of footsteps fractured her chain of thought, and seconds later Stipes appeared beside her. "Found anything, Guv?"

Rose held up the photo so that it caught the light from the window. "I found this caught in the cracks of one of the drawers. Here's Mrs. Sampson." She pointed her finger at a small woman standing at the photo's periphery. "And, if I'm not mistaken, this looks very much like Leah Fawcett."

Stipes took the photo from her and walked across to the window to view it in better light. After a few moments, his expression changed. "My God, I think you're right."

Rose took the photo back and looked at it again. She had butterflies in the pit of her stomach. "Do we know anything about Fawcett's parents?"

Stipes shook his head. "There was no reason to look."

"Then that's something we need to get onto ASAP."

There was a moment of silence while they both considered Fawcett's potential relationship with Mrs. Sampson. It was Stipes who broke it. "Perhaps Fawcett didn't see anything the night of Finlay's murder after all. She *did* seem an odd candidate for a witness. She seemed to be enjoying herself a bit too much."

His sentiments echoed Rose's own, but she tried not to sound as anxious as she felt. "Whatever the case, we need to bring her back in. We didn't even show her Sampson's photo. For all we

210

know, she might admit freely to knowing her. She might even be able to throw some light on her activities during recent months."

Stipes walked back to the window. "I wonder if she'll give her DNA."

His comment struck a nerve and Rose reached for her phone. "I'll call Blake and see if they've tried her yet. If they haven't, we'll ask her when we get her back in."

For once, Blake's phone went unanswered. Rose left a message, then placed her mobile back in her pocket. "Typical. The one-time Blake doesn't answer his phone. Let's finish up here and get back to the station."

The rest of the house revealed nothing that hadn't succumbed to their previous search. Other than a few outdated ornaments, and, of course, the box of files, it seemed that Sampson, like Finlay, wasn't one for sentimental keepsakes. As Rose descended the staircase and headed for the front door, she shot one final glance at the white chalk figure inside the kitchen door. It sent a shiver along her spine. Was Sampson somehow responsible for helping them find the photo? She shook the thought off and headed for the exit. This case really was getting to her.

As they headed toward the car, Stipes shot a glance at the house next door. Even though it was a good distance away, its sizeable façade was easily identifiable. He stepped up alongside Rose. "D'you think we should question Ms. Mills again? She might remember something she forgot on the night."

Rose continued toward the car. "I'll send Banks around later. I want to see how the guys are getting on with the DNA samples first."

As if in answer to her statement, her phone sounded in her pocket. She pulled out her keys to deactivate the car's central locking, then reached for it. She could see it was Blake before she answered. "Blake. How are you getting on with the samples?"

His voice sounded distant. She guessed his signal was compromised. "We've done Frederickson, Broom, Brannigan, and Dyer Junior. Perhaps we should've got a sample from Simmons before she flew back to Germany."

His statement prickled her. Hindsight was a wonderful thing. She ignored it. "Well, make Fawcett next, will you? In fact, we need to pull her back in. Can you do that?"

"Sure thing, Guv. Any particular reason?"

"We've reason to believe she knew Sampson. So perhaps she had an ulterior motive in coming to see us."

"I'll get onto it now."

Before he had a chance to break off, Rose added, "So you've had no refusals yet…for the samples?"

"No…no refusals."

Rose ended the call and turned back to Stipes. "Let's just hope Fawcett hasn't done a vanishing act."

CHAPTER THIRTY-THREE

When they got back to the station, Rose's first priority was to task Sherman and Reece with researching Fawcett's family tree. That done, she sought out Banks. "Any luck with the psychiatrist?"

Banks put down the pile of papers he'd been holding. "He was very helpful, Guv. Though I don't know if what he told me has any relevance for the case." Rose shot him a look that urged him on. "Apparently it *was* Campbell that went. But he only went a few times, the last time being a couple of months ago. He had anxiety issues and was referred by his GP."

Rose raised her eyebrows, recalling Campbell's slightly nervous disposition. Still, it hadn't seemed particularly out of the ordinary, considering the reasons for his questioning. She nodded, again urging him on.

"There's not really a lot more to tell."

She shook her head. "Why was he anxious? And in what circumstances?"

Banks leaned back on his heels. "The psychiatrist, Dr. Miller, seemed to think it was a general problem, something brought on when Campbell was particularly stressed."

"And did he have any reason to be particularly stressed?"

"If he did, he didn't elaborate on it. At least not during his sessions."

Rose bit her lip. Was she missing something here? "I thought you said the psychiatrist was helpful."

Banks flushed slightly pink, seeming to realize where she was coming from. "Perhaps I should've used the word cooperative instead."

A uniformed officer brushed past with a pile of paperwork and Rose took a step back, cursing him for his rudeness. "Perhaps you should've. Because Campbell didn't seem anxious enough to warrant a psychiatrist when we spoke to him. Can you get hold of his GP? See if he can elaborate on his reasons for referring him?" Banks nodded. "Oh, and speak to the girlfriend again as well, will you? You never know, she might be better informed than the doctor *or* the psychiatrist."

"Sure thing, Guv."

Once she was back at her desk, Rose's mind drifted back to Blake. She'd heard nothing from him since she'd instructed him to bring Leah Fawcett back in. She hoped he wasn't experiencing any problems.

She recalled Fawcett's lithe figure and canny disposition. If she *was* their killer, she might well have flown the nest by now. They'd had no contact with her since her interview which, looking back, had been surprisingly lacking in any real detail. The thought concerned her.

She reached for her phone and dialed Blake's number. For the second time that day it went unanswered. She put it back down and sank into her chair, recalling how Fawcett had made quite a deal of savoring her cup of coffee. It would've been easy for them to have hung onto that cup for future analysis. But they'd had no grounds, or even reason to believe that it might be necessary. After all, Fawcett had come in voluntarily.

She shrugged the thought off. As with Blake's earlier comment, it was easy to envisage ideal scenarios after the event. But that wouldn't help them now. What they needed was a more tangible reason for Fawcett to have wanted to murder Sampson, Finlay, and Campbell...and for that, they needed a whole lot of background information.

As if reading her mind, Reece appeared with a printed file containing information on Fawcett's closest relatives. Only one was still alive...her estranged father. Rose sighed at the lack of data. Nevertheless, she pulled out a photo of Fawcett's deceased mother and studied it carefully. She did the same with the photo of her father. An anomaly immediately leapt out at her.

"If these are Fawcett's parents and Fawcett's never been married, how come she doesn't have one of their surnames?"

Reece shrugged. "I was getting to that. Fawcett changed her name by deed poll a few years ago."

"Did you not find that strange?"

"I did, but I couldn't find any reason why. She's never served time or been given as much as a parking ticket. Maybe she just didn't like her parents."

Rose placed the photos back in the file. "Have you checked her original name with the Criminal Records Bureau?"

"Sherman's doing it now."

"OK, let me know if she finds anything. If someone's dissatisfied enough with their name to change it by deed poll, there's usually good reason." Reece turned to leave, and Rose changed tack. "Have you had anything back on the DNA samples you've taken yet?"

He let out a loud sigh. Even he was beginning to look frustrated with their lack of progress. "Not yet, Guv. Shouldn't be long though. I was thinking...should I contact the hospital and see if I can speak with Mrs. Dyer yet? We might be able to get a sample from her."

Rose dismissed the thought instantly. A fuss at the hospital was bound to attract more media attention, and she was in enough trouble with the chief already. "Not yet. Besides, we have her son's DNA. If the hair belonged to her, her son's sample will flag up as being related."

Reece drifted off and Rose tried Blake again. When there was still no answer, she drummed her fingers against her desk and glanced at her watch...three-fifteen. If Blake hadn't made contact by three-thirty, she'd send out a search party.

Blake finally walked into the incident room at three twenty-eight, minus Fawcett, and Rose was instantly on her feet. "Where the hell have you been? I've been trying to call you for over an hour."

Blake pulled out his phone as though he'd been blissfully unaware of the anxiety he'd caused. "Sorry. I've been busy trying to find Fawcett. She hasn't shown up at work for a couple of days, and she didn't appear to be at her apartment. A neighbor gave me a couple of her local haunts, so I tried those as well. She seems to have vanished into thin air, and the phone number she gave us is an old pay as you go that's not in operation anymore."

Rose was struggling to keep her calm. "And you were too busy to answer your phone?"

He looked slightly sheepish. "I had it switched to silent when I was talking with the psychiatrist earlier...I guess I forgot to turn it back up."

It took all of Rose's strength to maintain her cool composure. She took a deep breath. "Well, get down to the magistrate's office, will you? See if you can get a warrant to check out Fawcett's apartment."

When he was gone, Rose stared out into the busy street. It wasn't yet four in the afternoon, but darkness was already descending. Within the next half an hour, the whole of London would be cloaked in its ominous blanket, and it was those impenetrable hours of darkness that she dreaded the most. For it was during that period that most crimes were committed. Particularly those culminating in murder.

Reece reappeared, and she shook herself back to reality. "Preliminary DNA results are back, and none of them are a match with the hair Weller recovered."

"Great." She placed her hands behind her neck. "Maybe we need to widen the net to include Campbell's friends and work colleagues."

"On it, Guv."

Reece walked away, and she carefully digested his words. Maybe the hair didn't belong to the killer after all. Campbell could've been in close contact with any number of individuals prior to his death. The hair could simply have been transferred.

Stipes seemed to appear from nowhere. "So there's nothing on Fawcett or the DNA samples?"

"Nope. And the fact that we can't find Fawcett concerns me."

Stipes moved in closer. "Because you think she might be the killer, or because you're thinking she *could* be a victim?"

Rose fiddled with a pen at her fingertips. "At this point, I guess it's a bit of both." She released the pen and flicked it across the table. "You know, Stipes, unravelling this case is like unravelling one of those Russian dolls. The deeper you get, the more complex it becomes."

He pulled up a chair and sat down opposite her. "I know what you mean. But there can only be so many layers. Sooner or later they're gonna lead us to the killer."

Rose leaned back, raising her eyes to the dull cream ceiling. Generally Stipes's words placated her. But right now, she was beginning to think that nothing would lead them to the killer.

With every step forward, they seemed to take two steps back. If Fawcett *had* had anything to do with the murders, she was probably miles away by now. And if not....

CHAPTER THIRTY-FOUR

Within an hour of Banks having left the station, he was back with a search warrant for Fawcett's apartment. Rose grabbed her jacket and summoned Stipes. The sooner they established whether Fawcett had absconded, was hiding out in her or apartment, or, worst case scenario, was lying somewhere with a needle sized hole in her neck, the sooner they could go about the business of unravelling her connection with Sampson.

When they reached the small cul-de-sac which, as Fawcett had described, was situated a short distance from the end of Violet Crescent, Rose stared out into the growing darkness. The properties, essentially a collection of three bedroomed semis that had been converted into tiny apartments, were less well maintained than those a short distance away. Grimy curtains hung in the small, stained windows, and most of the gardens were overgrown. She guessed that people who shared their amenities with others had little reason to take pride in those amenities. She pulled out enough gloves and boot covers for herself, Banks, and Stipes, and stepped anxiously from the car.

When they reached the property where Fawcett lived, Rose pushed the door. Surprisingly, it wasn't locked. She shot a glance at Banks, who held out his hands in a "tell me about it" motion.

219

"Same as earlier, Guv. I guess people don't worry too much about security round here."

Rose shook her head in disbelief. Given the depravity of the neighborhood and the slippery nature of many of its inhabitants, it was surprising there weren't more incidents. Especially those involving burglary. Then again, perhaps there were and they just weren't reported.

When they reached Fawcett's apartment, Rose knocked on the door. When there was no reply she knocked again, this time harder. After a third attempt, she gave up knocking and resorted to shouting through the keyhole. "Miss Fawcett! This is the police! We have a warrant to search these premises!"

A short, stocky man from the apartment next door stepped into the corridor, clearly keen to see what the fuss was all about. He was wearing stained nightclothes, and Rose wondered if he'd been wearing them all day...or, indeed, if he ever took them off. She turned to face him, flashing her badge so that there was no mistaking her identity.

"Do you know the young lady who lives here?"

The man shook his head, turning to go back inside. Rose moved quickly, blocking his path before he had a chance.

"Have you seen her in the last couple of days?"

The neighbor took a step back, clearly surprised by her forthrightness. "No. Sorry. I haven't seen her in a while. We generally come and go at different times."

"And you haven't heard anything? The door closing maybe... or any sounds inside?"

"No. Nothing."

"Is that unusual?"

"No. She's pretty quiet. Why, what's she done?"

Rose headed back to Fawcett's door and the neighbor retreated into the safety of his own living space. Stipes knocked on the door again, repeating Rose's words. When there was no response, Rose finally gave the signal for him to force the door. One swift push and it yielded. She took a deep breath and stepped inside.

Fawcett's apartment was essentially one room housing what could only loosely be termed a living area, along with a narrow single bed. It had one tiny window that looked out onto the property beyond, and, judging by the smell, it wasn't opened often. However, it wasn't the smell that caught Rose's attention. It was the crumpled body that lay sprawled across the room's center.

"For Christ's sake!"

She instinctively dived to the floor, placing her fingers around Fawcett's neck and feeling for the carotid artery. But there was no pulse, and the skin felt waxy and cold. Realizing that the young woman had probably been dead a while, she pulled back, taking a moment to catch her breath. When she'd recovered her senses, she stood back to examine the scene.

Fawcett was lying on her front, her long blonde hair matted with blood. Like the other victims, she appeared to have been struck from behind, possibly shortly after entering her flat. Rose eyed the worn black ballet pumps that still clung to her tiny feet, and the faded green parka that shielded her body. It ran to just above her knees and reminded Rose of a body bag.

She scanned the immediate surroundings. It was impossible to tell whether the incident had caused any disruption or not due to the chaotic nature of the environment, but she guessed it hadn't. Fawcett appeared to have made no attempt to break her fall. One arm was tucked awkwardly beneath her torso, while the other lay twisted and outstretched, as though it had simply landed as it had fallen.

As with Campbell and the others, Rose wondered if there was

221

a needle mark. But there was so much hair, it was impossible to tell without closer inspection, and the scene was already making her feel nauseous.

She looked to Stipes and Banks, who, in that order, were phoning the incident in and checking the nearby vicinity for signs of an intruder. When she felt calm enough to decipher her thoughts, she turned to Stipes. "What in God's name's going on? Someone might've had a good motive for killing Sampson and Finlay. But what the hell could Campbell and Fawcett have had to do with it?"

Stipes ended his call, the look on his face reflecting the darkness of his mood. "She said she saw the killer that night. Perhaps she did. Perhaps the killer saw her too, and they were worried she might be able to identify them."

His words struck Rose like a brick to the chest. She'd never really taken Fawcett's claims seriously. If she was honest, she hadn't taken *Fawcett* seriously. If they'd viewed her more closely, as she'd originally planned, they might have realized her vulnerability before the killer had struck. She glanced down at the young woman's twisted torso. Could all this have been avoided if she'd simply done her job properly?

She walked across to the window and Stipes followed behind. His heavy boots echoed noisily against the bare floorboards, but she was too preoccupied to notice. She considered the likelihood of Stipes's theory. Fawcett coming to them *could've* been the act that had signed her death warrant.

As if sensing her concern, Stipes placed a friendly hand on her shoulder. "We couldn't have known, Guv. She didn't seem genuine. Besides, we still don't know if that was the reason she's dead. If she was connected to Sampson, the motive could've run much deeper."

Rose stared blankly at the dull brick wall that faced her.

As usual, Stipes was right. They couldn't disregard Fawcett's connection with Sampson. The reason for her death could well reside in the nature of that connection, rather than in anything they could or couldn't have done to prevent it. If only they'd found that photo before.

She turned from the window and looked again at the pitiful remains of Leah Fawcett. In death, she had a peacefulness about her, an eerie sense of calm that had probably evaded her in life. As with Sampson and Finlay, Rose wondered if anyone would miss her. Judging by the absence of family members and her careless, solitary lifestyle, the answer was most likely no. It was a dispiriting fact, a sad failing of modern society.

She listened to Stipes as he summoned Weller, then, after a brief search of the property that yielded nothing of interest, signaled for him to follow her back to the station. Banks would stay behind and secure the scene until the cavalry arrived. Until then, there was little they could achieve here. Uniform would begin work on house to house within the hour, then they might have something more to work on.

As they stepped back out into the ferocious evening, Rose scanned the vicinity for any sign of surveillance cameras. For the second time that day, she found none. She guessed there hadn't been enough reported incidents to warrant the cost. Either that, or this tired little backwater had simply been forgotten.

They headed for the car and she took one last look at Fawcett's building. She wondered if they'd have any luck with the neighbors; though, even as she thought it, she very much doubted it. In places such as this, people tended to keep to themselves, for self-preservation as much as anything else.

When they finally got back to the station, Rose left it to Stipes to update the rest of the team. She needed to take a good long look at her spider-gram, and to go back through the interview transcripts before deciding on her next course of action. Besides, it was already nearing six-thirty, and she needed to inform the chief of the new development. A prospect she wasn't looking forward to.

Sherman had been tasked with seeking out Fawcett's estranged father, who had left the family home when Fawcett was a child and subsequently had little contact with his ex-wife or daughter. As far as they could ascertain, Fawcett had no significant partner. As with Sampson and Finlay, informing the relatives *wasn't* going to be complicated.

CHAPTER THIRTY-FIVE

That following morning, before Rose had chance to get her head together, an anomaly in Fawcett's post-mortem led to her being summoned to the pathology lab by an ever-cautious Dr. Weller. She sought out Stipes and they headed there together.

When they got to the pathology building, Weller was waiting for them in a small side room adjacent to his lab. As always, he was wearing his standard white lab coat, which looked tattered and stained. It sent Rose's mind drifting back to the murder scene, and she quickly proceeded with the reason for their visit.

"So, what do you have for us, Doctor? And *please* let it be good."

Weller smiled. It was the first time she'd seen him relaxed since all this had begun. "Oh, it's good. You see, despite the similarities to your other recent cases, your latest victim died of a cerebral hemorrhage, resulting from a severe blow to the head."

Rose took a moment to digest what he was saying. "You're saying she wasn't injected with potassium chloride?"

"I'm saying she wasn't injected with potassium chloride."

Rose shot glance at Stipes, who looked as confused as she was. "So are you saying this could've been a different killer? That it might not have been related to the others?"

The doctor raised his hands in the air. "I'm not saying any such thing. I'm simply stating the facts." His words had a familiar resonance. He lowered his hands back down to his sides. "There are clearly very distinct similarities between this victim and the others. Namely, there were no signs of forced entry, and the attacker struck from behind…with a blunt instrument, I might add, which hasn't, as yet, been found. Plus, there were no obvious signs of disruption to the property. In fact, the only *difference* between this one and the others appears to be the lack of an injection."

Rose sighed inwardly. Surely that was the most significant part, for the killer at least. It was his or her way of exacting a very specific form of revenge.

Weller pressed on, oblivious to her train of thought. "Of course, it's possible her attacker hadn't intended to kill her. Or, at the very least, that her death hadn't been premeditated."

Again, Rose shot a glance at Stipes. "So this *could've* been the result of a discussion that turned sour?"

Weller merely shrugged. "Her killer might not have come equipped with the potassium chloride if he or she hadn't been intending for this to happen."

Rose shuffled her feet against the hard tiled floor. The scenario seemed feasible enough, but it just didn't feel right. If Fawcett's death hadn't been premeditated, how come there appeared to be no forensic evidence and a murder weapon had just happened to be on hand? She voiced her concerns aloud.

The doctor raised his eyebrows. "I never said I had all the answers. If I did, I'd be a miracle worker."

After a few more minutes of discussion, during which Weller promised to email the report, Rose thanked the doctor and stepped out into the corridor. Stipes followed behind, his heavy footsteps echoing her mood. Whenever she felt she was getting somewhere, something new leapt out of the woodwork. It seemed this case had hidden depths she just couldn't get to. She paused for a moment, resting her back against the cool tiled wall.

"If Fawcett's part in all of this was just opportunistic, the killer might not have felt she deserved death by potassium chloride. This wasn't an execution, Stipes. It was murder. Pure and simple."

Stipes stepped up alongside her. Small beads of sweat had formed on his forehead, and when he spoke his voice was quiet and labored. She hoped he wasn't coming down with something. "I agree. We need to find out how well she knew Sampson and establish whether or not she really *did* witness anything."

Rose tapped her head with the palm of her hand. "Like that's gonna be easy."

She pulled herself from the wall and continued along the corridor. Stipes followed suit. "Of course, her connection with Sampson *could've* been recent. That photo couldn't have been more than a few years old. Fawcett might not have even been aware of the old lady's past."

Rose kept walking. "They might've just run into each other and struck up a friendship, you mean?"

"Stranger things have happened. They were both probably lonely. Perhaps Sampson saw something in Fawcett that reminded her of herself."

Rose turned a corner and headed toward reception. "What about the shop Fawcett worked for? The charity shop? They could've met there." Stipes screwed up his face as though he'd just heard something particularly offensive. Rose continued regardless. "I'm not saying Sampson might've shopped there. I'm saying she might've donated things. Surely it has to be worth checking out."

"OK, Guv. I'll check it out."

As they stepped out into the freezing parking lot, Rose pulled her jacket tightly across her chest. She was about to make a dash for the car when, for what seemed like the umpteenth time, her phone sounded in her pocket. As she pulled it out, Reece's name appeared on the screen. She scrolled to answer. "Yes Reece."

"I just had a call from uniform. One of Fawcett's neighbors saw her stepping out of a red car early yesterday morning."

A flash of anticipation flooded Rose's brain. If Weller was right, Fawcett's death had occurred not long after that time. She reached the car and stopped. "Any idea of the make or model?"

"She thought it could've been a Fiesta. One of the new ones."

"She didn't happen to notice the number plate? Or any distinguishing marks?"

"I'm afraid not. She said it was dark and she only noticed it 'cos she was having trouble sleeping. She'd walked over to the window to have a cigarette."

"She didn't happen to notice the driver?"

"No, Guv."

Rose opened the car door and climbed inside. The freezing air was already chilling her to the bone. She continued the conversation from the comfort of the driver's seat. "So she couldn't tell if they were male or female?"

"No."

"And did the car hang around? Or was it driven straight off?"

Reece paused for a moment. "That's the thing. You see, she stubbed out her cigarette and headed back to bed. So she didn't know if the car hung around or not."

"But she didn't *hear* it drive off?"

"No. But she wasn't particularly listening for it, and she hadn't actually heard it arrive either."

Rose attained the neighbor's address and ended the call,

turning the key in the ignition. Then she turned to Stipes, who'd already settled into the seat beside her. "One of Fawcett's neighbors saw Fawcett arriving in a red car, possibly a Fiesta, in the early hours of yesterday morning. I don't s'pose that rings any bells?"

"Not off the top of my head. But we can check it out. Shame there's no CCTV round there."

The fact still surprised Rose.

As she exited the parking lot and pulled out into Main Street, she tried to recall if she'd noticed a red Ford Fiesta recently, specifically at the home of anyone she'd interviewed. But, as with Stipes, it didn't ring a bell. She gripped tighter to the steering wheel. The roads were precariously slippery at this time of the morning, and the last thing she needed was to prang the car.

She negotiated a particularly tight bend, the previous thought still playing on her mind. The car might not have had anything to do with the killer; and even if the killer *had* been driving it, that didn't mean it hadn't been borrowed or stolen. Nevertheless, it was imperative that they rule it out. Whoever had been driving it was likely to have been the last person to have seen Fawcett alive. And whether they realized it or not, they could well have information pertaining to her death.

When they got to Fawcett's neighbor's residence, the door was answered by a short, slightly chubby woman, with tousled brown hair and what looked like a partial moustache. She appeared to be in her early to mid-twenties, similar to Fawcett's age, yet she had a look about her that way exceeded her years. Rose guessed that was down to her lifestyle.

They held out their badges and Rose stepped forward. "Good morning. Miss Tillet, isn't it?"

The young woman nodded. She was clearly aware of the reason for their visit, yet she made no attempt to invite them in.

Rose took the initiative.

"It's pretty cold out here. D'you mind if we step in for a moment?"

Reluctantly Tillet moved aside, though the minute Rose entered the property, she wished she hadn't. Like Fawcett's meagre living space, the room served a multitude of purposes — those of lounge, dining area, *and* bedroom — and the pungent smell that seeped through its crevices reflected that. She looked to Stipes, scrunching her face in a "God, this is disgusting" expression. If she'd had a face mask with her, she'd have been tempted to put it on.

Instinctively she headed for the one tiny window, which wasn't open, and looked out into the narrow road. This would've been where Tillet had stood that previous morning. Her eyes scanned the vicinity for any sign of lighting that might have aided her view. There was one streetlamp ten meters or so along the road. It was a wonder Tillet had even been able to identify the car as being red.

She turned back to the young woman, who had just closed the door and was perching herself on the edge of a stained grey armchair. "You told one of our officers you saw Leah Fawcett getting out of a red car early yesterday morning."

Tillet nodded. "That's right. I woke up. I hadn't been sleeping well, so I walked across to the window for a cigarette."

Rose noticed Stipes shielding his nose with his hand and signaled to him to refrain. "Did you know Miss Fawcett well?"

"I didn't know her at all really. I just bumped into her every now and again; y'know, when we were coming in or out."

"So you didn't speak to her?"

"We said hi sometimes. When I first moved in, there was kind of a get together in one of the other apartments. That was how I knew her name."

"How long ago was that?"

Tillet thought for a moment. "About four years or so, I guess."

"So you haven't spoken with her recently?"

"No. Not recently."

Rose shifted her weight from one foot to the other. Her lack of sleep over these past few days was taking its toll. Every bone in her body ached. She tried to stay focused. "Did you ever see her with anyone?"

"Like a boyfriend, you mean?"

"Anyone."

Tillet glanced up at the dirty brown ceiling. "No. I don't think so."

"And you never saw her be dropped off by a car before?"

"No."

A noise outside in the corridor fractured the intensity of the moment, and Rose glanced at her watch. Time was moving on and she had no wish to waste it. She asked a few more questions, getting equally repetitive answers, then gave up and decided to return to the station. If Fawcett *had* arrived in a red Fiesta, the identity of its driver wasn't to be found here.

She stepped out into the corridor, breathing an audible sigh of relief. If she'd been subject to that smell much longer, she was certain she'd have thrown up. Tillet closed the door behind them and Rose looked to Stipes, who appeared to be experiencing a similar such sensation. "How the hell do people live like that?"

Stipes rubbed his nose with the back of his hand. "I guess they don't have much choice, Guv."

Rose shook her head with accentuated vehemence. "Don't give me that, Stipes. Cleanliness isn't something that requires money or advantage. Just a good old-fashioned sense of self-respect."

As they made their way back to the station, Rose reflected

231

on their forthcoming tasks. They were still awaiting news on what Campbell's doctor and girlfriend had to say regarding the psychiatrist. And it was about time they spoke with Mrs. Dyer. She was one of the only people in the box of files they hadn't managed to speak to yet, and her testimony *could* prove invaluable. She just hoped the doctors would deem her fit enough.

When they reached the incident room, Banks was waiting. He marched toward them. "I've spoken with Campbell's doctor, Guv. As the psychiatrist said, he came in complaining of anxiety. She prescribed some pills, but it seemed to be increasing. So she thought he might benefit from counselling."

Rose proceeded towards her desk. "Did he give her any reasons for this anxiety?"

"Apparently, he just said he was having a few problems at work, stuff he didn't really want to talk about."

"So she just wrote out a prescription? Seems to me doctors are a little too keen to dole out pills and counselling these days."

She reached her desk and Stipes leaned his elbow on a nearby chair. "Don't forget his last visit to the psychiatrist was a couple of months ago. He could've resolved whatever it was that was making him anxious. It might not have been related to his death."

Rose sank down into her chair. It was one more thing they didn't have an answer to. "OK. Well, when we discover Campbell's role in all this, perhaps we'll find out." She'd been hoping it might have worked the other way around. She waved Banks away and turned back to Stipes. "We need to speak to Mrs. Dyer. She had motive *and* opportunity, and she still hasn't been questioned. Can you check in with the hospital? See if she's up to having visitors yet. Even a few minutes could help us enormously."

Stipes drifted to his own desk to make the call and Rose leaned forward across the table. The more she thought about it,

232

the more crucial Dyer's testimony seemed. OK, so it would've been impossible for her to have killed Campbell and Fawcett. She was in the hospital at the time. But they still couldn't be certain this was the work of just one killer. Plus, there was always the possibility that she'd gotten her son to do her bidding for her. After all, he had pretty crap alibis for the first two murders.

Her mind drifted to Dyer Junior, and she recalled his odd, slightly childlike disposition. Was it the disposition of a killer? Initially she'd thought it out of the question. He'd seemed far too naive to have been able to coordinate such seamless acts of violence. But, for some reason, she was starting to rethink that initial hypothesis. It *had* been known for serial killers to draw on other personalities when carrying out attacks.

She recalled Dyer's stint in a juvenile unit when he was younger. Was it possible that he possessed such a condition? At this stage in the investigation, she was willing to contemplate anything. She called to Stipes. "Come to think of it, let's get Dyer Junior back in too! Perhaps we dismissed him a little too easily!"

CHAPTER THIRTY-SIX

The hospital agreed to allow them ten minutes with Mrs. Dyer during the early afternoon, provided their questioning wasn't too intense. They still hadn't discovered the cause of the former bank clerk's illness, but apparently her condition was slow to improve.

Rose decided to check in with Campbell's psychiatrist, Dr. Miller, in the meantime. He *had* to have more information on Campbell than he was letting on. Psychiatrists generally had a close relationship with their patients. Even if Campbell *had* been reluctant to divulge his innermost secrets, it was likely the doctor knew more about what made him tick than they did.

She climbed into the car alongside Stipes and fastened her seat belt. Dyer Junior could wait until after they'd spoken with his mother. After all, it was probably better to gain her side of the story before getting him back in. That way they'd be better prepared.

As they headed along Dew Street, Stipes seemed restless. He fiddled with the buckle of his belt. Rose put it down to frustrations associated with the case. When he finally spoke, the sudden interruption made her jump. "Are you sure this is worth it, Guv? I mean, Banks *has* already spoken with the psychiatrist."

Rose nodded her head but maintained her focus on the road. "Yes. I do. I think Miller knows more than he's letting on. He was pretty vague with Banks. Besides, I'd like to get an idea of what he considers *anxiety issues.*"

When they arrived at the practice, Miller was waiting for them. Stipes had called ahead to warn him of their impending arrival, news the doctor hadn't been best pleased about. Nonetheless, he hadn't kicked up too much of a fuss. Perhaps because he felt it was better to cooperate with the police than risk them turning up unannounced. After all, any hint of scandal wouldn't be good for business.

Rose stepped forward and made the formal introductions. Miller was a tall, stocky man, with dark brown hair that was fast succumbing to the onset of grey. He wore brown cord trousers, which Rose considered typical attire for a psychologist, and a green barber jacket with a brown collar. Overall, he had the look of someone who cared a great deal about image, a detail Rose found strangely discomforting.

The introductions over, Miller led them to his office, where he seated himself behind his vast wooden desk. Rose presumed the oversized piece of furniture was some kind of status symbol, something to signify power and professionalism to prospective clients. The idea made her smile. She sat herself opposite, alongside Stipes.

As she settled into the firm wooden chair, she noticed that the desk's surface held several photos of teenage children, but none of a female counterpart, and again she smiled to herself. Perhaps even psychologists were bad at relationships. She straightened herself up. She *had* to focus. She took a long, deep breath.

"Dr. Miller, before we start, I'd like to thank you for agreeing to see us on such short notice. I realize you've already spoken with one of our colleagues but, to be honest with you, we were hoping for a little more detail with regard to Mr. Anthony Campbell."

Miller shot her an unnecessarily wide smile, displaying an immaculate set of shiny white teeth. Life had clearly been good to him. "I totally understand. The problem is, I really don't think there's much else I can tell you. Anthony Campbell was quite a private young man. He had his share of problems, like any other young person, but there was nothing out of the ordinary."

Rose forced a thin smile. "I see. So you wouldn't consider a person in their early twenties requiring counselling as out of the ordinary?"

Miller leaned back in his seat, seemingly getting into character. "Not necessarily. Campbell had been referred for counselling because of anxiety. It's actually quite a common disorder in this day and age."

Rose could feel herself growing hot. "And why do you think that is?" Her words sounded more aggressive than she'd meant them to, but Miller didn't seem to notice.

"Well, I guess there could be a number of reasons. Peer pressure, pressure to succeed, concerns over not fitting in.... Young people have a lot to cope with these days. People have high expectations. However, in Campbell's case, I think it was just in his DNA. When things were running smoothly, he didn't have a problem. But as soon as something didn't go the way he planned, he couldn't deal with it."

Rose shot a glance at Stipes, then turned back to the conversation at hand. "You said the last time you saw Anthony Campbell was a couple of months ago?"

Miller fiddled with a paperweight on his desk. "That's right. I checked my notes again before you came. October 9."

"Do you think his anxiety was decreasing?"

The doctor paused for a moment. "It's most likely, yes. Although I'd only seen him three times altogether, and he never really opened up to me. I think he was hoping I could give him some kind of miracle cure. Unfortunately, it doesn't work like that."

Rose bit her lip. Just like Banks, they were getting nowhere. She decided to get straight to the point. "Can you tell us exactly what Campbell said to you? When you first questioned him over the nature of his visits?"

Miller released the paperweight and placed his hands down in his lap. "Again, I *have* consulted my notes over this. He told me he was experiencing an increased heart rate and breathlessness when in certain situations. When I asked him what those situations were, he was very vague. He said that sometimes it was happening at work and sometimes at home, specifically when he didn't feel in control of a situation. I asked him if there was anything particularly stressful going on in his life...anything that might've triggered such symptoms, which were essentially panic attacks. He finally *did* admit to having been put under unexpected pressure, but he didn't wish to elaborate."

Rose sank back into her chair and Stipes leaned forward. She hoped he'd have more luck than she was having. Stipes cleared his throat. "Did he say if this pressure was related to home or work?"

Miller smiled. "I'm afraid not. Although, as he said, it *was* affecting him at both places."

"But how could you treat him if you didn't know what the underlying cause was?"

The doctor leaned forward slightly. "My treatment for anxiety would've been the same no matter what its cause. I taught him some coping mechanisms for when the symptoms struck. Basic relaxation and distancing techniques. If his anxiety had persisted, I'd have suggested hypnotherapy."

Rose decided to change tack. There had to be something

237

they were missing here, and it seemed Miller wasn't likely to divulge it unless they specifically requested it. She pulled herself up straight again. "Did Campbell mention anything about his family? Or his girlfriend?"

The doctor reverted to his earlier rigid position. "He said things were good at home. He had no quarrels with his relatives or his girlfriend. He led me to believe that, whatever it was that was troubling him, he was dealing with it alone, which was probably one of the reasons he was finding it hard."

"Did he mention if he had any health concerns?"

"He didn't. It was the first thing I asked him."

Rose's phone sounded in her pocket and she reached in to retrieve it. She could see the call was from Blake. "I'm sorry, you'll have to excuse me."

She left Stipes in Miller's office and stepped out into the waiting room. On realizing it wasn't empty, she headed for the exit and stepped out into the busy street. She just caught the phone before it rang off. "Blake?"

Blake's voice resonated clearly along the line. "I just got a call from SOCOs, Guv. They found three mobile phones in the drawer of a closet in Fawcett's apartment. I'm off to collect them now."

A spark of electricity shot through Rose's spine, but she managed to keep the excitement from her voice. "OK, when you have them, run the SIMs against the details we have for Finlay and Campbell's phones, will you? If any of them come back as a match, call me. Then get them down to Forensics and see if they can find any prints. They could just be items people had brought to the charity shop. Fawcett might've stolen them to make money. But we need to rule out her involvement in our other crime scenes."

She could sense Blake nodding down the line. "Got it."

"I don't suppose you have anything on Fawcett's change of name yet?"

"Not yet. But we're working on it. Since she had no record and pretty much no family or friends, it's proving difficult."

Rose placed the phone in her pocket and walked back to the office feeling a hundred times lighter than she had when she'd left it. If the phones found in Fawcett's apartment proved to have belonged to their victims, it was likely Fawcett had been in recent contact with their killer, and that *might* make it easier to narrow down their list of suspects. She knew she was being optimistic. But, at this point, what else could she be?

When she re-entered Miller's room, the look on Stipes's face informed her that there was little more to be gained here. Not that she hadn't gathered that much herself. She thanked Miller and they headed back out the way they'd come, much to the psychiatrist's relief. Now that they were gone, he could get back to something resembling normality. Not that a psychiatrist's lot seemed particularly normal to her.

When they stepped back outside, the sky had turned a deathly shade of white. It made Rose shiver, despite the fact that she'd put on two extra layers that morning. She quickened her pace, updating Stipes as they headed to the car. With any luck, Blake's news *could* bring them one step closer to understanding what was going on.

She glanced back at the modern red brick building. Their conversation with Miller had proved as futile as Stipes had warned her it might be. Nonetheless, she felt better for having made the effort. It was the job of every good detective to leave no stone unturned, and she was determined to prove she *was* a good detective. She would break this case if it was the last thing she did.

CHAPTER THIRTY-SEVEN

On their way to the hospital to speak with Mrs. Dyer, Rose's mind turned again to Fawcett's mode of death. The fact that it hadn't been an execution told her that, whatever it was that Fawcett had done, it hadn't been connected to Samson and Finlay's sideline…at least not directly. It was more likely that Fawcett had discovered something and become a threat to the killer, and her connection with Sampson could've facilitated that discovery. Not that they'd discovered how the two had become acquainted yet. No one at the charity shop had recognized the photo of Sampson. Then again, they probably had a lot of customers. It was possible Sampson had been there and they'd simply forgotten.

She tapped her fingers against the steering wheel. The sooner the phones were checked out, the sooner they'd have a clearer idea of what it was Fawcett had been up to.

The call from Blake came quicker than she'd anticipated. She reached forward and switched on the hands free. "What have you got for me, Blake?"

Blake took a moment to catch his breath. Rose guessed he'd probably just hot-footed it back from scenes of crime. "Two of the phones are a match with Campbell and Finlay's, Guv."

For a brief moment, Rose was so overwhelmed she couldn't

speak. When her words finally left her mouth, they didn't even sound like her. "Are you *serious*?" Even though she'd been half expecting the news, it still astounded her.

"I'm serious."

Rose took her eyes off the road for a moment to glance at Stipes, who was listening in on the conversation. "Do we know who the third phone belonged to?"

"Not as yet. It's a pay as you go, so unless someone reported it missing, there's probably no way of finding out."

A thought struck Rose and she voiced it aloud. "Check it out with the call emergency services received after Finlay's death. You never know, Fawcett *could've* been our anonymous caller." She disconnected the call, then remembered something. She switched her attention to Stipes. "Get him back on the line, will you, and remind him to get those phones to Forensics ASAP if he hasn't already done so. We need to know if there are any prints on them." Stipes reached for the hands free, and she added, "For all we know, Fawcett could've been blackmailing the killer."

Stipes shot her a look that suggested she was mad. "If she was blackmailing them, why would she come to us?"

"Perhaps she thought it would give her more leverage. Who knows? Let's just wait 'til we hear back from Blake."

When they reached the hospital, Rose felt too wired up to focus. She had to stop at the coffee machine to get herself a drink before their meeting with Mrs. Dyer. Not that it was likely to calm her down. Stipes followed suit. It had been a long morning and, the closer they seemed to get to the truth, the more complicated things became.

When they *did* finally get to see Sampson's elusive ex-patient, she looked old and frail, a state that had no doubt been exacerbated by her stint in the hospital. Rose walked along the side of the bed, carefully negotiating the many wires that surrounded it. Stipes stepped up alongside her.

When they'd shown their badges, it was Dyer who spoke first. "I knew you'd come. Andrew told me about how he'd been interviewed…but he's a good boy, you know? He had no clue about what she did in her private life; he still doesn't."

She reached out her hand for the glass of water on the cabinet beside her. Her voice sounded croaky and dry. Rose picked up the glass and handed it to her. As she lifted it to her lips, her hands were shaky, and a few drops spilled onto her clean white gown. Rose reached forward to retrieve the glass, placing it back on its resting place.

"So you know what we've come to speak to you about?"

Dyer nodded. "You want to know if I killed Mrs. Sampson because she helped me get an abortion thirty odd years ago."

Rose looked her in the eye, astounded by her bluntness. "And did you?"

Dyer smiled for the first time, the action causing the wrinkles around her eyes to broaden. "No. I didn't."

There was a short pause while Rose struggled to digest the directness of Dyer's words. Before she had chance to comment, the latter continued.

"Are you sure Dr. Sampson's past had anything to do with her death? I mean, a lot of people must've been grateful for her help. I know I was. Besides, she must've retired years ago. If someone wasn't happy with what she did for them, why wait until now for revenge?"

It was the question Rose had been asking herself. Still, she hadn't been expecting it from Mrs. Dyer. She stepped forward in the hope of taking control of the situation. Somewhere between entering the room and opening her mouth, it seemed to have gotten away from her.

"At this stage, we're not sure of anything. What we *are* trying to do is rule out anyone who might've had a motive. By the way, what made you think we considered you a suspect?"

Dyer fiddled with the pillow beneath her head. "I've seen the papers. Her death was suspicious. Then you want to speak to me. What other reason could you have? Plus, I've spoken with my son." She exhaled a cynical sigh. "But I wouldn't have a motive. Dr. Sampson saved my life. Literally. If I'd have had a child at that point, I don't think I'd be here today. I simply wouldn't have coped."

Rose decided to dig a little deeper. "Did you know she lived at Amber Court?"

"No. I had no idea. At least, not until Andrew told me he'd been questioned."

She fiddled with the intravenous drip leading into her arm. The action made Rose shudder.

Oblivious to the discomfort she'd caused, Mrs. Dyer added, "Even then, it didn't really click. It wasn't until I saw the papers that it really hit home...not that I really knew her. I only met her once, and it was very brief. To be honest, I was surprised she was still alive, and not because of anything she'd done. In my opinion, she never did anything wrong."

"So you didn't know your son was working for her?"

"No. My son doesn't give me a list of the people he works for. Why would he?"

Her voice was becoming croaky again, and Rose handed her the water without her having to ask for it. When she'd taken a sip, Rose took it and placed it back on the cabinet.

"Did you ever tell anyone about the abortion?"

Dyer hesitated. "Not for a very long time. A few years ago, I told my husband. He couldn't understand why I hadn't told him before, but it's not something you tend to want to revisit."

Rose tried to look sympathetic. "I can understand that. You

243

don't think it's likely your husband confided in your son?"

Dyer held out her hand for the water again. Rose obliged. "You're thinking Andrew might've found out I had an abortion and decided to eliminate the woman who'd helped me? No, I don't think my husband would've told him. He had no reason to. It was personal. Even if he had, why would Andrew have been bothered about something I did before he was born? Believe me, Detective, you're barking up the wrong tree."

Rose stared ahead at the peeling white wall. Like the other women she'd interviewed from Sampson's files, Dyer wasn't what she'd expected. Her cynicism and forthrightness were enough to rival her own, and hers had been nurtured by many years on the police force. She reached inside her jacket for the envelope she'd placed there, pulling out a photo and handing it to Dyer. It was a photo of Finlay.

"Do you recognize this man?"

Dyer stared at it for a long time before finally replying. "I'm not sure. It's possible this was the man who referred me to the doctor, but it was such a long time ago. I'm really not sure. Sorry."

Rose let out a deep sigh. "I don't suppose you'd remember his name...the man who referred you?"

"I only met him once, and I don't think he ever told me it."

Dyer handed the photo back to Rose, who tucked it back into the envelope.

A nurse wondered in to check on the patient, and Rose waited until she'd gone before continuing. "So you haven't had any recent contact with Dr. Sampson?"

Dyer shook her head. "No. I haven't had any contact with her full stop. Not since...well...."

She cleared her throat, which was followed by a bout of coughing, and Rose realized her time was running out. She requested Dyer's alibis for the times of Sampson and Finlay's murders, which, as with the other women, were by no means rock solid, then shot a glance at Stipes. She'd had her phone switched off for the last ten minutes due to the sensitive machinery surrounding them, and if she hadn't had a call from Blake by now, she'd be extremely surprised. The thought was distracting her to such an extent, she could barely think of anything else.

She thanked Dyer for her cooperation and headed out into the corridor. The moment she'd pulled the door closed behind her, she pulled out her mobile. As she'd expected, there were two missed calls from Blake. She could barely move her fingers fast enough to click on the redial button.

When she finally got through, Blake answered almost immediately. "Guv. I had the third phone checked out as you asked, and guess what? It *was* the phone used for the anonymous call."

Rose glanced at Stipes, who was hovering expectantly beside her. For the first time since being assigned this case, it felt like things were really falling into place. She ended the call and addressed her partner. "The third phone from Fawcett's apartment was the one used to make the anonymous call."

Stipes exhaled a deep breath. "So perhaps Fawcett *was* conflicted. She wanted to do the right thing, but the opportunity to make a little money was too tempting."

Rose merely shrugged. "Perhaps. And perhaps she somehow stole Finlay and Campbell's phones for leverage. Blake and Sherman are going through the call logs as we speak. If the killer's on them, we'll find him. Or her."

They stepped from the building into the busy hospital parking lot. If they were right about Fawcett and she was merely a pawn in all of this, she'd been playing a very dangerous game, one she'd probably always been destined to lose. If the killer had already killed in cold blood, they'd have had no qualms about killing a blackmailer. But what was Campbell's role in all of this? They still had no clue as to the motive for *his* murder, which, unlike Fawcett's, was of an execution style.

Rose unlocked the car doors and they climbed inside. Once seated, Stipes turned to face her. "Are we still off to pick up Dyer Junior, Guv?"

She placed the key in the ignition and started the engine. "Yep. Until we have a definite suspect, we carry on as normal. I don't care what his mother said, Andrew Dyer had crap alibis for the times of Sampson and Finlay's murders, and he would've had knowledge of Sampson's security cameras. Plus, he had the opportunity to case out her house. If anyone could've gotten in uninvited, he could've. He might come across as a bit simple, but that doesn't mean he's not capable of murder."

Stipes fastened his seat belt. "You've changed your mind about him then?"

She pushed her foot on the accelerator and slowly pulled away. "I haven't changed my mind. I'm just being pragmatic."

In truth, she'd seriously re-evaluated Dyer's capabilities, despite his mother's glowing recommendation. He'd had opportunity *and* potentially motive. At this point, he was probably one of the best candidates they had.

CHAPTER THIRTY-EIGHT

When they arrived at Dyer's place of work, he was out on a job, which was hardly surprising considering it was two o'clock in the afternoon. Rose left Stipes to wait for him and got Sherman to pick her up and take her to the station. There was plenty for her to be getting on with, particularly as developments were occurring at an almost unprecedented rate. Plus, she needed to take another look at her spider-gram. Relationships between the people it concerned seemed to be changing by the minute, and she wanted to get a clear idea of the dynamics in her head.

As she headed for her desk, she spotted a copy of the Brackley Times laying on the table in front of her. Its headline read, *Four Deaths in Brackley, and the Police are Still Clueless. Does DI Rose Have What it Takes to Catch a Killer?* As before, the words made her cringe. She picked up the paper and tossed it into the rubbish bin. If there was one thing she didn't need right now, it was bad press. It wasn't going to make her job, or her life, any easier.

When Andrew Dyer was finally brought back in, he looked tired and harassed. Rose guessed he'd had a busy day and being brought back into the police station hadn't improved it. She asked Stipes to take him to the same interview room as before. It was fast becoming her personal meeting space. Then she went to get herself a coffee. After her recent run-in with the chief, she needed the caffeine. It was the only thing she could think of to take the edge off.

Once she'd gotten the coffee, Rose went over the details of her recent meeting in her mind. The chief had told her, in no uncertain terms, that if she didn't get a suspect soon she'd be removed from the case. Words that, despite having been expected, had both angered and saddened her. This case had become her baby, and she was damned if she was going to let someone else see it through to its end. She gripped tightly to the polystyrene cup and made her way back along the corridor. If Dyer had anything to offer, anything at all, she was going to make damned sure she got it out of him.

When she finally entered the interview room, Stipes was waiting. She placed her coffee on the table in front of her and glanced across at Dyer. He'd already been furnished with a hot drink, which was currently going cold on the table beside him. She guessed that he was peeved at having been called in a second time. Perhaps he'd also learned of their visit to his mother, and that had angered him further. Still, she wasn't about to apologize for either.

She leaned forward in her seat and shot him her most casual smile. "Good afternoon, Mr. Dyer. I hope we're not putting you out too much. We just needed to discuss a few things with you."

Dyer merely grunted. Rose glanced up at the two-way mirror. Perhaps she should've placed her colleagues behind it again. Still, it was too late now. She pressed on.

"I wanted to ask you a few more questions regarding your meetings with Mrs. Sampson. The lady who lived at Six Amber Court."

Dyer screwed up his face. "I told you, I didn't *know* her. I just did her garden."

His cheeks had flushed pink, probably from the pressure of being cross examined. Even innocent people tended to feel the pressure in such circumstances.

Again, Rose pressed on. "Did you consider her to be a likeable person? From your brief encounters with her, I mean."

Dyer shrugged his shoulders. "She was OK. Normal, I guess. Like I said, I just knocked on the door when I arrived and gave her the sheet to sign when I left. We barely spoke."

"You didn't find her rude? Or arrogant in any way?"

He shuffled in his seat. "Of course not. She was an old lady."

Rose was trying to ascertain if Dyer had harbored an underlying grudge against the former doctor. If he had, it wasn't obvious.

She glanced across at Stipes, then reached for the envelope on the table in front of her and pulled out photos of Campbell and Fawcett. She pushed them across to Dyer, explaining her actions for the tape.

Dyer visibly stiffened. "Do you recognize any of these people?"

He rested a finger on the image of Campbell. "This one. I've seen him before. When I was at the house."

Rose felt her heart quicken. "Six Amber Court?"

"Yes."

There was a short pause while Rose deliberated over the best way to proceed. The last thing she wanted was to scare Dyer into thinking he needed to hide things from them. In the end, she decided just to follow her instincts.

"Can you tell us what he was doing at Six Amber Court?"

Dyer fiddled with the corner of the photo. He had that child-like look about him again. "He was doing the same thing I was. Working. Only he had a delivery of logs."

Rose smiled. It made sense so far. She tried to keep an even tone of voice. "Did you speak to him?"

Dyer shook his head. "No. I was busy."

For the first time since Rose's arrival, he took a sip of his drink. Rose guessed the questioning was making his throat dry. When he'd placed the cup back down, she continued.

"Did you see him speak with Mrs. Sampson?"

Something seemed to click in Dyer's brain. His face lit up and there was a sudden eagerness in his demeanor. When he spoke again, his voice was lighter. "Yes. I remember now. He spoke with her for quite a while. I was watering the tubs in the front, so I could see them standing in the doorway."

Rose nodded, urging him on. "Did you hear anything of what they were saying?"

He paused for a moment as though deep in thought, then replied. "No. I was too far away. But she didn't look happy, and when she closed the door, he was still standing there."

Dyer was holding his hands together and there was a glimmer of excitement in his eyes, like a child on Christmas morning. He was clearly enjoying his new-found usefulness. Rose was glad he was starting to relax.

She was about to question him further when there was a knock on the door and Blake poked his head around. He was waving a piece of paper in the air to show that he had something important. She paused the interview for the recording, her frustration evident in her voice. Then she signaled for Stipes to follow her out.

"I'm sorry," she said to Dyer as she headed for the door. "We won't be long. Can I get you another drink?"

Dyer sank back into his chair, his previous excitement having dissipated. He merely shook his head.

A minute later, Rose was standing in the corridor, finding it hard to stay still. They'd just been getting somewhere with Dyer, and she wanted to get back in there. She looked to Blake.

"What have you got?"

His expression told her it was good. "I think I know why Campbell was killed, Guv."

"And?"

"Well, I found an article that was published in the Brackley Post last October." He handed her the piece of paper in his hand. "It's about doctors who abuse their power. It doesn't mention Sampson and Finlay by name, but it *does* include doctors who help women abort their babies. And look at the name of the writer."

Rose's eyes scanned the small black print until they reached the name at the bottom. *Anthony Campbell.*

Blake hovered in front of her. "It didn't come up before because Campbell didn't actually use the words 'obstetrician' or 'abortion.' He was a bit more creative with his writing. But as soon as I typed *his* name in...."

Rose ran her eyes over the article again, her mind ticking over at a hundred miles an hour. She hadn't had Campbell pegged for a would-be journalist. Then again, perhaps the opportunity had come about by accident. His friends *had* said he hadn't had much of a social life. Perhaps he'd stumbled upon the information unwittingly and felt it was too important to keep to himself. Plus, it had possibly earned him good money.

She mentally took a step back. "So maybe Campbell *did* discover something while working at Sampson and Finlay's houses." She glanced at the date in the top left corner of the article. "It coincides with his anxiety issues, so maybe he dug a little too deep and found himself getting into something he didn't want to be part of. Maybe he unintentionally alerted the killer to Sampson and Finlay's identities."

Stipes stepped forward. "If the killer had thought he wanted

251

to profit from what had happened, it *could* explain the way he was murdered."

For a few moments the three detectives stood in silence. Events were unfolding at such a rate, it was becoming virtually impossible to keep abreast of them. Finally, Rose shook her head and let out an exasperated sigh.

"So Campbell and Fawcett could both have gotten in the killer's way. For totally different reasons."

Stipes smiled sarcastically. "Let's just hope no one else gets in his or her way."

The thought disturbed Rose. It appeared that their killer had insecurity issues and wasn't averse to taking radical actions to eliminate them.

Again, she thought back to Campbell's interview. "What I don't understand is why Campbell didn't tell us what he knew. We told him there'd been an incident at Six Amber Court. And yet he neglected to inform us of the killer's possible motive. Even though he'd published it in a newspaper."

Stipes stretched his arms behind his back. "When you first mentioned it, he probably thought there'd been a complaint. From the sounds of things, it's likely he'd been snooping around. Perhaps he was worried that Sampson might've noticed and reported him. After that, he probably just didn't want to incriminate himself. Finding out you're a murder suspect must be pretty scary, and we already know he had anxiety issues."

Rose shook her head. "The ironic thing is, if he'd told us, we might've been able to save his life." She felt her phone vibrate and reached for it before it sounded, instinctively scrolling across the screen. "DI Rose."

Weller's voice greeted her. "Good afternoon, DI Rose. I have some information for you."

He seemed to have said that a lot lately. Rose just hoped that, this time, it proved useful. She pushed the phone closer to her ear, praying for him to get on with it.

"Forensics discovered a fiber on Fawcett's coat. It contains DNA, and it doesn't belong to the victim."

Rose sighed. She was beginning to get a sense of dèjá vu. "But can we link it to her murder? I mean, couldn't it have got there while she was going about her daily business?"

She thought back to the hair found on Campbell and how she was certain it hadn't belonged to the killer. It reminded her how, sometimes, too much information just got in the way. Plus, Fawcett had worked in a charity shop, so she must've been subject to all manner of fibers.

Weller made a loud, deliberating sound with his throat. "It's possible. The coat *is* pretty old. Nevertheless, we ran it through the system and something pretty interesting came up. The DNA belonged to a lady who was convicted of murder twenty-eight years ago. She was only nineteen at the time and, as the circumstances were considered extenuating, she was released after serving just ten years of her sentence."

Rose could feel her pulse rising. "What were the circumstances?"

"That's the interesting part. The victim had performed an abortion on a close friend of the perpetrator, but there'd been complications. Severe ones. The young woman died as a result."

Rose shot a glance at Stipes. The significance of what Weller was telling her was almost too great to comprehend. She paused to catch her breath. "But the perpetrator was considered mentally stable?"

"Yes. Her lawyer tried to get her off on grounds of diminished responsibility, but the judge was having none of it. The killing was premeditated, and the perpetrator had been meticulous in the planning."

"So how was she caught?"

"She left a piece of jewelry at the crime scene. She must've dropped it when she leaned forward to strike the body. Anyway, her prints were all over it, and since she'd been arrested for theft the year before, her details were in the system. It was an open and shut case."

Rose shook her head. "How was the woman killed?"

"The victim suffered a fatal blow to the head."

"No potassium chloride?"

The doctor paused. "No. But it's possible she's honed her skills since then."

The sigh that left Rose's body was one of release. Was it possible they'd finally identified their killer? When she'd recovered enough to gather her words together, she asked, "What's this woman's name?"

Her heart was pounding so hard, she was having trouble breathing. Weller let out a long, self-satisfied sigh.

"It's a Miss Alice Fox."

In the seconds that followed, confusion clouded Rose's brain. It wasn't a name she recognized. For some reason, she'd felt sure that their killer would turn out to be someone they were acquainted with. Perhaps she'd wasted too much time on the box of files after all. Then again, that *was* what had led them to uncover Sampson and Finlay's connection, so the effort hadn't been entirely wasted.

She pulled herself together before the doctor rang off. "Do we have any details for this Miss Fox?"

"Other than her date of birth and her national insurance number, I'm afraid not. At least, *I* haven't been able to come up with any. You might have more luck." He was referring to her ability to access databases he wasn't privy to.

Rose was about to end the call when Weller added, "There's

254

something else I think you should know. A couple of years before Miss Fox was released, her parents died in a car crash. As she was an only child, she inherited their estate, which amounted to quite a considerable amount of money."

Rose closed her eyes, shaking her head. "So she's not only free from prison, she's got the money to live pretty much anywhere she chooses. And possibly change her identity."

The doctor sighed. "Pretty much."

The fact that Fox had the money to move around wasn't going to help them find her. Still, if her DNA was on Fawcett's coat, it was likely she was in Brackley. They just had to hope she'd hung around long enough for them to track her.

Rose tightened her grip on the phone. "Do we have a photo of Miss Fox?"

It was likely she'd changed her image quite considerably in the last twenty-eight years, but the photo would at least give them something to go on.

"I have her original mug shots. Though it's possible she's changed quite a bit since then. I've already emailed them over to you, along with the other details."

Rose ended the call and relayed the entire conversation to Stipes and Blake. Stipes was first to respond. "So what do we do now, Guv?"

He looked as wired up as she felt. This case was turning out to be a real rollercoaster ride. Just when they thought they might've found their killer, another suspect had arisen from the ashes.

She turned to Blake. "Blake, could you update the rest of the team? Let them know that finding Miss Alice Fox is now our number one priority. I'll forward you a copy of her mugshots in a moment, along with her date of birth and her national insurance number."

Blake nodded before disappearing down the corridor.

Rose turned to Stipes. "Can you finish up with Dyer? I'm going to see Campbell's girlfriend again. If Fox *is* our killer, she could've been someone who was known to both of them, if by a different name."

Stipes stepped forward. "What I don't understand is, if she killed the abortionist, how come Sampson and Finlay's names never came out?"

Rose ran her hand along the ridge of her brow. Her previous headache was returning. When she spoke, her voice sounded labored. "If the process of recruiting patients was cloaked in secrecy, it's possible the names were never revealed. Until Campbell started writing that article."

Stipes shot her a strained smile. "Still, it all seems a bit odd, don't you think?"

"What does?"

"I don't know. The whole thing I guess. The fact that this woman, Miss Fox, killed someone twenty-eight years ago, then suddenly turns up in Brackley and kills Sampson and Finlay, then Campbell and Fawcett, without even appearing on our radar."

If Rose was honest, the same thought had occurred to her. But the fact that Fox's history was so pertinent, and her DNA was on Fawcett's coat forced them to take her seriously. She shrugged her shoulders. "That's probably just because there was no reason for us to look at her."

Stipes raised his eyebrows as though not convinced. "I guess you're right."

He turned and headed back to the interview room. As he drifted away, Rose called out behind him. "When you're done, give me a call. If the girlfriend recognizes the mugshot, we might have an address for our killer!"

Even as she said it, she doubted they'd be that lucky. Still, it had to be a possibility. Stipes turned briefly, then disappeared from sight.

CHAPTER THIRTY-NINE

Less than a minute later Rose was back at her desk, bringing up her emails. She found the one from Weller and clicked on it. The young, dark haired woman staring back at her didn't look familiar. Still, she forwarded the image to every member of her team and instructed the printer to print two color copies…one for the murder board and one for herself.

When she finally left the incident room and turned to head along the corridor, she felt dizzy with excitement. For so long they'd been searching for answers to the fundamental questions surrounding this case. Who'd killed Sampson and Finlay? Why now? And, how did those incidents involve Campbell and Fawcett? If they really *had* uncovered the killer's identity, they'd soon have all the answers.

She envisaged how Fox might've felt if, after all these years, the people who'd sent her friend to be butchered were revealed to her out of the blue. Could reading Campbell's article really have turned her back into a killer? Or could Campbell have spoken with her before it had even been published? After all, the article had contained no real details. She'd have needed to gain more information from somewhere in order to have fitted the puzzle pieces together.

The concept of a puzzle sent her mind back to her Russian doll analogy. It was the perfect comparison for this case. Right from the start, she'd known it was going to be complicated. But she could never have known just how twisted and tangled the path to its conclusion would be.

She picked up her pace, her mind switching back to Fox. After Sampson and Finlay had been revealed to her, had she immediately had the urge to kill them? Or had she considered the possibility over time, eventually deciding that they *had* to pay for their sins? She was a mature woman now, as opposed to the naïve nineteen year old she'd been when she was arrested. Was her friend's death all those years ago really still that raw for her?

As she stepped out into the parking lot, Rose barely even noticed it had begun to snow. As tiny white snowflakes clung to her face, she reached for her phone and dialed the estate agency where Campbell's girlfriend worked. When it turned out that she hadn't returned since Campbell's death, she climbed into her car and dialed the apartment.

The phone rang for several minutes before Rose eventually hung up. She tried the mobile number they'd been given, but telephone contact wasn't to be. She put the phone away, deciding to visit the apartment anyway. If *her* life had been turned upside down, she probably wouldn't want to speak to anyone either.

When she reached the apartment block she couldn't jump from the car fast enough. If anyone had been watching, they'd have been forgiven for thinking it had been fitted with some sort of explosive device. She found the right apartment and knocked on the door. As she'd expected, there was no reply. But that didn't mean the tenant wasn't in. She knocked again, this time harder, then accompanied the knocking with shouting through the letter box.

"This is the police! Miss Lyons, are you in?"

She placed her ear to the door. There were no signs of movement, but again that meant very little. She wished Stipes was here to force entry, then realized that wouldn't be a good idea. Miss Lyons hadn't committed any crime, and there was no justification for them to break into her apartment without a warrant. She mightn't even have *known* the former Miss Fox.

As she lingered in the corridor, Rose recalled the last time she'd been here. The door had been ajar then, the pungent stench of death seeping from the apartment's thin plasterboard walls. She shook the thought off and returned her mind to the present. The notion that Alice Fox was their killer was still prickling her, and she wasn't sure why.

She raised a hand to her temples. Perhaps it was because there were a lot of aspects to this case that hadn't panned out the way they'd seemed. Or perhaps it was Stipes's earlier comments starting to needle her. The question was, was she doing the right thing by putting all her eggs into one basket?

She shuffled her feet against the hard concrete floor. The fiber on Fawcett's coat was certainly incriminating, as was Miss Fox's past, and her likely hatred of the first two victims. She'd have certainly had a motive for wanting Sampson and Finlay dead, and the motives for Campbell and Fawcett's murders could've come to her later. The question was, after all this time, would she really have wanted to kill again?

Rose pulled herself together. She was torturing herself unnecessarily. It was their duty to act upon Weller's discovery, regardless of where it might lead them. Whether Miss Fox was their killer or not, she needed to be identified, and either ruled out of the investigation or arrested for multiple murder. She knocked on the door one last time.

When there was no reply, she was on the phone to Stipes. He'd dismissed Dyer ten minutes previously and, like every other member of her team, was in the process of trying to trace their latest suspect. So far, their searches had proved fruitless. Fox seemed to have kept a very low profile since being released from prison all those years ago. Her name hadn't come up on the electoral roll, and she wasn't listed as ever having been married. Nor were there any records to show that she'd ever had children or held down a steady job. She hadn't even applied for a passport. Which at least meant that the chances of her fleeing the country were minimal.

Rose leaned back on her heels. Of course, Fox could've chosen to change her name, perhaps to free herself from any association with her previous life. And if that *was* the case, it wouldn't be impossible to find her; but it would be difficult.

She hovered on the line, silently contemplating her next move. She considered going back to the station, but there didn't seem much she could do that wasn't already being done. She let out a long sigh. "Stipes, is there anything we've missed in this investigation? Anything at all."

Stipes hesitated. "I can't think of anything, Guv." The sound of paper rustling echoed down the line. "No. There's nothing that springs to mind."

Rose tried going through the investigation in her head. It was a virtually impossible task—so much had happened since the day they'd been summoned to Sampson's house—but gradually she envisaged each step, like a random collection of images on a carousel. When she could think of nothing they hadn't followed up on, she switched her attention back to Stipes.

"Are you absolutely certain?"

There were further shuffling sounds on Stipes's end. Rose envisaged him digging, up to his elbows in a mass of paperwork. The thought made her smile. When he spoke again, his breaths were more rapid.

"Actually, there *is* one very minor thing, though I can't imagine it'll be much help to us now."

Rose's pricked up her ears. Any anomaly could have significant consequences. "Go on."

"Well, you never got around to questioning Sampson's neighbor again. I doubt she'd have remembered anything she didn't tell us on the night. It's just the only thing I can think of that we didn't follow up on."

A young man stepped out of a nearby apartment, and Rose let him pass before considering Stipes's statement. He was right, there was probably nothing to be gained from questioning the neighbor again. Nevertheless, it was a line of inquiry she hadn't pursued, and she couldn't say she'd given this case one hundred per cent until it had been done. Again, she let out a long sigh.

"You're right. I'll pop round there now. It'll only take me ten minutes. Then I'll meet you back at the station."

She was about to hang up when there was a further shuffling along the line, and Stipes's voice shot through it. "Come to think of it, we didn't get a sample of the neighbor's DNA either, Guv. Since there were no prints found at the scene, it wasn't imperative we rule her out."

Rose nodded silently to herself. She always kept a DNA testing set in the car, in case of emergencies. It wouldn't take much for her to get a sample of Mills's DNA. Provided she was at home. That way, at least they'd be secure in the knowledge that they'd covered all bases.

"OK, I'll do that at the same time. That way, no one can accuse us of not being thorough."

She ended the call and exited the apartment block. There'd still been no sounds from Campbell's apartment so, if his girlfriend *was* in, she was probably unlikely to have been of much use anyway. They'd just have to speak to her another time.

261

When she got back to the car, Rose considered calling Ms. Mills, then decided against it. Forewarning her would only give her time to censor her reactions, and she wanted the answers to her questions to be instinctive. Besides that, she didn't want to cause the woman any unnecessary distress. She stepped on the car's accelerator and headed for Amber Court.

CHAPTER FORTY

Ten minutes later Rose was sitting by the roadside opposite Sampson's house. The location was becoming strangely familiar. Slowly her eyes scanned its magnificent exterior. Its sheer size still astounded her. It was like a great monument, piercing the late afternoon lull. She shifted her attention to the neighboring property. Even though it was slightly smaller, it projected a similar sense of awe. Despite working a night shift, Mills clearly had money.

Rose turned away, rummaging in her glove compartment for the DNA testing kit and placing it in the inside pocket of her jacket. She'd get it out once the conversation was flowing. That way, she could always pass it off as an afterthought. She straightened her collar and stepped from the car.

When the door wasn't answered on the first ring, Rose felt an uncanny sense of dèjá vu. It was beginning to feel like no one wanted to talk to her. She stepped forward slightly and pressed the bell again. This time a shadow shifted in the hallway. She took a step back and prepared to greet the owner, just as her phone sounded in her pocket. As usual, the timing was impeccable.

She rolled her eyes, then pulled out the phone and scrolled across the screen. Stipes's familiar voice boomed along the line.

"Where are you?"

Despite her frustration, Rose kept her voice to a dull whisper. "Where do you think I am? I'm at Sampson's neighbor's house."

She heard the sound of a latch being unfastened, then a dead bolt, and wondered if Mills had heightened her security since Sampson's death. After all, unlike the Sampson house, there were no electric gates here. She turned her attention back to the call.

"I've gotta go. I'll call you when I'm done."

She was about to hang up and put the phone back in her pocket when Stipes's voice burst through again. This time it sounded more urgent.

"Don't go in there, Guv. It could be dangerous."

Before she had chance to reply, the door opened and Mills's face peered around it. Consumed by confusion, Rose switched off the phone and fixed the woman with a strained smile.

Mills stared in bewilderment and Rose held up her badge. She supposed the woman didn't get many visitors, particularly as she worked nights and presumably wasn't around much during the day. Mills nodded and moved aside to welcome her visitor in. Despite her apprehension, Rose obliged.

As she stepped cautiously into the heavily carpeted porch, Rose recalled Stipes's last words to her. What the hell did he mean by "it could be dangerous?" She recalled the fact that they hadn't taken Mills's DNA. It unnerved her so much that she felt the waistband of her trousers for the small pocket knife she always kept there. It had saved her life on more than one occasion. Hopefully it would do so again, should the need arise.

Mills ushered her through to a tastefully decorated lounge, which was almost totally dominated by a large log fireplace. Its decorative shelves held the most delicate of ornaments, and its grate was so clean, it looked like it had never been used, despite the time of year. Rose's thoughts turned to the sturdy wood burner in the Sampson house, which was much more her style.

Mills followed her into the room, stepping a little too close and causing her to shiver unexpectedly. She offered her a seat in one of the plush purple armchairs and sat herself opposite. There were a few moments of slightly awkward silence, while Rose struggled to make sense of Stipes's call. Should she have heeded his warning and turned back? By the time she'd gotten it, it had been too late. Or had it? She could still have made an excuse and walked away.

Mills was eyeing her cautiously as though she was wondering if something was wrong. The woman pulled herself forward in her seat. "Can I get you a drink? Tea or coffee? Something cold?"

Her voice was polite enough, but her eyes were expressionless, and suddenly all Rose could think was, *Are they the eyes of a killer?* She decided to accept the offer of a drink. It would give her time to send Stipes a text and find out what in God's name was going on. Though, if she really *was* in danger, he'd surely be on his way. She flashed her host her most gratifying smile.

"Tea would be lovely, thanks. White, no sugar."

Mills drifted off and Rose reached into her pocket for her phone. When she found it, she was surprised to find that her hands were shaking. She unlocked the keypad and typed a few short words. *What the hell's going on?*

She clicked send just as her host appeared back in the doorway.

"The kettle's on. So how can I be of help?"

Rose switched her phone to silent and placed it on the chair's arm, where she could see if Stipes replied. Then she leaned forward in her chair.

"This is just a follow-up call, really. I wanted to see how you were doing after the shock of the other day. Plus, I wondered if you might've remembered anything you forgot to mention at the time. It's hard to string two words together when you've just been through something like that. Let alone recall every minor detail."

Mills perched herself on the edge of the other armchair. She looked pale and emaciated, not at all like a cold-blooded killer. "To be honest, I've been trying my best to push it from my mind."

Rose nodded. "I completely understand. Still, if there *is* anything you've remembered since, even something that might seem insignificant...."

"There isn't."

Mills was quick to reply, and Rose wondered if there was a reason for that. As if reading her mind, her host added, "I'm sorry. As you said, it was a hell of a shock, and I've been trying my best not to dwell on it. I stayed at my sister's for a few days... you know, just to get away from it all. I'm sure all the neighbors are talking about it."

Rose thought it slightly odd that she'd be bothered about the neighbors, since the houses were so far apart. Still, she guessed that everyone had their vulnerabilities.

The kettle started to boil, and Mills rose from her seat. "I'll make that tea."

Rose waited until Mills was back in the kitchen before checking her phone. There'd been no reply from Stipes, which did nothing to ease her tension. She contemplated making an excuse to return to the station, then spotted something resting on a nearby sideboard that instantly captured her attention. It was an old silver hammer that looked like it'd seen the inside of a mechanic's workshop. It seemed out of place amongst the shiny ornaments. More than that, it matched Weller's description of the blunt instrument used in Finlay's, Campbell's, and Fawcett's murders.

She considered pulling an evidence bag from her pocket and dashing over to retrieve it. How long did it take to make a cup of tea? But by the time she'd thought about it, Mills was back, cup in hand. She passed it to Rose, who placed it on the coffee table beside her. She was afraid to drink it for fear it might contain something lethal.

Mills eased herself back into the armchair opposite, apparently oblivious to her guest's anxiety. Rose glanced at the phone through the corner of her eye. Still nothing. She decided to take the bull by the horns and get out the DNA testing kit. If Mills *was* their killer, it might provoke a reaction from her. Anything had to be better than pussy footing around like this. Besides, she was prepared. She had her pocket knife.

The creaking of a floorboard outside in the hallway stopped her in her tracks. She presumed it was Stipes. He still hadn't replied to her message and, if she really *was* in danger, he'd undoubtedly come to her aid. She leaned back in her chair and pretended not to have noticed. Mills was staring off into space, apparently oblivious.

The thought that Stipes was nearby relaxed Rose slightly, and she held off on retrieving the DNA testing kit. If assistance was imminent, there was no point in rushing things. They'd find out if Mills was the killer soon enough. She took a deep breath, preparing herself for the chaos to come, just as the door swung open and a familiar figure appeared in the doorway. But contrary to Rose's assumption, it wasn't Stipes.

For a brief few seconds, Rose wasn't sure what was happening. When she realized Brannigan had a syringe in her hand, she felt all the blood physically drain from her face. For a fleeting moment, she froze. Then her survival instinct kicked in and she leapt from the chair. But by then, Brannigan had covered the distance between them and was standing directly beside her.

Rose felt a sudden hard shove against her shoulder, which temporarily put her off balance. When she'd regained her footing she spun around, desperate to gain the advantage. Her heart was beating so fast she could hear its rhythmic thumping through her eardrums, and the pain in her shoulder was excruciating.

She raised her arm, desperate to fend off her attacker. But Brannigan was too fast for her. The woman clenched her fist, striking Rose's bone with one almighty crunch. The pain shot through her arm with the intensity of a head-on collision. She winced in agony. What the hell was going on here? This woman was like a machine.

Rose made one more attempt at defending herself, but nothing she did seemed to have an impact. All her years of training and she couldn't deliver when it mattered. She tried to reach into the waistband of her trousers for her pocket knife, but Brannigan had a grip on her upper arms and she had no way of reaching it. She caught a glimpse of the syringe as Brannigan raised it to her neck. It stirred something within her, and she somehow found the strength to force it away. But only temporarily. The woman's stamina was just too overpowering.

As she felt herself weakening, Rose envisioned the key moments in her life, flashing before her like the montage of a Hollywood movie. She tried to push them away, but she could feel herself drifting further and further from reality. Was this how it was all meant to end? Had her life really been destined to lead to nothing?

She felt the pressure of Brannigan's hand against her neck. She braced herself, anticipating the cold metal of the syringe piercing her skin. She'd almost resigned herself to an agonizing fate when, for no apparent reason, Brannigan loosened her grip. Rose took the opportunity to seize her hand and push her off balance.

As the syringe fell to the floor, Rose reached into her trousers for her pocket knife. She was about to plunge it into Brannigan when she realized they were no longer alone. Stipes's familiar face was the last thing she saw as she fell to her knees. The room was spinning, and she could feel herself drifting away. Then her entire body went cold, and everything faded to black.

CHAPTER FORTY-ONE

When she finally came around, Rose was lying on a rug in the center of the room and Stipes was hovering over her. It was a few seconds before she could find her voice and, when she did, it was faint and croaky.

"What happened?"

Stipes shot her an unusually wide smile. "You passed out. The doctor says it was a combination of shock and exhaustion. You'll be OK. As long as you rest."

She pulled herself up onto her elbows, suddenly recalling the events of the last thirty minutes. When they finally made some semblance of sense, she asked the first question that entered her head. "Where's Mills?"

Stipes signaled to the right of him. Mills was sitting in the corner of the room with her head in her hands. A uniformed officer was speaking to her. "From the looks of things, she didn't have anything to do with the murders."

Rose was confused. "Then how come you told me I could be in danger?"

A wry smile struck Stipes' face. "We finally managed to trace the elusive Miss Abigail Ross. You know, the one woman from the box of files we hadn't managed to trace."

"It's Mills?"

"That's right. But, ironically, I don't think she realized who she was living next door to, at least not until now. She said she met Brannigan at a local charity event and, when Brannigan found out where she lived, she probably couldn't believe her luck. No doubt she used this house as a base to help plan Sampson's death."

"But you *thought* Mills was the killer?"

"When we found out who she was, it certainly seemed a possibility. Plus, she hadn't been tested for DNA. We had no idea about Brannigan until ten minutes ago."

Rose closed her eyes. So *that* was how the killer had entered Sampson's property so easily. Brannigan had probably visited the Sampson house with Mills a few times and taken the opportunity to check out the old lady's security. She could've planned Sampson's murder over a period of time, working out how she could get in without setting off the burglar alarm. She could even have discovered the security code for the gates. Either that, or she'd simply knocked on the door. They may never know.

She opened her eyes again, seeing aspects of the case as though she were viewing them for the first time. It was clear now how the killer had known Finlay would be home, and how they'd known their way around his property well enough to disable the fuse box on entry. She wondered if Finlay had discovered Brannigan's intention before his death.

She turned her gaze to the sideboard. As if reading her mind, Stipes added, "We found the hammer. Brannigan probably left it here to incriminate Mills, who was in such a state of shock, she hadn't even noticed it. Forensics are examining it as we speak."

A SOCO walked by and Rose instinctively lowered her voice. "But why did Brannigan want to kill Sampson?"

She might've had reason to kill Finlay, as a result of their closeness. But Sampson was a stranger to her. Wasn't she?

Stipes hesitated before answering. "I think she probably found out what Finlay had been up to, and Sampson's part in it. After he'd shielded his activities from her for all those years, finding out that he'd been involved in something so unsavory probably just made her snap. We'll know more once we've interviewed her."

Rose was suddenly consumed by an odd sense of satisfaction. She was looking forward to looking Brannigan in the eye and charging her with multiple murder.

The SOCO drifted off and she resumed her usual voice. "How did Brannigan become so forensically aware?"

Stipes shrugged. "She's a journalist. At least in the loosest sense. Who knows how she comes by her information?"

It was a simple answer but valid nonetheless.

"And what about Campbell and Fawcett?"

"It's likely they'd threatened to expose her. We already know that Campbell wrote that article, probably from information he'd gained while at the Sampson house. He could've inadvertently run into Brannigan. If he talked to her and happened to mention it…. As for Fawcett, it probably *was* a simple case of blackmail. Whether or not she saw Brannigan at Finlay's property that night, we may never know. But she had the stolen phones in her possession, so she must've been onto her."

"And she knew Sampson."

"Right. For all we know, she could've been helping Brannigan. Until Brannigan's insecurity got the better of her."

Rose shuddered. This case had given her the greatest challenge of her life. But who could have known that the killer had been right in front of them the whole time? A thought struck her, and she furrowed her eyebrows.

"What about Alice Fox?"

Stipes lowered his voice. "It doesn't look like she had anything to do with the murders either. Her DNA showing up on one of our victims was probably pure coincidence, albeit extraordinary. It's likely she donated that coat to the charity shop and Fawcett later commandeered it."

Rose sighed. Forensic evidence had hindered them again. It certainly wasn't turning out to be the miracle of science it was purported to be.

Stipes's phone beeped in his pocket and he reached in to retrieve it. He stared into the screen, then put it away again. "I guess it's a good thing Brannigan showed her hand when she did. If she hadn't, we could've ended up arresting the wrong woman, for totally the wrong reasons."

Rose smiled inwardly to herself. She wasn't sure she'd describe her near-death experience as fortunate. Still, Stipes was right. If Brannigan hadn't shown her hand, Mills would definitely have been in the firing line. But why had Brannigan come for *her*? And how had she known she'd be there? Stipes didn't have an answer. She guessed it was something else they'd have to hope to uncover in the interview.

She pulled herself up into a sitting position. Her head was thumping and the pain in her arm was making it hard for her to put weight on it. Still, their case had finally reached its conclusion, and she was suddenly filled with an extraordinary sense of euphoria. It imbued every nerve in her body with a strange, electrifying warmth. She was just beginning to relax when another thought struck her.

"What about the red Fiesta?"

Stipes shrugged. "It probably had no relevance. It could've belonged to anyone. And we have to bear in mind that Fawcett's work at the charity shop was voluntary. Who knows how she chose to top up her benefits?"

Rose sighed. There'd certainly been no shortage of dead-ends in this case. She looked Stipes in the eye. "Yeah. I guess."

Another SOCO appeared from nowhere, and Rose was reminded of the need to get moving. The team needed to be updated, if Stipes hadn't already done so, and she was looking forward to visiting the chief and giving him the good news. She let Stipes help her to her feet and, deliberately bypassing Mills, headed for the door.

CHAPTER FORTY-TWO

Twelve hours later, when Rose and Stipes entered the interview room, Brannigan was seated with her hands in her lap and her head facing the window. Contrary to expectations, she looked cool and calm. Rose imagined it would take a lot to get inside her head, to unravel all the layers and ascertain what really made her tick. Then again, would anyone really want to? If justice prevailed, she'd be safely behind bars for the rest of her life.

She switched on the tape recorder and recited the words she'd recited so often over the past few days. When she was done, she looked Brannigan square in the eye.

"Miss Lucy Brannigan, you've been charged with the murders of Mrs. Elise Sampson, Mr. Zack Finlay, Mr. Anthony Campbell, and Miss Leah Fawcett."

Brannigan merely nodded. She seemed to have lost the will to pretend. Perhaps she'd always known this day would come.

Rose leaned forward across the table. "Could you tell us *why* you did what you did?"

For the first time since their arrival, Brannigan turned to face them. When she spoke, her voice was strangely monotone. "Like I told you, Zack and I ran into Sampson on a day out. Of course,

I didn't know who she was then. But I knew that something significant had occurred between her and Zack...he was so unnerved after seeing her. So when we got back, I made him tell me."

Rose recalled her first interview with Brannigan. She'd seemed so believable when she'd told them she had no idea who Sampson was. She was clearly a good actress. Perhaps that was why she'd found it so hard to make a judgement on her character. She shook her head as Brannigan continued.

"When I found out the kind of thing he'd been keeping from me all those years, I was horrified. I thought he was a decent man. Not an accomplice to murder." She paused for a moment, as though the words stuck in her throat, and when she spoke again, her voice was quieter. "I found the hammer in his toolbox. They both needed to pay for what they'd done. But simply striking them over the head didn't seem enough. I wanted them to suffer, to experience the pain those women must've experienced when their babies were pulled away from them."

Rose looked at her incredulously. "But those women *wanted* their babies aborted. They paid money for the surgery."

Brannigan merely shrugged. "They might not have done if the procedure hadn't been laid on a plate for them. If people hadn't preyed on them when they were at their most vulnerable. I think that's what got me most of all. The fact that Zack and that doctor profited from those baby's deaths."

Stipes pulled himself forward, ready to interject. "So you decided to use potassium chloride? Because it had been used in the abortions?"

Brannigan managed a thin smile. "I looked it up. It seemed appropriate, and it wasn't hard to get ahold of." She turned her head toward the window again, and when she turned back there was a sense of melancholy about her that hadn't been there

276

before. She fumbled with a button on her blouse. "I couldn't have children, you know. It's an inherent condition. I was born that way."

Rose shot a glance at Stipes. Suddenly Brannigan's motivations were clear. For years, she'd probably been desperate for a child. So when she'd found out that Sampson and Finlay had been making money by helping women get rid of their babies.... If only they'd possessed that information at the outset. But why would they have had reason to ask? Like every other aspect of this case, they'd been one step behind all along.

Rose sat back in her seat, studying Brannigan as though she were seeing her for the first time. Had it really been Finlay's actions that had turned her into a killer? Or had she always had the propensity inside of her?

She drummed her fingers on the table in front of her. "OK, so we know why you killed Elise Sampson and Zack Finlay. What about Anthony Campbell and Leah Fawcett? They hadn't committed any crime. Had they?"

Brannigan's expression turned hard again. "They thought what I was doing was wrong. Can you believe that? What *I* was doing."

Rose shook her head in disbelief. "And they deserved to die for that?"

Her question went unanswered, and Rose had a feeling that Brannigan wasn't sure herself.

There were a few minutes of uncomfortable silence whilst Rose deliberated over her next question.

"Why were you at Amber Crescent today? And why did you attack *me*?"

Brannigan let out a deep sigh, leaning back in her chair.

"You were beginning to connect the dots.... I could sense that when you brought me back in. I can't go to prison. I don't think

I'd…. She trailed off, sinking her head in her hands as though finally admitting defeat. But Rose wasn't finished.

"But how did you know I'd be at Mill's house?"

The question was really niggling her. Brannigan looked up. Her face was red, but there were no tears, and Rose couldn't tell if she was remorseful or not. She concluded that she was probably just peeved at having been caught.

"I was there when you turned up." Her words caught Rose by surprise.

"You mean….?"

Brannigan shrugged her shoulders. "Andrea lets me stay sometimes. She had no idea how helpful her living next to that doctor was. When I found out, I saw it as a sign. Fate intended for them to be punished for what they'd done."

Rose had no answer. The woman was clearly unstable. She just hoped she didn't get a reduced sentence on medical grounds. She'd not only known what she was doing, she'd probably do it again if the opportunity arose.

Twenty minutes later, when they'd gotten all they could from Brannigan, Rose ended the interview and switched off the recording. Brannigan would be taken to the cells, where she'd have ample opportunity to reflect on the severity of what she'd done. Not that it would make any difference. Four people were dead as a result of her actions, and it would be a long time before the quiet suburb of Brackley returned to normal again.

As she stepped into the corridor alongside Stipes, Rose felt a shudder of relief wrack her body. This case had taken such a toll on her, it would be a while before *she* returned to normal again. What she was looking forward to the most was a good nights' sleep. She'd earned it.

As they headed to the interview room for a celebratory drink, Stipes turned to face her.

"Well, you were right, Guv. Everything *was* connected to that box of files, even if the killer *wasn't* in them."

Rose shot him a cunning smile. "So I guess I won't need to buy that hat now."

He shook his head, a mischievous expression adorning his lightly tanned face. "That's a shame. I was looking forward to watching you wriggle your way out of that one."

Rose stopped in her tracks, looking her partner square in the eye. "Stipes, you should know me by now. I *never* wriggle my way out of anything."

A BIT ABOUT ME

Since the release of my first two books, *A Chilling Fate* and *A Fitting Finale*, I've spent a great deal of time engaging with other writers and sharpening my writing technique. I've also completed a short course in Forensic Psychology, which allowed me fascinating insights into the dilemmas associated with identifying a criminal. This new-found knowledge definitely helped inspire me to write this book.

A Natural Killer? was tremendous fun to write, particularly as I tried to envisage it as a modern day whodunnit. I've always been a fan of Agatha Christie and I love to weave my way through a complicated story-line or an intricate plot. There's nothing more rewarding than reaching the end of a particularly satisfying thriller, to find an unexpected twist in the tail. I just hope the book was as much fun to read as it was to write.

As I reach the end of this journey, I'd like to thank my husband and children for their patience in trying to get through to me when my mind was continually elsewhere. As much as I hate to admit it, there are probably few things more frustrating than living with a writer.

is what it does: it predicts the finite, more fascinating than being wild bacon.